MW00643280

ANOTHER
PRESENT
ERA

ANOTHER PRESENT ERA

ELAINE PERRY

Farrar • Straus • Giroux

NEW YORK

Copyright © 1990 by Elaine Perry
All rights reserved
Designed by Victoria Wong
Printed in the United States of America
Published simultaneously in Canada by Harper & Collins, Toronto
First edition, 1990

Library of Congress Cataloging-in-Publication Data
Perry, Elaine.
Another present era.
I. Title.
PS3566.E6958A83   1990   813'.54   89-71528

For my parents,
Archie W. and Bertha M. Perry

Acknowledgments

I WISH TO THANK my literary agent, F. Joseph Spieler, for eons of encouragement, insight, and inspired support; my editor, Elisabeth Dyssegaard, for her editorial engineering and unlimited humor; my architectural adviser, Lawrence H. Mason, R.A., for invaluable assistance; and Judith A. Czelusniak for providing time and resources. Special and enduring thanks to my parents and Steve Bryant. Further thanks to Colette Inez, Michael Stephens, and Stuart Friebert, who helped me get started on this journey to alternate realities.

E.P.

Contents

PART I ANOTHER PRESENT ERA

Still Life with City   3

I Don't Believe in Magic   17

Haunted by the Visible   25

Meeting Her at the Potzdamer Platz   42

Little White Lies   51

The Borderline   63

She Was Reading *War and Peace*   77

Dangerous Ground   90

Mirrors   109

Transients   129

I've Got My Love to Keep Me Warm   139

The Wrong Men   154

A Rainy Sunday   169

PART II AN INTERLUDE: NIGHT PASSING
(ALL CLEAR)

Drôle de Guerre   187

Second City   202

Contents

PART III   DO NOT TURN TO GHOSTS

Body and Soul   213

What I Desire   220

Do Not Turn to Ghosts   236

ANOTHER PRESENT ERA

On or about December 1910 human nature changed.

VIRGINIA WOOLF

Still Life with City

THE FOG IN NEW YORK HARBOR casts a nebula around the dying city. Wanda is alone on the fifty-eighth floor of the Savings of America Tower, listening to footsteps. But everyone left hours ago and no ghost could haunt a skyscraper like this, ninety stories of smoke-gray glass and steel, and windows that can't be opened. It's past midnight, she should be alarmed, the financial district isn't safe after hours. Nor is this suite, with its curving glass-block walls, airy offices with scarlet-red Barcelona chairs and August Sander photographs, and a cluster of computer terminals, plotters, and oval viewphone screens, where she's working. The suite is small compared to the London headquarters, but the Architects Consortium needs this New York address. The city is strong in the memory, no matter how much it decays and gives way to the sea.

She's been absorbed in the late-night rebroadcast of *Suspense*, as if she doesn't know how it will end. Because of storms and the interference of skyscrapers, the loud static and radio voices sound like hand-clapping. She forgets about the footsteps and keeps working until the radio, the computers and plotters shut down with a high whine. The downlights fade quickly and the emergency lights come on, uselessly faint. The integrated system's soothing baritone voice tells her where the exit doors are and estimates how long the power shutdown will last. She ignores it, as she

3

looks through her black Danish schoolbag for the photovoltaic flashlight she is never without. The blackouts and brownouts are so frequent she anticipates and sometimes predicts them. She picks up her bag and throws her black sweater coat across her shoulders and is about to leave when she hears a man calling her name.

"Bradley?" she says, looking around, clutching her bag and moving into the dim reddish light of the exit sign at the corner stairwell. She can't imagine why he's here.

"None other," he whispers, and swaggers out from behind the glass-block wall, his hands in his trench-coat pockets, the collar upturned. She shines her flashlight on him and he is so tall he startles her, tall and elongated like the shadow looming above him. "The man who's building you a dream house," he adds, and stops a few meters away from her.

"You scared me. What are you doing here?" She is puzzled, but smiles at him anyway. She walks closer, shines the flashlight up at the ceiling, and turns it off. She puts her arms around him, but he keeps standing stiffly against the wall, like a child whose height is being measured.

"Haven't you heard the forecast? They're predicting flash floods tonight," he says, sounding so anxious she could believe he's not used to the constant floods and flood warnings.

"Then the fifty-eighth floor is the place to be." She picks up her bag, puts her flashlight in it, and slings it across her shoulder, where it catches her long, wavy hair. He steps closer to the exit door, presses the handle, but she pulls it back shut.

"Let's take the emergency elevator," she says. He stands with his hands against the door handle, so silently he begins to unnerve her.

"I'm forty years old." He repeats himself twice in a voice so strained and breathy all she can think of is how fragile vocal cords are. He doesn't look forty, though she isn't sure what forty is supposed to look like. He still has a full head

4

of dark blond hair and the sort of thin, colorless face that reminds her of photographs of unsmiling Left Bank intellectuals. His eyes are strong and dark, like those of a visionary or a great musician.

"Honey, you've been forty for months. And I'll turn thirty one of these fine days if I don't die first." She reaches up and touches his face. He grips her hand tightly. She knows it's not his age he's upset about. She wishes he would tell her the truth. "Let's have a drink at O'Sullivan's and celebrate," she says. He frowns, seeming to mistake her cheerfulness for sarcasm. The power comes back on, lights flickering, computers humming. The radio blares loudly with a shaving-cream jingle sung barbershop-quartet style.

He reaches into his coat pocket, takes out a black-and-gold pouch of pipe tobacco. "I keep trying to quit." He tosses the pouch across the floor, reaches into his pocket again, pulls out a revolver. He spins the cylinder and fingers the barrel. She's never known him to carry a gun. "What's with the gun, lover man?" she asks, trying to sound nonchalant.

He turns away from her and steps into one of the offices, closing the door behind him partway. She follows him, pushes the door open. The power fails again and the emergency lights trace his outline in ice blue as he puts the barrel into his mouth.

She can't believe what she's seeing, faint and hallucinatory in the blue light. She moves toward him. "Bradley, stop it!" Both his hands, shaking, are on the gun, which he is tilting toward the roof of his mouth. Standing just a few steps away, she calls his name over and over. He doesn't seem to hear her. He takes the safety off, his hands no longer shaking.

"At least tell me"—her voice wavering now—"why you want to splatter yourself all over the walls."

He takes the gun out of his mouth, lets it dangle on his thumb. "I don't want to hear about the walls, sister," he says, with what could be mock exasperation or extreme anger.

"Put the gun away and come here," she says, almost

shouting at him. She's perspiring, too warm in her sweater coat and black shirtdress, and still afraid but trying not to show it. She doesn't stop looking at him as he cradles the revolver like a heavy stone in his hands and walks slowly toward her. He slides on the safety, puts the gun back in his coat pocket, and kisses her forehead. His hands and face are so cold she shivers. "I'm sorry," he whispers. He leans his back against the door and slips out of the office. In a few seconds, she hears his footsteps echoing down a stairwell. He refuses to answer her or to stop. She rushes through the suite, past the reception area, and takes the emergency elevator. Powered by a generator, it drifts slowly, green diode digits ticking off the floors. He could be anywhere in the building; she knows she's lost him. The synthesized voice talks about the power failure, assuring her she has no reason for panic.

She looks through the cavernous lobby for him, waits several moments at the stairwell door. The power comes back on. He doesn't show up. She leaves the building finally and walks through the deserted streets, arc lamps hopelessly dim, layers of asphalt worn down to the brick and cobblestone as old as the nation. These horse-and-buggy trails are too narrow for the elevated trains and the masonry and glass-and-steel colossi that span the night. Many of the buildings are abandoned or covered with scaffolding that rattles alarmingly when the trains pass by. They run even this late, stopping at Park Row, Wall Street, the South Ferry Terminus, no one boarding or exiting, shrill whistles disrupting the night. Street fires burn in garbage cans and gutters of uncollected trash, amber light in the dark streets. They burn strongly in the fog, sending up thick, noxious fumes. She wonders if she's saved his life. Or is he out here wandering the streets, still trying to kill himself?

She should have called for car service. She keeps walking uptown until she reaches her Chambers Street loft. It's the entire third floor of a five-story cast-iron building, with a charcoal-gray palazzo façade. She takes off her clothes, throws her dress into a wastebasket in the upper level bedroom. She designed and renovated the loft, put in all the electrical wiring and plumbing by herself. Once a nut and spice warehouse and wholesale store, it had been abandoned when its owner was assassinated by a rival crime family. The entire district, of these cast-iron industrial buildings built in the previous century, is notorious for underworld violence and contrabanding: pharmaceuticals from South America and the Balkan States, electronics from Korea and the Philippines, Chinese-run garment and print sweatshops in the basements of condemned loft buildings on Warren, Chambers, and Murray Streets. Now the contrabanding has expanded a few blocks southward, to Battery Park City, and even to the plazas and skywalks of the World Financial Center and around the towers of the World Trade Center.

She opens the gray silk-tulle draperies and peers between the Venetian blinds, looking for him futilely. But no one is out on the streets. Searchlights sweep across the sky and the fog above the neighboring blocks of four- and five-story buildings and the hypnotic stream of headlights and taillights on multilane West Street. Civil Defense klaxons wail, indicating the severity of the flood warning. Four long blasts followed by a brief silence, repeated endlessly. On her nightstand is the booklet every New Yorker has, explaining why and when the klaxons sound and what to do.

She sits down at the vanity in the corner, beveled rectangular mirror and black lacquered surfaces she has to dust every day. The stale lemon furniture buffer scent never goes away; she sprays Chanel No. 5 to mask it. She watches herself brush her hair, but it's so dark in the room all she sees are the white sparks of static electricity. She places the brush back down carefully, afraid of waking up Sterling in the adjacent bedroom. Sometimes she doubts he's really there.

No one else sees him, knows him. He wants nothing, expects nothing, or he's altering her life so deftly she doesn't realize what's happening to her.

She's too tired and shaken to think about Bradley or anyone else; she goes to the bathroom and runs hot water in the shower stall. The water roars, spraying out wide and full. She had to search diligently for a fixture like this and for the black-and-white mosaic tiles to make the pattern of pyramids and ankh symbols that covers the walls. She closes the shower stall door, stands under the hot water. It should be purging, healthful, erasing everything. It hurts the way good medicine always does.

•

Sterling turns on the chromed-metal task lamp beside the bed. Steam drifts across the bedroom, molecules colliding into the white enamel walls and the beamed ceiling. The sound of the water soothes him; he listens to it the way he imagines people listen to waterfalls. But he has trouble imagining what other people do, not even knowing what he's been doing here in Wanda's loft, where he sometimes spends the night, lying awake in the tiny makeshift bedroom cordoned off by shoji screens, waiting for her to return. She draws him back again and again; he doesn't understand how or why. He is too old to care about finding friends and too fearful to find a lover. But she knows him, knows who he is, and no one else does. He puts on his maroon satin robe and looks for the waterfall. The bathroom door is ajar; he opens it and steam covers him. The stainless-steel fixtures and the pendant lamp of the same nickel alloy as coins are gleaming in starbursts.

He knocks on the sliding door of the shower stall. She is shadowy and distorted behind the sanded glass, but he can see her trembling. He slides the door open, finds her under the shower nozzle, arms folded tightly. The water is fiercely hot, hissing against the tiles, steam blinding him as he turns

8

the faucet off. She looks around frantically as if the water has shut itself off.

He reaches for a towel, wraps it around her, and guides her to the bed. "You could have died from that scalding water." He puts an arm around her and she shivers.

"Don't talk about dying," she says, rubbing her arms, shocked at how red they are. She pulls the zebra-patterned blanket around her shoulders and pushes her wet hair away from her eyes. She tells him about Bradley.

"I hate guns," he says.

She expects him to say more but he doesn't. She leans her head against his shoulder. "They remind you of the war," she says, wanting to run her hand through his thick, silvery hair. But her hands are so swollen she can barely move them.

The war? Revolvers don't make him think of the war. It was a war of air-raid sirens, blacked-out cities, the terrible roar of bombers passing overhead, and later, the uneasy peace in a country collaborating with the enemy. The war has become a movie to him, the celluloid deteriorating in splotches like raindrops. He lived through the war, but now he watches from outside the frame. "I'm sure you saved Bradley," he says. "I'm sure of it." He smiles the sad smile of someone slowly becoming inebriated after a long evening alone.

●

Wanda Higgins Du Bois wanted to know his name. He told her to call him Werner Schmidt and she pronounced the name with the proper German accent. But László Moholy-Nagy's book *Painting, Photography, Film* had already told her what she wanted to know. She showed him the book one day as they sat together on the ebonized beechwood sofa in her living room, two white plaster Ionic columns and a tall utility steel bookshelf separating it from the kitchen. Afternoon sun poured in heavy and dusty white through the

Venetian blinds covering the front, street-facing windows at the far end of her loft, the studio consisting of her drafting table, computer, plotter, and scale models, scattered and in varying stages of completion.

Her copy of the book was a contemporary paperback reprint, but Moholy-Nagy's layout and typography were intact, in facsimile. Lower-case letters, asymmetrical columns, horizontal rules, large dots in place of asterisks; typographical innovations that never quite caught on. She turned to a center inset of black-and-white photographs and pointed out a photograph he'd seen many times. A man stared back at him, his overcoat misted with rain, his hair dark against the cloudy, bright sky. Moholy had taken this photograph of Sterling Cronheim, his friend and colleague, on the roof of the tallest building in Weimar, not tall at all really, and destroyed in the war. He had stood at a distance and focused the camera downward at Sterling, who was restless and shivering, flanked by piping and the bold, jagged shadows they cast on him, looking back at the camera like a silent-movie actor trying to tell the audience he was in sudden danger. He was not smiling. It didn't occur to him or anyone else he knew to smile in front of a camera. Now all he saw in photographs were tense, wide smiles.

"It's almost like portraiture," she told him. He kept looking through the book, carefully turning the pages from the top corner like an archivist. "By a man who disparaged photography that strove for painterly effects."

He didn't say anything for a while, as he pondered her succinct analysis of his friend's aesthetics, and looked her over, subtly. She wore a pearl-gray tailored dress with white piping on buttercup collar, cuffs, and jet-buttoned shoulders; seamed stockings with a cluster of rhinestones at each heel; gray-and-black pumps of a high-quality imitation alligator. Always immaculately glamorous in tailored suits and dresses, though a bit too slender to be truly curvaceous. Her wavy, side-parted hair, falling well past her shoulders, was a dark

10

and unusual blond. Her face resembled that of several legendary screen actresses. He couldn't stop looking at her, not then, not now. Everything about her reminded him of a place and a time. And a woman he tried his best not to think of.

"Moholy used to say photography was a medium that could and should stand on its own. He thought it had possibilities way beyond reportage and realism—" He stopped himself, but she smiled knowingly.

Wanda, he whispers, but now it is morning and she has left for work. His hands have a memory of her hair. He feels the color on his hands, warm as the rest of him shivers. Once he could feel the colors of walls, recognize them in the dark. He closes his eyes and tries to forget her, but the rich harvest-gold of her hair surrounds him. It is like a tundra disappearing under an azo sunset and he is so far away now he doesn't understand the idea of four directions. There are thousands of directions to go. Only walls and doors are keeping him in place.

Later that day he flips through the channels on her telescreen, credit-card thin and covering most of the living room wall opposite the sofa, like a large painting. He watches a few moments of the colorized version of *White Heat*. Colorization is a dreadful, childish fad to him, like drawing mustaches on magazine photographs. His eyes are already tiring themselves out colorizing the world which has nothing at all like color. There is only motion and light.

●

"I remind you of Lenore Hayden, don't I?" she asks him when she returns home from work. She's wanted to ask him this for weeks. A thunderstorm outside, she leaves the draperies and Venetian blinds wide open. The rain hits the bedroom windows, leaving long, blurry trails on the floor-to-ceiling Securitglas. Bradley is still missing. She wonders what else she could have done.

"That was so many years ago," he says, leaning against the headboard, a herringbone-veneer bookshelf stacked with monographs of artists he knew.

She notes his refusal to answer. "I've always liked your photographs of her," she says, remembering Hayden the scientist busy at work in the lab, in the midst of his dramatic, atmospheric lighting. "She has an incredible gravity in those photographs." Wanda sits on the Cesca chair by the window, draping her red silk kimono sleeves on the tubular-steel chair arms. The thunderclaps are becoming louder, more frequent, and the room flashes from dark to light. She hopes Sterling will really talk to her tonight.

"The gravity, as you call it, was hers." He thought he wouldn't want her to talk about Lenore. He tries not to think of Lenore at all, but it's impossible. He remembers the day they married on a whim, after years of living together in Saint-Germain-des-Prés. An abrupt civil ceremony early in the morning, and they drove to the South of France, hundreds of kilometers, through Limoges and Toulouse and all the villages along the way. The rain was falling on top of a thin covering of snow.

"I loved her," he says. "I don't see why it takes a published volume of correspondence to prove it to the world. Or why anyone should care."

"That's our century for you," she says, looking out the window again. She's known about Lenore Hayden and Sterling Cronheim since she was ten years old, when she would spend hours in her room reading all the encyclopedias and biographies she could. She was becoming curious about other lives, other times.

He still doesn't know she hardly has any friends, though she isn't shy or antisocial. Some have died, left the city, stopped calling, or shown themselves to be racists. She goes to receptions at galleries and museums where people she knows linger for hours, talking in lobbies or on sidewalks. They scatter, not seeing one another till the next event. It's

12

the phones, some say. Phones are too expensive. The world isn't shrinking so much as disappearing.

Later, as she drifts to sleep, she remembers how she met Sterling in Battery Park City, at Hurricane Principia Gallery, with its triangular and hexagonal rooms on the penthouse floor of a red granite high-rise, walls covered with neon art, long needles of light. She was alone in the gallery when the tall, slender man in Levi's, white Oxford shirt, and gray tweed suit jacket stepped in. He took off his fedora and began to sketch as he looked at the exhibit.

She walked up beside him and they talked about the exhibit. She tried to look at the leather-bound sketchbook in his hand, but he closed it. She asked him what sort of artwork he did.

"I was a Modernist," he told her, so solemnly she believed he was joking at first. "I believed that art could change the world."

She knew right then he was Sterling Cronheim. Born in Wisconsin, spent most of his life in Europe. Disappeared one day, body and soul, no proof that he'd ever died. He looked and sounded just like the Cronheim she'd seen in an old NBC broadcast, rerun not too long ago on one of the art channels. He and the interviewer sat in a library, Cronheim in a dark, two-button suit, legs crossed, as if trying to contain his height within the television screen. His hair shimmery and bright in the key lighting; lighting so balanced there were no shadows anywhere. He was recapping his career, fending off the interviewer's harsh questions about Modernism's alleged failures, speaking softly, with the slightest trace of a German accent, never smiling.

"I have to get back to work. But could you meet me later, say around six?"

He nodded. She told him where she worked and he jotted down only the suite number in his sketchbook.

That night, after she had dinner with him, she took him to her loft and showed him her portfolio. Most of the buildings she had designed were earth-sheltered houses and apartment-office complexes with two or three sublevels. But the soil was eroding, building codes were strict. They were paper buildings for now; she and everyone else at the Consortium were too busy with corporate parks and planned communities to pursue visions. And all the infrastructure projects: restoring the elevateds and subways, rerouting trolley lines, constructing skywalks, rebuilding seawalls, platforms, bridges, overpasses, and landfills.

She turned off the lights as they sat across from each other on the aquamarine chintz chairs in the living room, a threadbare Spanish Berber rug between them. A remastered Pablo Casals recording of a Bach cello suite played softly. She told Sterling in detail about the restoration projects. He said very little but listened carefully, his silhouette nodding generously.

"We've got something in common, Werner. Neither of us really belongs in this era," she said. He was calling himself by his middle name and had adopted Schmidt as a surname. She kept talking about the past, trying to get him to talk about his. "I've always wanted to be a flapper. I used to have a white silk sheath dress. I wore it to a party and it fell apart. There I was, shivering out on a terrace sixty stories above the street in nothing but somebody's raincoat. I kept the pieces and my mother said she was going to make doll clothes out of them. But she hasn't got time, now that she's responsible for the mental health of everybody in the South Bronx." She paused, thinking of how much she missed her mother, who'd been in Washington, D.C., at a conference all week. "Sometimes I think she's my only friend in the world."

She took an old black-and-white photograph of her mother from the rosewood sideboard behind the sofa. She turned on the halogen uplighter beside his chair and stooped next to him with the photograph. He looked at it closely, fingered the beveled silver frame. In the photograph, her mother wore a dark V-neck dress and a single strand of pearls, a

14

marcasite tiara in her upswept hair. Twenty-six years old, gazing into the middle distance, the way the photographer told her to.

"Your mother is—"

"African-American. And so am I. My father isn't. He left my mother for a twenty-year-old Swedish model, whiter than Snow White. But I shouldn't talk, seeing as I look like some kind of Nordic." It still astounded and saddened her that she looked nothing like her mother. She frowned at her pale hands, turned off the uplighter.

"A biracial heritage isn't something to be ashamed of. You're beautiful," he said.

She took the photograph from him and put her hand on his knee. "Does that mean you want to stay here tonight?"

His silhouette drew up its angular shoulders, exhaled a loud, nervous breath.

"Well, *I* want you to stay. You shouldn't live in a hotel. Not even the Parker Meridien."

The storm is so forcefully disruptive it seems wrong to close windows and doors, fall asleep and ignore it. It will overtax the drainage systems and muddy water will flood the streets around the harbor. She gets up, puts on her kimono, goes to the kitchen, and turns on the recessed fluorescent tubes above the center island storage unit. Pots and pans hang from the ceiling racks, casting no shadows in the artificial light, which gives the black-and-white-checker-board tiled kitchen walls a blue-white glow. She pours herself a tall glass of orange juice and sits down at the table, four squares of black-and-white-lacquered pinewood, like the corner of a giant chessboard. She has a loft full of exquisite furniture: antiques, designer samples, heirlooms. Most of it from men who thought the way to woo an architect was to give her furniture. She can hardly remember who most of them were.

But now it's Sterling she's thinking about, trying to decide what he is to her. She wants to do the deciding. He sat up with her and listened to her talk most of that night and almost every night since. They didn't make love. She doubts they ever will. She turns on the tabletop shortwave radio on the counter, tunes in the Voice of Kenya, trying to improve her Swahili. But the signal is weak and the words a rumble, a mysterious liturgy.

I Don't Believe
in Magic

WANDA GOES TO THE Manhattan Starlight Ballroom, on 125th Street in Harlem, after work. It's around the corner from her hairdresser on Lenox Avenue, a benevolent woman in her eighties who wears floor-length calico dresses and speaks in an obscure Caribbean accent. She was dismayed that Wanda wanted her to cut her long hair today. But Wanda likes it, believing this short hairstyle will give her the credibility and maturity she feels but can't always project. She's tired of being a blonde, tired of people's hasty perceptions of her.

She sits at one of the round tables near the dance floor, which sparkles with tiny inlaid white lights flashing on and off in sequence. The ballroom, crowded with mostly retirees and dance students this early in the evening, was once a movie palace. She looks around at the lingering traces of elegance—a pipe organ that covers the wall to the left of the stage, and six-branch crystal chandeliers. On the stage, a big band plays a virtuoso arrangement of "That Old Black Magic" and people rush to the dance floor. She sips a club soda and turns down four offers to dance, shaking her head at the men, all of them more than twice her age. She takes out a sketchbook and works on detailing for a corridor of one of her earth-sheltered buildings.

All day, she's been sensing someone thinking about her. It could be Sterling. So enigmatic: a man too old to still be

17

alive, whom no one has seen for years. A man frighteningly complacent with his new identity, speculating on the global art market, living like someone who could never create art. Trying to hide all his sadness from her.

Or it's Bradley thinking of her. They used to come here almost every Friday, dance till three or four in the morning, drive upstate to his cabin in the Catskills for the rest of the weekend. A small cabin, in the middle of the woods, several kilometers away from anyone else. She always liked the isolation, completely different from East Hampton or Fire Island, which were overpopulated with weekending New Yorkers. They could relax in the cabin and forget their demanding careers for a while. But everything's changing. She would never have believed Bradley would try to kill himself.

Wanda thought it would always be perfect, because meeting Bradley was perfect. Like destiny.

She met him at the cobblestone streets and restored piers of the South Street Seaport at a private party thrown by a well-known New York entrepreneur. Hundreds of the city's elite gathered in the open air around Pier 17's multileveled boardwalks, outdoor cafés, cedar-paneled specialty shops, and boutiques. No one was poorly dressed or much over forty. She spotted a few motorcycle jackets, strategically torn, and faded blue jeans, black minidresses, and rainbow-colored mohawks.

He stood along the matte-black railing of the pier, his back to the harbor. He was dressed in a white linen suit with peaked lapels, and he was smoking a pipe. She was a few meters away, leaning against the plankwood stairway to the upper levels. They kept glancing at each other, smiling, but there was another man close by, intruding, trying to talk to her—an influential developer and a Consortium client, so she couldn't be too rude. She looked at the sunset, more fiery and blazing than most; the air choked with toxins that lured the warmest colors of the light spectrum. Thinking about complex chemistry helped her appear even more bored. She stared at the red brick incinerator smokestacks: three of them in view along the Brooklyn waterfront, pouring so much black smoke into the sky they threatened to turn the sunset into premature darkness. But the man still wouldn't leave her alone. He looked as if he'd stepped out of a war-bond poster in his navy-blue suit, slicked-back brown hair, and constant smile. He told her about his plans to replicate the design of the Flatiron Building in a 120-story office tower on a site in downtown Pittsburgh. She told him she disagreed on principle with the idea—the replication would be pretentious, unsound planning. She reminded him of how costly, if not impossible, it would be to find a contractor to execute the French Renaissance façade in rusticated limestone. Still, he asked her to come back with him to his apartment that evening to make preliminary sketches. She was disgusted enough to start laughing out loud, but instead, she coolly suggested he speak with the general manager of the Architects Consortium and muttered some well wishes.

She walked away, slipping past a group of tall women in silk dresses and strings of pearls, searching for somewhere to stand along the railing. The man followed her and tapped her shoulder.

"Listen, I'd really like to get to know you," he said, smiling. He paused, as if expecting thanks from her. She didn't say anything. Flustered, he said, "A friend of mine says you're black. I told him I had to get a close-up look and see for myself."

"Well, this is as close a look as you'll ever get." She glared at him long enough to make him blush and grin. She'd met literally hundreds of men just like him; she could almost laugh at how charming and complimentary they thought they were. Even her current beau, a divorced cardiologist eighteen years her senior, wasn't so much different from these others. A reluctant socialite, he really wanted no life outside of his work at Cornell Medical Center. He bought her Art Deco jewelry, collectibles, and Japanese stocks, all of which were escalating in value. It was invariably the same, the same conversations, the same gifts. She was to meet him later that evening for dining and dancing at the Rainbow Room. Well, he was an excellent dancer, she reminded herself, and she liked the spectacular views from the sixty-fifth floor, the city magically serene. She found a quiet spot on the pier and looked out at the harbor. The other man walked up to her, the lighted pipe in his hand.

"I don't mean to intrude, but I couldn't help overhearing. It's terrible what they put us through," he whispered.

"Us?"

He nodded, with weary emphasis. They looked at each other closely, not smiling, not feeling the usual social necessity. He was as white as she, and like her had brown eyes. He had wavy hair combed straight back from his high forehead and widow's peak, a slightly darker blond than hers, which was truly the color of tupelo honey. She used to try to explain her hair color as luminous, harvest moon, or a mystical color she never saw in real life except in some medieval frescos of the Madonna and Child. Not a white person's head of hair, in other words. But she knew she would never have to explain this to him. They were both Hollywood blacks, the way Elizabeth Taylor was once a Hollywood Egyptian and Burt Lancaster a Hollywood Indian. She wondered if he carried a wallet photo of a parent or grandparent as she did, like a membership card to the club he didn't apparently belong to.

She motioned him to follow and they walked away from the crowds, to where the pier faced the Brooklyn Bridge, its lighted arches sparkling in the distance. The crescent moon was rising above the span like someone's perfect dream of New York.

He puffed on his pipe, filling the air with a pine-like aroma. "You know, I'm sure I've seen you at the Architects

Consortium. I drop in every once in a while to check up on my friend Mackenzie Johnson. He's been designing an active solar house for me. But I can't build it now."

"Bankruptcy, divorce, or death? Do you want to talk about it?" she asked in the direct but empathetic style of her psychiatrist mother.

He looked away and puffed on his pipe for a moment, an almost imperceptible tremor in his hand. "Let's go somewhere," he whispered, clasping her hand with both of his own. He forgot he'd been holding his pipe and it fell into the gray water around them.

It gets later and later. Bradley isn't here, but she was afraid he wouldn't be. Her sketches frustrate her. She's never drawn freehand as well as she wants to, and the mathematics of perspective are too taxing in the dim light and smokiness of the ballroom. She wonders if it's time to really worry, to call the police or even Bradley's attorney parents, Eleanor Langford and William Stewart, who, with their international connections, do what ordinary investigators can't. She can't forget that night at the office and how she let him run away. How ugly and deserted the streets were. Nowhere for him to go.

•

The next day, she walks from the Port Chester Metro North station to her mother's house, past ostentatiously restored Victorian houses with trellises, miniature willow trees, pines. The house is at least the eleventh one her mother has lived in; she and Wanda moved all over the South and Southwest, wherever Charles's Air Force career took them. Whether at Edwards, Maxwell, Cape Canaveral, or elsewhere, Wanda would sneak outside to look at the flat and endless airfields beyond the tall steel fences, and the mysterious security system. She and the other children believed the laser sweeps would disintegrate a person. The memories are faint, riding along with the swing melodies on her Walkman, broadcast live from the Statler Hotel Ballroom. A light rain begins as she rings the doorbell, puts the wireless earphones in her pocket.

Francine opens the door. "Wanda! I'm so glad to see you." Her mother hugs her and leads her into the Georgian foyer, the pale olive walls decorated with framed presentation drawings Wanda has done of buildings under construction in Montreal and Osaka. Francine has changed very little over the years. She has the stature and poised presence of a great concert singer. Elegant, as usual, in a gray pinstripe suit and mauve silk high-collar blouse, her jet-black hair pulled back in a French twist; silver streaks at her temples like a perfectly placed theatrical flourish.

"You're looking well, slim and trim as ever," Francine says, hugging her again. "And I like your haircut. You look just like Rita Hayworth in *The Lady from Shanghai*."

"Rita Hayworth? This is your African-American daughter you're talking about," she says, pulling away from her mother and glancing at herself in the round Trafalgar mirror above the oak banister, its frame a carved giltwood snake swallowing its own tail. The mirror distorts like a fish-eye lens, and she hates what she sees, herself so pale and white. Not glamorous at all. She doesn't have the patience for makeup except the Ebony Fashion Fair powders she layers on sometimes, trying to give herself some color. But she will never have even a hint of her mother's beautiful dark coloring. She puts her coat across the table in the foyer.

"Honey, I can't exactly say you look like Cicely Tyson," her mother says, hanging the coat in the closet.

Wanda turns away and steps into the living room, with its rosewood and gauffraged velour sofa and matching *bergères* in delicate shades of aqua. A mantel full of cameo glass vases and sepia-toned photographs of great-grandparents, aunts and uncles Wanda never knew, all staring out from their silver frames as if they are frightened and uncomfortable in their starched Sunday best. She sits down on the sofa. "You never visit and you compare me to dead movie stars."

22

Francine sits beside her, taking a cigarette from a pack of Salems on the sofa table, lighting it. She pinches one of the sleeves of Wanda's Gibson Girl blouse. "Well, you wear dead people's clothes, so what's the difference?"

"Estate auctions are the only place to shop." Wanda stands, twirls, making her black trumpet skirt flare, and sits down. "Not that I have time to shop. Too busy at the Consortium. I'm learning all about project management and liability these days. Architecture's a lot like psychiatry, don't you think? You don't want your clients jumping out of windows and we don't want our windows falling out of buildings. And none of us wants our clients pushing us out the window."

Francine laughs. "That's for sure."

Wanda takes the cigarette from her mother and puts it out. "Save *my* lungs if you can't save your own. It's too bad I don't see that cardiologist anymore," she says. Not normally a passionate man, he could go on for hours, eloquently crusading against smoking, not with statistics, but with stories of his dying patients.

Wanda fingers the textured velour of the sofa as she tells her mother about the night Bradley tried to kill himself.

"I hope he turns up. Alive." Francine puts an arm around her daughter and speaks soothingly: "But, honey, I honestly don't understand what you see in him."

"I need him in my life and you know exactly why." But from the beginning Francine considered Bradley too unstable. Why, Wanda doesn't know. Francine's met him only once, the three of them exchanging anecdotes about their respective years in academia, their voices and smiles complementing the swank Art Deco decor of an East Side bistro. "He's the only one who understands what I go through, and vice versa. People, even *our* people, take one look at me or Bradley and assume we have no right to sing the blues."

"I'm not blind to your pain, Wanda."

"Yes, you are. Everybody is." Her father most of all, though she doesn't know why she thinks of him now. She

23

tries to forget him. But when she closes her eyes she is a child again, with long blond ringlets and the pretty cotton print dresses with matching pinafores her grandmother made for her. She's in her father's office at the Air Force Station at White Sands, New Mexico, and he introduces her to his superior, the general, a man with hair whiter than she'd ever seen and rows of colorful medals on his uniform. He stooped and patiently explained each one to her. Then he turned to her father and kept saying over and over in his Southern drawl, A damn shame she's lost her mother. Her father nodded abruptly and looked down at his feet. The general put a consoling hand on his shoulder.

No, the seven-year-old Wanda told them, my mommy's not dead. She goes to school at night and we don't see her much.

Her father glared at her. Flustered, he told the general about Wanda's fantasies of her mother being alive. But Wanda interrupted and insisted she was. Finally the general left, puzzled, shaking her tiny hand. Her father used a steel ruler on her, right in the office. It wasn't the first time she'd forgotten to pretend her mother was dead.

Now she doesn't know what the lies were or why she had to tell them. Charles and she couldn't have been pretending Francine was dead, not in the closed environment of the Air Force bases. She wishes she could remember those days more clearly.

"Wanda, you've gone silent on me," Francine says.

"I started thinking about Charles, and I don't know why." She hasn't seen him for five years. She decides right now that she doesn't ever intend to see him again.

"Is it that hard to believe? He's your father, after all."

Wanda shrugs. She thinks of what she hears people say. That the naming of something is the beginning of its reality. If she says it enough, it will be true. She will never see him again.

24

Haunted by
the Visible

AT LUNCHTIME, Wanda takes a long walk in Battery Park
and the adjacent landfills. The rain keeps drug dealers,
panhandlers, and muggers away and draws in the Coast
Guard. Dressed in their Day-Glo orange ponchos and boots,
they ride through the waterfront streets in white vans with
chains draped around the tires. She frowns at them, overly
loud and rude, harassing her as she walks along the makeshift
boardwalk in Battery Park. The rain makes it even more of
a swamp spilling into the harbor. WPA crews are bulldozing
piles of garbage, swerving around trees and benches, unin-
tentionally grinding most of it into the mud. Clustered
around the fireboat house are more shanties and tents than
she can count, constructed of old rags, cardboard, large
empty cable spools, all kinds of discarded materials. Their
residents hide during the daytime, under seawalls and in
abandoned subway stations, staying away from the Coast
Guard and the Port Authority police, both so vicious that
Amnesty International has cited them for human-rights
violations. A huge sign near the concession booths in front
of Castle Clinton and the ferry landing has an airbrushed
photograph of the mayor and a controversial developer and
promises: AN EXCITING, ALL NEW JEWEL OF THE HARBOR,
BATTERY PARK, in eighteen months.

Through her transparent bubble umbrella, everything is
distorted, a blurring of light and dark. Crowds of tourists,

Wall Street professionals, day laborers from nearby loading docks, and Coast Guard officers stand along the rebuilt cast-iron gangways. Seagulls perch on the railings, their electronic-sounding chirps louder than the rain. The WPA is always busy, but the sea level is rising too quickly. They import material for seawalls and platforms from Appalachia, truck caravans rolling down the West Side Highway every other day. She knows New York will have to become a canal city or eventually be abandoned. Twenty years, two hundred years from now?

She's waiting here for Bradley. He left a terse message, audio only, on her answering console. *One o'clock at the Reformed Church of Battery Park.* It's what he calls this collection of steel-gray park benches arranged like church pews on either side of the East Coast War Memorial, graffiti-covered stone monoliths so acid-rain-damaged the names etched on them are completely illegible. The rain turns to hail, feels like broken glass on her hands. No Bradley and her lunch hour almost over. She isn't surprised, really; how can she be, after that night?

He's beginning to remind her of one of her father's subordinates at White Sands Missile Range in New Mexico. His name was Chad and he was quite tall, towering over everyone. She was ten years old and he was the first person she'd ever met who, like her, looked white but wasn't. He showed her pictures of his family; he wasn't ashamed of who he was. She wondered what her father thought of this, but she never asked. Chad would read to her on Saturday afternoons, those hot desert afternoons, outside the barracks, her mother nearby studying for exams or writing papers.

During the Memorial Day parade in Alamogordo, Chad suddenly eased his rifle from his shoulder, put the barrel in his mouth, and pulled the trigger. She was among the crowds on the sidewalks, at most ten or fifteen meters away from him. A terrifying crack of sound, Chad tumbling to the ground, his fellow airmen surrounding him, others fending off the crowds. The first and last time she'd ever seen someone die right in front of her.

She sits down on one of the benches and tries to put that day out of her mind. Bradley, too. She thinks about an arts and cultural center for a site on the Toronto harbor. It's an international design competition and she dreams of winning, with or without her colleagues, two architects from the Consortium's Guam office. They are identical twins; she and everyone else call them the Brothers Guam. Originally from Harlem, dropouts from the Army Corps of Engineers, about her age, swearing they will never return to the mainland. She has twice-weekly viewphone conferences with them; they tell each other political jokes, invent rumors to pass along the Consortium's communications networks, agree on nothing at all. They want to design a tall, needle-like structure like the CN Tower to enhance Toronto's Futurama skyline. She wants to build low or entirely underground, if the topography is suitable. She's been studying computer-generated images and engineering studies of the site taken from satellite data and the World Geological Congress's latest fractals. But building is still risky, and no computer analysis can predict all the rainstorms and flooding that go on for weeks all over North America. Tectonic plates shifting, topsoil vanishing in windstorms and floods, the ocean swallowing the coastlines.

She thinks of joining the Design Brigade, architects based in Pennsylvania and upstate New York who are converting downtown business districts in decaying industrial cities into residential areas, helping homesteaders in abandoned high-rises and shopping concourses. Or going to what's left of rural America, way out West, to build Architerra complexes in the mountainous, rocky land the local governments are trying to turn into toxic waste disposal sites. She is tired of working on Consortium projects, planned communities and corporate parks that sprawl for hundreds of kilometers, districts with no zoning laws or official names, with private police squadrons and motion-detecting lasers sweeping the land.

It reminds her of what a critic from Yale said on the Art, Architecture, Antiques Channel the other night. The Only One World concept of the global corporation is entirely inappropriate for an architectural firm. With its ninety offices worldwide, a firm like the Architects Consortium has no focus, no understanding of context, and builds the same kinds of projects anywhere and everywhere, like fast-food franchises, irrespective of local environmental and social conditions. The critic drew parallels to what agribusiness conglomerates do: taking away more than thirty nutrients from a grain of wheat, putting back four, and calling the final product "enriched." This is how the Consortium "enriches" the environment.

Wanda had always wanted to be an architect. She remembers the tremendously large buildings she used to see on Air Force bases: hangars, silos, transport stations. Monumental structures of steel-reinforced concrete rising out of the flat land. She wanted to be able to do that, make the buildings rise out of the land. Now she doesn't want to admit it's why she became an architect. Better to talk about being overwhelmed with the magnificent ruins of Pueblo Bonito at Chaco Canyon in New Mexico and reading all she could about both the pueblos and the Anasazi who built them.

She's achieved her goal after years at Harvard: it's all that anyone has to know. And that the Architects Consortium hired her immediately after her graduation. Then the licensing ordeal, two years ago. In an enormous customs hall, near the South Street Seaport, in long and perfect rows of banquet tables and folding chairs she sat with hundreds of fellow architects, with her credit-card-sized computer, agonizing over complex problems of design, structural technology, and construction. And integrated systems; helping the computer help you, one of her design studio professors used to say, with heavy irony. It was frightening sometimes, designing a system that adjusted the ventilation when you lit a cigarette or turned on lights as you walked from one room to another. She passed the exam, all eleven parts of it, designing and presenting a super-insulated five-story apartment building in the allotted twelve hours. Impressing the exam board with her grasp of structural and environmental requirements, and with the unusual design: a low, sloping roof full of skylights and trapezoidal windows that cut into the red brick and corrugated iron like relief sculpture. Afterward, she kept dreaming about the building; she was the stationary one and the building crept around her.

Leave the planet for good, buy an L-5 condo, her academic adviser told her, and took her own advice. But outer space is for the rich, the military, and the global corporations. Just another form of escape. She could do what Cronheim has done: crack the information networks to change her identity and collect art. Years of unrestrained speculation have already made art many times more valuable than oil or precious metals.

She hasn't lived long enough to understand pain, Cronheim keeps saying. It's no use telling him what it was like growing up on the Air Force bases in the South, the names children called her, or the lies her father made her tell that fooled no one. Building was her escape, her way out, she told Cronheim. And if she were a little more bitter, her buildings might be taller, starker, more foreboding than she could stand.

She walks back to work, slowly, on Broadway. The traffic is backed up, as usual, weaving around delivery vans, parked near the back offices of brokerage firms and investment banks that occupy the decaying Art Moderne buildings. The Ninth Avenue El speeds by, sending a shower of soot and cinders down on her and the rest of the street. People shove each other, umbrellas in the way.

Back at the office, she finds Mackenzie, asks him if he knows where Bradley is. But Mackenzie is distracted, trying

29

to videofax some drawings to Tokyo. He says he's stayed up two nights in a row and she can tell he isn't exaggerating. He's leaning against the terminal table, gripping the back of an ergonomic chair. His hair, usually spiked so acutely it looks like jet-black florist's wire, is falling down over his face and he's thinner than his usual anorexic thin.

He tells her Bradley is having conflicts with one of his Frankfurt clients, and thus working and fretting more than usual.

"Bradley's suicidal," she says.

"To state the obvious. He reads too much Sartre, Dostoevsky, and Eldridge Cleaver. That's enough to make God suicidal."

His attempted wit irritates her. She's afraid Bradley's in trouble, going off the edge. She leaves Mackenzie to his work and goes back to her terminal, tugging at the large turquoise-and-silver Navajo ring on her left forefinger. It was a surprise gift from Bradley. What will happen, she wonders, when he finds out about Cronheim?

●

The next day, she is sitting in her mother's office at the Sara Josephine Baker Medical Center in the South Bronx. Narrow, with floor-to-ceiling bookshelves, large windows behind the pale birch Aalto desk. Part of the office is set up with a classic black leather psychiatrist's couch, a Carver chair, and a halopane uplighter beside it. A spiral notebook with Francine's tiny, ideographic handwriting is on the desk beside an ozone journal, large as an unabridged dictionary. It must be from Tyler, her father's younger sister, an environmental lobbyist and the only Stoller whom Wanda has been able to befriend. Outside the fifteenth-floor window is a view of the hundreds of destroyed and derelict city blocks of the South Bronx.

Francine walks in, carrying a stack of files. Her maroon

shawl-collar suit jacket and her dark hair glisten in the diagonals of sunlight pouring in through the Venetian blinds. She looks distracted and tired, and Wanda wonders if this surprise visit was a good idea after all, and will her mother, so immersed in saving the South Bronx, really listen to her? Francine kisses her and sits down at her desk. Wanda leans on one of its corners.

"I see Tyler's got you reading about the ozone layer."

"Well, you know Tyler. She's always trying to reach out to me. Now, what's so urgent that you braved the El to come way up here?" Francine toys with the half-moon reading glasses around her neck. "Does this have to do with Bradley?"

Wanda paces the office. Her ankle-boot heels click loudly on the peach-red quarry tile. "I don't want to talk about him. I don't know where he is. I've got something really important to tell you. But you can't ever tell anybody, all right?"

"If it's that important to you, of course."

"It is. It's about this man I met." Wanda sits down on the Eames chair in front of Francine's desk. She tugs at her gray knife-pleated skirt, feeling uneasy. She knows she shouldn't tell her mother about Sterling, but she's got to tell someone. "He's Cronheim. The artist."

"The one who disappeared a long time ago?" Wanda nods. "Now, honey, it's been quite a few years since Cronheim disappeared, hasn't it?" Francine says, clearly skeptical but amused.

"I know. But he's still alive." Wanda leans closer to the desk, lowers her voice. "I met him at a gallery downtown and I just knew who he was. By the end of the day, I felt completely comfortable with asking him to move in with me. It's taken weeks of pleading, but he's going to do it."

"Well, this is a . . . surprise." Francine laughs. "I'd hate to think what poor Bradley will say."

"And I suppose you really care about poor Bradley."

31

Wanda laughs in spite of herself. "Listen, meeting one of the great artists of our century doesn't happen every day," she says.

"You'd better be careful, girl," Francine says, gesturing with a fountain pen for emphasis. "Sounds to me as if there's an element of fantasy at work."

"You don't believe me, do you? I'm telling you, he's Cronheim and he's never looked better. Kind of like those leading men when they start getting older and they still look so good it doesn't matter if they're sixty or seventy. I just wish you could meet him, he's so—" She pauses, looking for the right word and wishing her mother weren't so disbelieving. "Well, he's *Cronheim*."

"I never knew you had all this adulation for Cronheim. Maybe a bit more than mere adulation? You're up here saying he's leading-man material." Two calls come through on Francine's phone; she quickly forwards them away.

Wanda reconsiders what she's said. She doesn't really think "leading man" when she thinks of Cronheim. More like the last survivor of a dead era, as quaint or romantic as that seems. But it's neither, she thinks, remembering Cronheim's reticence and pain. She knows her mother won't understand or believe her. "That's just him. I don't have any say over how good or bad he looks," she says.

"Well, let's talk about what you *do* have some say over," Francine says, leaning back in her chair, steepling her chin. "I don't like the idea of you picking up strange men and I don't care who they tell you they are. The trouble is, you've been too isolated lately. You need to get out and meet some real people, not viewphone images."

"I just met one is what I'm trying to tell you. But you don't hear me," Wanda says. She's profoundly disappointed that her mother hasn't really listened to her. There's no one else she can tell. "You're too caught up in all your psychologizing."

32

"It's the best thing I know," Francine says, sounding much more self-assured than she feels. She's thinking of how a month ago she could drink too much champagne at the birthday party in East Hampton of her latest beau, a U.S. Court of Appeals judge, and lean against a Steinway grand and sing "The Man That Got Away" in her uncertain contralto. Of course there have been plenty of men, all distinguished, devoted to her; she keeps letting them go. But she didn't sleep for most of that night, thinking about the lyrics and the man she met more than thirty years ago in southern Florida when she was walking along the highway near her grandmother's house in Belle Glade, where she was staying the summer before her senior year at Spelman.

There he was, Major Charles Stoller, on the shoulder of the road, a few hundred meters from the city-limits sign, the hood of his sky-blue Volkswagen up, emergency lights flashing. Looking like all the other Air Force men who passed by on their way to the Cape: the same regulation haircut, so short it was impossible to tell what color the hair was, crisp dress uniform, a row of medals, shoes polished to a high shine. He looked ceremonial and distressed all at once. She didn't hesitate to walk up to this white man and try to help him. Her charity surprised him and he was too flustered to smile or look her in the eye at first. But she insisted he come along with her to the house. It was a long way back to the Cape on U.S. 441 and she was already starting to worry about him. Treacherous 441 was dubbed "highway to heaven," white crosses erected along the sharp curves where people had died in accidents.

They sat on the porch, waiting for the tow truck, and listened to the radio, to big bands playing at the Surf Ballroom. Her grandmother kept to herself in the living room, caning a chair, barely speaking to Charles. The neighborhood, with its prefabricated houses built on plat-forms, enclosed yards filled with dirt instead of grass, was crowded that evening with people having barbecues in the sweltering late afternoon. Across the street several children leaned their elbows on the fence and stared at Charles, the first white man some of them had ever seen.

She assumed she'd never see him again; they lived in different parts of the state and had nothing in common. But he started calling her every day and visiting her on those summer weekends. They would go driving. Charles loved to drive; he'd bring his jeep and they would go far into the Everglades and camp out on the high grounds or on the remote, undeveloped beaches near Cape Coral. They were always hiding, always way out in the wilderness, far from the Jim Crow diners and motels and the county sheriffs who would try to arrest them for miscegenation.

"You just be careful, young lady," Francine says finally, realizing she has been staring past Wanda, toward the bookshelves. "Be careful with this 'Cronheim' of yours."

"You're getting too motherly for words," Wanda says. Or judgmental, she thinks. All she can expect from her mother, it seems, are these homilies on the dangers of fantasy and social isolation. "Too motherly," she says again.

But Francine barely hears her. She's disgusted with herself, for remembering the past the way it never happened, forgetting the struggles. She and Charles spent a night behind bars in Clewiston. The charge was speeding, but that didn't put them in jail. The deputies searched the car for contraband and when they found a box of condoms they upped the charge to miscegenation, held them overnight without bail. Poorly ventilated, mildewed cells empty because prisoners (not criminals, just ordinary people like Charles and her, caught in the technicalities and the hatred that were part of living) were en route to the penitentiary near St. Petersburg. But there was no trial; the charges were dropped the next morning. Charles had chosen his one phone call well. He never told her whom he called or what happened. She didn't know it then, but his silences had begun. Places and people he would never talk about. Shy, he'd tell her.

•

Sterling is packing the last of his things, leaving the Parker Meridien for good. The suite is too fussed over, jade-green Hepplewhite wing chairs and sofa, formal dining room with a mahogany refectory table, reverse diamond-match rosewood veneer walls. White velvet draperies covering the view of nothing but the windows of other people on West Fifty-sixth Street trying to look out. He's never felt comfortable here and he can't pack up and leave fast enough.

All his sketchbooks, suits, shirts, jeans, and the stacks of catalogues from Sotheby's and Christie's fit into a gray Pullman and matching garment and carry-on bags, reminding him of too many transatlantic flights, part of his joyless art collecting. Buying and selling the art of the Modern era, works by his friends and contemporaries. Managing his sizable collection with the help of his financial advisers at Nomura Securities and Deutsche Bank AG. Lending most of the art to galleries and museums around the world, stashing the remainder in Geneva in his many safe-deposit vaults, never seeing it. He is wealthy, embarrassed with wealth, moving further away from who he was.

He has nothing but an endless succession of hotel rooms to look forward to, and his tiny postwar houses in Berlin and Geneva. He realizes how much he wants to stay with Wanda, listen to her talk. He couldn't have known half as much when he was her age. He was a law-school dropout, trying to decide whether to be a dancer or a painter, floundering around in Munich and, later, in Berlin. Joining Novembergruppe and Arbeitsrat für Kunst and other organizations of artists, designers, and architects anxious as he to find some truths. But Wanda is completely on her own, too brilliant for the Architects Consortium and its impersonal and empty agenda.

35

He turns on the telescreen in the bedroom, sits back down on the bed, and leans across his lap, in the position that remedies fainting.

Spacious, comfortable living . . . with a view like no other, says the off-camera corporate spokeswoman, her voice mixed on multitracks of sound coming through the Surround speakers discreetly installed in the ceiling. He sits up and watches the stars, supernovas, and quasars drift by, steadily as grains of Morton Salt, reliably falling in the rain. But now the girl on the package has grown up, left her umbrella, left the planet. *Suntel makes the stars your home.* The lush and expansive synthesizer music lingers after the voice-over. *You are tuned to the Art, Architecture, Antiques Channel,* says another announcer, who proceeds to list the channel's corporate underwriters.

Waiting for the auction to begin, he stares at the painting on the opposite wall, of the Grand Canyon at sunset. He would still like to ride a mule down the canyon, as he wanted to years ago, but now he can only watch television and marvel at the haunting whiteness of the wall fabric and wainscotting. He could keep living in this hotel, or another one like it, and never see dirt and dust. Pretend the revolutions, wars, and epidemics on television will never touch him.

The auction begins, live from Sotheby's in London. He reaches for the teletext link-up console, a tiny hexagonal screen on a swing arm attached to the nightstand, to signal his bids to the auctioneers. Paintings fill the telescreen: Picasso, Matisse, Klee, Kandinsky, Mondrian, Moholy-Nagy, O'Keeffe, Cronheim.

"Mine," he mumbles. The bidding on his four paintings escalates. *Composition with Gray,* he called each one, numbering them successively. He painted them in Chicago, right after the war. For years, the war made canvas so scarce he and his colleagues had to paint on boards. But these canvases were large, so large each brushstroke was a gestural dance, and the energy released itself in colors, muted and somber.

The paintings were somehow about Lenore, about losing her.

Lenore, Lenore, he whispers, trying to forget. Forget Lenore and forget his own life. Let the world sell his paintings to private collectors, corporations, and foundations who will hire designers to plan color schemes accordingly. He can't help but be curious about who purchases them; his canvases peering at flawlessly decorated homes, offices, atriums, and lobbies, or in warehouses, unseen. But wherever the paintings go, they will continue to rise in value with the global art market, each one worth hundreds of times more money than he ever had in those years.

He makes his bid for Moholy-Nagy's *Jealousy*. The pale green digits on the teletext change so quickly they are blurs. He's competing with two other bidders from Tokyo, for a photomontage Moholy began over a long weekend in Weimar and completed a few years later. Sterling feels unnerved, placing the highest bid, buying his friend's photomontage. Sotheby's will ship it from their vaults in Madrid to his safe-deposit vault in central Geneva, a short trolley ride away from his modern, flat-roofed house. *Jealousy*, sealed away, appreciating by the hour.

He changes the channel to Australia International. Two genetic engineers in Melbourne talk about stacking and reshaping the building blocks of life and about their experimental group of five-year-olds, whom the press call Millennium Babies. One of the children, in a crisp white shirt and short pants, tells reporters he will live forever. He tells them forever means he will be able to play outdoors so long his parents will let him live there. He doesn't know he was once a frozen egg, left unclaimed for years. Sterling changes channels.

Modern architecture died the day in St. Louis that the Pruitt-Igone housing projects, designed by Minoru Yamasaki, were demolished less than thirty years after they were built. Yamasaki is, as we

37

know, the architect of the World Trade Center in New York. And why were the projects destroyed? Well, the structure of the buildings themselves, the so-called Le Corbusierian streets in the air—extra-wide corridors and play areas for children—encouraged a criminal and back-alley life within the buildings. A clear example of architecture adversely influencing behavior. There is overwhelming evidence suggesting that the projects were built this way intentionally, to destroy minority communities.

You lost sight, all of you, he thinks. The panel of experts on the Art for the People Channel are surrounded by scale models of Wright's Johnson Wax buildings and Mies van der Rohe's Seagram Building. A British and an African-Caribbean woman and two Japanese men; color coordination, Wanda cynically calls it. Re-Visionists, on a channel run by Re-Visionists, the only ones who would care about the death of Modernism. More Modern than the Modernists, they have the excitement and exuberance he once had for technology. But it isn't the technology of global communications, computers, space stations, and satellites; they want to clean up the air and the ocean, understand the enigma of Gaia, the earth as a single, unified organism. The true technology, of planetary survival and harmony, not expansion and progress. Their artworks and architecture are sometimes mistakenly called Neominimalist, but he knows their work is all about the light, motion, and energy in the world.

●

"I was worried about you," she says. He's waking up on the sofa in Wanda's living room, not knowing how he got here. She tells him what happened. When she came home, she found him asleep in front of the telescreen, apparently having a nightmare. He reaches for her, touches the soft Kaska chemise she's wearing, until gravity pulls his hand back to the bed.

"Sterling, can you hear me?" She grabs his hand, squeezes

it tightly, and he looks up at her. His eyes are watery and unfocused, like an old man's. He *is* old, she thinks, and all his nostalgia and sadness could kill him quickly.

"You cut your hair," he says, sounding alarmed, as if the cutting has made her suffer. Her hair is very short and wavy and he has to reach too far to touch it. He takes his handkerchief from his pocket, wipes his eyes. She touches his shoulder so gently he wants to cry. He was dreaming about William, whom he hadn't dreamt about in years. Thanks to the explicit biographies, anyone could learn about his relationship with William Thompson, who was born into a wealthy Toronto family and left home for the United States at an early age. One of the few African-American architects in the Modern era. A Walter Gropius associate, a bright young star.

That night, he dreams about William again. He receives a letter from him. It is hot, Philadelphia in a heat wave, windows wide open in his large, Italianate villa house, ceiling fans tossing the humid air. He looks at the envelope, wonders if it is significant that William has misspelled his own name. Sterling reaches for the Zippo and the pewter ashtray on the end table. He unfolds the letter, tears the heavy cotton bond paper into small pieces, places them in the ashtray, lights them. He watches the paper slowly turn to charcoal-gray petals. The smell of smoke will linger in the room for hours. He stares at the flames, believing they will help him forget William. Forget the sneaking around, the lies, the terrible effort not to smile, not to touch.

He wakes himself from the dream. Gratified, as always, that he's learned to recognize when he's dreaming. William met him far, far too late, he's thinking as he clutches his hands, trying to stop their tremor. He gets out of bed, puts on his robe, goes downstairs to the kitchen. He likes how Wanda's designed it; the stark black-and-white enameled walls and counters look impervious to every possible destruction.

39

But it isn't so. Entire nations still vanish overnight. Like Germany between the wars. Not that he knew the worst of those days firsthand; he was in Paris by then, receiving letters from friends who were trying to flee the country. He remembers the early lean days in Germany, the billion-deutsche-mark notes that bought no more than a sandwich and a cup of coffee.

It isn't the deutsche mark he's thinking of right now. Wanda's convinced she discovered him in Hurricane Principia Gallery. She doesn't know he'd been following her for days, ever since the Saturday afternoon he saw her heading downtown on the Third Avenue trolley, dressed in an elegant black-and-white houndstooth suit. She was sketching in a spiral-bound notebook. He stood a few seats away, moved closer to peer over her shoulder. Her sketch was of an earth-bermed town house, crescent-shaped, with equidistantly placed gables. She conveyed the essence of the structure with an economy of line he thought phenomenal. He couldn't stop looking at the sketch. Or at her. A woman with an understated glamour. He wasn't a man to notice women.

She rode the trolley to the end of the line, Park Row. He followed her home. The street she lived on, in the gutted-out waterfront district, was full of debris. For days, he rose early, took a taxi from the Parker Meridien to the corner of Chambers Street and West Broadway. He'd stand outside the building and wait for her. He found out she worked at the Savings of America Tower on Broad Street and he'd follow discreetly behind her as she took long walks at lunchtime.

The day he followed her to Hurricane Principia Gallery he knew he'd finally talk to her. But what could he tell her? He had never known the proper lines, never tried to meet a woman this way. She was looking over the artwork. Neon art that didn't interest him. He appreciated the artist's originality in approaching light and color, but neon reminded him of all the cheap hotels he'd passed through in his lifetime. He pulled out his sketchbook, forgetting he made a point of never sketching in public.

Years ago he had met Lenore in a gallery in Berlin. But he had no time to float into memories; Wanda had started talking to him. He couldn't believe he told her he was a Modernist. A Modernist, as someone might call himself an accountant or a teacher. As if, being a Modernist, he fit properly and unremarkably into the social strata. He knew she would recognize him. He hadn't let anyone know who he was for years. He told her his name was Werner Schmidt, that he was an art collector and lived in New York on and off a few weeks during the year.

It happened so quickly, her knowing who he was and begging him to live with her. He's afraid it will all go wrong now, just as quickly. Bradley is still missing, but he knows he will return. And Wanda will start spending her nights with Bradley, leaving him alone to wander the streets of what used to be the greatest city in the world. He closes his eyes, thinks of Lenore. He wishes he could still dream about her.

Meeting Her at the Potzdamer Platz

Painting is an art, and art is not vague production, transitory and isolated, but a power which must be directed to the improvement and refinement of the human soul—to, in fact, the raising of the spiritual triangle.

WASSILY KANDINSKY

SHE WILL ASK HIM WHY he left America. Why he gave up law for dancing and dancing for art. Everything that is difficult to talk about. He is at a rolltop desk reading her letter under the dim light of the hobnail glass chandelier high above him. His drawings and paintings surrounding him here in Herwarth Walden's Sturm Gallery, three narrow, connecting rooms of a large stone house, on Potzdamer-strasse. The letter is handwritten in cautious, grammar-book German on perfumed parchment with a gold monogrammed *L*. By a woman who's bought two of his paintings and wants to meet him now. She assures him she understands and speaks German better than she writes it. He will keep silent and let her talk to him. In English.

He arranges to meet her later that day, and waits next to the stained-glass and ironwood revolving door of Café Josty, the ground floor of a building that resembles a miniature palace, with its limestone pilasters and segmental pediments above all the windows. Nearly dark and very windy as he waits, city lights beginning to glow through the branches of oak and linden trees along the streets intersecting Potzdamer Platz. Grand but decaying stone masonry buildings surrounding him, their soot-gray porticos and pillars turning black as night falls.

The young woman walks up to him. *"Guten Abend, Herr Cronheim,"* she says, smiling, her German precise. She is pretty in a soothing, tranquil way. He doesn't know how far from tranquil she is, that his entire life will change, irreversibly, after this evening. She is stylishly though not expensively dressed in a knee-length royal-blue sheath dress, cloche hat, muskrat coat draped over her shoulders, and long silk scarf so faded he can't tell what color it was supposed to be.

"I'm glad to meet you, Miss Hayden," he says, extending his hand.

"You speak English," she says, with clearly a relieved smile, and shakes his hand.

"Like quite a few people from Wisconsin," he says as they walk through the revolving doors into the tiny, cramped café, warmly lighted by the fireplace and opal glass pendant lamps. The walls are covered with large, framed daguerreotypes of Paris and Berlin street scenes. Many people sit alone at the round tables, writing or drawing, dressed in the leather bomber jackets and the lead-gray industrial work clothing the literati sometimes wear. Sterling and Lenore find a table opposite the fireplace, next to the windows.

"They didn't tell me you were American," she says, taking off her white gloves. "The Waldens, I mean."

"Herwarth tends to overlook my nationality. Being the forgiving sort," he says, laughing.

"Well, what can we expect from a man who says art is as inhuman as God?" she says, laughing with him. The young, black-haired waiter comes to their table and they order Viennese coffee. "But he and Nell certainly know talent when they see it." She leans closer to him and lowers her voice. "I like the juxtaposition of scientific clarity and spontaneity in

43

your work. It's so hard to put aesthetics into words. Much, much easier to say I'm thoroughly impressed." She smiles at him warmly and tells him she's heard he's a popular teacher at the Bauhaus. His colleagues and friends who know her say she's a brilliant scientist. It's all he knows about her, really, and that she likes to mingle among artists. She's a microbiologist at the Robert Koch Institute in Berlin, she says, before he has a chance to ask.

"Miss Hayden, you'll be glad to know word's gotten out in Weimar that you're a most intriguing woman," he says.

She laughs. "Possibly more *intrigued* than intriguing. By my work, that is. I happen to believe microorganisms are a sentient life form. They have a special kind of beauty all their own," she says, with a reverent intensity. "I don't think they mean to kill us. Most likely, they don't understand their effects upon us, or even that we're also life forms."

He doesn't know what to think of her and this talk of microorganisms. He'd tried to think of what she might ask him, but he hadn't thought of her or of her appearance. She looks very young in the soft light of candles and the pendulum lamp above the table; platinum-blond hair bobbed and finger-waved, a single-strand cultured pearl necklace and matching earrings. Heirlooms, he suspects. She's placed her brown leather accordion folder on the table, stuffed and overflowing with papers. It seems to double as a handbag. She's pale and fragile-looking (from living her life in laboratories, she will tell him), and he will always think he has to protect her from the outside world.

"Some of these microorganisms are tireless workers," she continues. "Putting the holes in Swiss cheese and other thankless jobs." She pauses as the waiter sets down their coffee. "But something tells me you'd rather talk about art."

"I feel a bit more qualified to talk about art, at least," he says, and she agrees, telling him she's read his article in Walden's art journal, *Der Sturm*. He's entitled it *"Farbe, Form, und Innere Notwendigkeit,"* or "Color, Form, and Inner Need."

His thoughts on the transcendental power of art and how this can be better expressed in abstract composition. That art must be more than wall decoration for the elite: it must comment dynamically and unhesitatingly upon modern life, society, and the human spirit.

"As Moholy-Nagy so succinctly puts it, art and life have had nothing to do with each other for much too long," he says.

"I've had a friendly argument or two with Moholy. His German is almost as bad as mine." She sips the fragrant coffee. "But art isn't life. Art simply *is*. The Bauhaus wants to throw its talented artists headfirst into the factories. Art and technology are headed toward collision, not unity. Just as we ourselves are. We'll build machines to do our factory work and thousands will lose their jobs. There's going to have to be a restructuring of society somewhere down the road. But that's getting into politics and you Bauhäuslers shy away from politics. Ironic since you're always accused of being Bolshevists. And your illustrious Herr Direktor Gropius wants to keep the Bauhaus politically neutral. I don't think he can do it; the whole political arena is moving so fast. Don't you sense it? The tempo of life itself is speeding up all the time."

"Of course. And your own tempo is quite something, Lenore Hayden. I can imagine you frighten more than a few of my fellow Bauhäuslers. Being so young and American besides."

"My Americanness will fade away, along with my youth." She laughs and lifts her cup toward him. "To my new American artist friend." She takes out a Turkish cigarette from a gold case and lights it with the candle on the table. She offers him a cigarette, but he takes the one from her hand and draws a deep drag. He surprises himself with this gesture of assumed intimacy. But he can't help it. Awkward as he feels right now, he knows he doesn't ever want to be without Lenore Hayden. Not understanding how or why this is, he shifts his attention to particulars: how well-spoken she is, a free thinker, and how they seem to be here in Germany for the same reasons. He glances away, toward the windows cut deeply into the stone masonry. He looks at her again and she is smiling.

"You seem quite young to be in Europe all by yourself," he says, pulling another drag from her cigarette.

"I'm twenty-four. You decide if that's young or not. And I'm not by myself; I live here with Kally Steiner, we've been best friends since our Barnard days. We work together at the institute. Her family's from Austria, so she speaks impeccable German. I probably depend on her too much in that way." She takes the cigarette back from him and puffs on it, silent for a moment, even a bit troubled. "How long have you been here?" she asks.

"Since I was your age."

"*Mein Herr,* you've gone from the sardonic to the elliptical." She smiles recondily and blows smoke rings. "I'll try another question. Are you married?"

"No. I've never married in my thirty-four years. And I've been known to be forthright, occasionally," he says, smiling back at her and sipping the coffee.

"How refreshing," she says, laughing. "Now, whatever is keeping you from marrying?"

He shrugs. This isn't a question he's anxious to answer. Or that he even knows how to answer. "I've hardly given it any thought. Besides, I'm completely immersed in the day-to-day matters at the Bauhaus. We can barely decide on a proper curriculum, let alone entertain all the Bolshevist notions we're said to have."

"So what kinds of notions are you entertaining? At the Bauhaus, I mean."

"I run the photography workshop, help oversee the metal workshop. Pass myself off as a photojournalist or a lighting-fixtures designer when I can profit from it. And yes, I am a *painter.*"

46

"At last, a Bauhäusler who calls himself a painter, with no apologies." She laughs until he joins in. "My opinion of you is growing by the second. But how can a man like you remain a bachelor?" He looks away as she casually leans back in her chair. Maybe she sees through him already, as if peering at the microscopic world makes seeing the world of humans painfully simple. He can't imagine he can keep his secrets from anyone.

•

He and Lenore have talked freely for hours, already like old friends at the café and later as they walked along Friedrichstrasse. The street was lively with music from the dance halls and cabarets, crowds of people drifting slowly about in their best furs and woolens. He realizes the evening has been like the beginning of courtships he has heard or read about; he's never had a courtship. After seeing *Fridericus Rex* at the Gloria Palast, they are standing in the ornate lobby of Meissen chandeliers and quarter-turn gilt stairways.

"Grim," she says, lighting a cigarette. "Putting aside for a moment that the film is propaganda for the restoration of the German monarchy. But still, it's that old story of the tyrannical father who sees his son not as a person but as an extension of himself." She leans against the wall. "The story of my life, too. My father always told me a woman should appear in the newspaper three times in her life: when she's born, when she's married, and when she dies. Not that I'm trying to be in the papers. Or that owning a newspaper gives my father the wisdom of the ages."

He puts a hand on her shoulder. He sees already how difficult it is for her to talk about her family in Connecticut, about why she left, forgoing her inheritance; choosing to struggle on a researcher's salary and the dividends from a few stocks. He wants to be as sympathetic as he can. "You're hardly lacking in wisdom yourself," he says.

"I do all right, don't I? But enough about my troubles. Finish telling me about your films."

"Moholy and I are working on some ideas. We won't use stories or actors. We want to explore the aesthetics of light and motion. You've noticed how film directors have been relying on the narrative and dramatic techniques of the theater. But we're feeling challenged to discover the unique possibilities of the medium."

"Sterling Cronheim, ever the Bauhäusler," she says. "That's a compliment, by the way. Walk me home, won't you? It's a pleasant stroll along the Spree. Why can't American cities be like Berlin?"

But he misses American cities, he's thinking, as they leave the theater and head slowly down Dorotheenstrasse with its impressively large linden and chestnut trees and brick-and-stone buildings with a permanence that is frightening. He misses New York, where streets and avenues are numbered and Central Park really is in the center of the world. Berlin is a rambling, imposing forest with wild boars, nightingales, and peacocks. A wilderness in the night, where the wealthy and the farmers live hidden away on their sprawling plots of land and the beggars lie, day and night, against tall iron fences, as if someone's chained them. He wonders how many times the city has been built and rebuilt over the same site, ancestors layered beneath him. So different from America, the New World, the towns west of Wisconsin abandoned when the life is all out of them.

It starts raining and they put their coats over their heads and huddle. Talking about politics and art till they reach her neo-Grecian stone house, three stories with a large, wrought-iron-fenced yard, thick with oak trees. She tells him she and Kally bought it for almost nothing when one U.S. dollar was worth two hundred million deutsche marks.

At the doorstep, she puts her arms around him and whispers against his ear, "The evening doesn't have to end now."

He pulls away from her, leans against the carved mahogany door, away from the rain dripping off the portico. He has to raise his voice above the loud staccato. "It's late," he says, looking downward. "And I've been alone . . . all my life." The words sound uneasy, false, even to his own ear.

"You don't have to be anymore," she says. She lowers her coat onto her shoulders, reaches up to touch his face.

"No, no," he whispers. He embraces her and they lean into the rain. She pulls him closer and closer, the rain soaking them both. When he releases her she is pale, as if watching someone die.

"I have to catch an early train back to Weimar." He hesitates a moment and kisses her forehead, holds her hands tightly. She looks at him, confused, but he has no better explanation for her. "I'll write you," he says.

"Tomorrow," she says.

•

He writes her a letter every night before he sleeps. The letter is part of a recurring dream. He hears her voice, in a room without light, windows, or doors. He must have stood patiently while someone built the room around him. He writes quickly, not knowing how he will escape from the room and get the letter to her. He tells her everything that happens here in Weimar. What he does in his new photography workshop, trying to make do with the inadequate materials and workspace. What he tells his students, what they tell him. Many of them fought in the war and have sketches and diaries all about death. More death than he's ever seen. They want to throw out their old lives and live for the camera; looking, as he always does, for the new vision, an objective reality the unaided eye can't see.

He spends hours at a time in the darkroom developing his prints. Under the safelight his hands are larger, blurred around the edges, as if all the strength in them has moved to the center and he can only pound with them, not grasp.

This is what happens to a leper, he thinks; he moves further into himself and his extremities wither.

He wants to photograph her. Standing over the developing tanks, glancing at his timer, he is a frantic man. He doesn't often photograph people and he doesn't think of anyone the way he thinks of her. If there were spotlights and photofloods all around her, he would make the light and shadow fall the way he wanted it to and she would sit patiently, silently, thinking of her work.

She tells him she dreams about viruses. She's as minuscule as they are. No sky or ground; only colors, shifting and moving toward her. She can't see the viruses but she hears their strange humming, like a crowd singing one note. While she listens to the note he will photograph her. She will pass through developers and fixers, become an image on paper. Grays, blacks, whites. Different from life. He will let her go and keep her image. Cry over it when he has to.

Little White Lies

IT'S TWO IN THE MORNING and Wanda's been sitting in the living room, unable to sleep, listening to the Voice of Kenya on the shortwave radio. A flute quartet, lulling, polyphonic harmonies. She shuts it off, turns on the small television by the end table that doubles as a teletext, its screen cut into a marbleized blue Bakelite globe on its own pedestal. She watches a symposium on orbital laser weapons technology on the Socrates Channel. The panelists are from Los Alamos Laboratory, where her father went to work after he left the Air Force. Los Alamos always sends its youngest, most soft-spoken men (always men) to appear on programs. They look and act like students on *College Bowl*, reciting long answers full of complex statistics.

She's drifted to sleep and wakes up suddenly in the closing moments of a rebroadcast of *Gender and Society*. Beryle Danner is addressing the camera directly, an out-of-focus bookshelf behind her. She's Bradley's ex-wife, an ash blonde with the wholesomeness of a child star barely grown up, wearing a gray mohair sweater dress. Bradley has told her Beryle is successful because she projects perfect neutrality. She is from a German-Hispanic family, well established in the Argentine oligarchy, and he says she is now atoning for years of privilege. With Beryle's broadcast English and perfect neutrality, Wanda can't imagine her living a life of any sort beyond the television screen. Certainly not her life

51

as Bradley's wife for twelve years, or the divorce that dragged on for more than two. Beryle talks about death, genocide, the end of the world, the decay of civilization; frightening and unthinkable abstractions. She makes them soothingly sad, like the death of someone's pet.

She turns and a second camera picks up a wide shot of her and a panel of guests, three professorial-looking older women in dark suits, seated with her at a round dark-wood table. *But I'll say this: Subjugation of women cuts across all cultural, ethnic, and social groups everywhere. Or, to paraphrase John Lennon, we women have always been the niggers of the world . . .*

Wanda shuts the television off. She picks up the phone headset by the sofa, thin bendable black wires like an operator's, and calls Bradley, though she doesn't expect him to be home and she's already called more times than she can remember. But his voice and image on the small oval screen startle her. White paint on his forehead and cheeks, and he looks as if he hasn't slept for days. "Please come see me," he says, and hangs up before she can answer.

PARTY HAS VOLUNTARILY DISCONNECTED flashes across the screen when she tries to call him back. She has to go. She rushes uptown in a jitney to the Seventy-ninth Street Marina. This was once a desirable place, with a stone terrace, rotunda, and fountain at the edge of Riverside Park, overlooking the Hudson River. Now, built above the fountain, a boardwalk disfigures it and there are layers of ink-black mud and garbage below. Strong odors merge—ammonia, urine, alcohol, and rotting food—as she walks down the steps to the marina. Hundreds of houseboats sway and creak, their portholes shining with light. A floating shantytown, Bradley calls it, but some of the houseboats are luxurious, white fiberglass and chrome or exotic veneered wood. It was the only place he could live in the city after the divorce, he told her. He lost the Fifth Avenue apartment to Beryle and he didn't want to sell any of his other properties to buy another cooperative in the city. Still, Wanda thinks he could have done better; the marina has a notoriously high crime rate and little charm or quaintness left.

She unlocks the gate, walks down the long pier where Bradley's houseboat is moored. The hatch is unlocked and music rushes at her when she opens it. Bradley is painting in the dark. He works quickly, painting on a large canvas with a palette knife, gestural strokes, thick and heavy. *A world in white gets underway*, sings a voice from the Surround speakers. *And I want to be with you, be with you night and day.*

She steps farther into the cabin and looks at the painting. In the dim light she makes out an abstracted figure in muted blues and grays. The figure appears to be an old woman standing by a window filled with a brilliant white light. She has told him over and over to give up economics, but he never listens. He'd become a successful stock analyst while still an undergraduate at Yale, where he and a few classmates started an investment club. He picked the London School of Economics over law school and became a mergers and acquisitions wizard at J. P. Morgan. He gave it up five years ago for a less stressful life as economic adviser and consultant to an impressive roster of global corporations and an occasional adjunct professorship at nearby Ivy League colleges.

Now he works here at his houseboat: opposite the Pullman kitchen and its curtain of sapphire glass beads is a wall of computer screens and Quotrons with the latest on commodities, currency, stocks and bonds around the world. What he misses most of all, he tells her, is speculating on the markets. He can't, now that professional ethics dictate that he keep his assets in a blind trust. Though some would have trouble feeling sympathy for him, she feels it acutely. She knows he has yet to learn that what he truly wants is to be a painter. His paintings are stark and sometimes frightening, different from any she's ever seen. He paints abstract compositions in powerfully somber and dark colors, juxtaposed with washes of silvery brightness. Never the tranquil landscapes and still lifes of dilettantes.

53

And so we are told, this is the golden age, the voice sings. *And gold is the reason for the wars we wage.*

He looks up from the easel, reaches over to a storage wall of stereo components, and shuts off the music. He tiptoes across the cabin, dodging stacks of architectural drawings on the gray linoleum floor, and kisses her, holding his arms wide in back of him, exaggerating his care not to get paint on her. She embraces him tightly, unconcerned with the paint. "I thought something had happened to you," she says. She's almost crying. Right now, she understands how people can faint from relief.

"That's a story and a half," he says, clearly trying to sound more calm than he is. With a gesture of his hand, he lets her know he likes her haircut. He kisses her again. "Let me get you something to drink." He rubs his hands on his paint-covered white shirt and reaches for vodka in a cabinet underneath the beechwood terminal table. He pours the drink, putting blue fingerprints all over the fluted highball glass.

She glances outside, at the distant George Washington Bridge lighted in red, white, and blue for a holiday whose name she can't remember. She sits with him on the gray Dover sofa. He's drinking straight from a bottle of Johnnie Walker Black. His hair has gotten shaggy and his face is gaunt and grayish white with several days' growth. It disturbs her how oblivious he is. "Bradley, tell me what happened. I haven't seen you since—"

"I'm sorry. This stalwart Langford-Stewart really lost it that night." He drinks the last of the Scotch. "He was overcome with misery and self-pity. He hasn't quite recovered from running into his ex-wife at Saks a few weeks ago."

"What happened?" she asks him, as gently as she can.

"No scenes. No nothing. She just stared at me. A hate stare. The stare that white women give black men. It says: You are an animal, you have no right to even look at me." He throws the empty bottle; unbreakable polymeric glass, it

54

bounces off the stove. The sapphire beads clatter and sway. He takes out another bottle of Scotch from the liquor cabinet, opens it, and fills a tumbler.

"Bradley," she whispers. She takes the glass from him and sets it on the end table. "Don't drink any more." He sits next to her, lets her hold his hand. She knows how devastating those last years with Beryle were for him. He has told her the trouble began when he quit J. P. Morgan. Beryle, champion of a more balanced, humane work life for both men and women, couldn't accept his decision. It wasn't only concern about loss of income and status; Bradley was disappointing her in every way: she didn't realize until they'd been married for years that he was a black man who'd had himself sterilized at twenty to keep his secret. "I've been worried about you. I'm worried *now*," Wanda says.

"I know. I'm sorry I couldn't meet you for lunch that day. I was up in the Catskills, neglecting my work and missing you." He lies across her lap, hands over his face. "I thought the fresh air would do me some good, but it didn't. I still couldn't get out of bed half the time."

She strokes his face. "Why did you want to kill yourself that night?"

He sits up and finishes his Scotch. "Because I hate my life, melodramatic as that sounds." He picks up his pipe and taps it against the glass ashtray so hard he shatters it. He curses under his breath and shoves the pieces to the floor.

"You don't mean that."

"Yes I do, sister, yes I do." He gets up and pours himself more Scotch, staring at the Tokyo stock exchange Quotron as he drinks it. He sits back down beside her. "I can't keep living like a fraud. My brothers and sisters are out there, dying, they can't get jobs or decent housing. They're getting shot and beaten to death. And if you're an African-American man, forget about walking around on the Upper East Side, even in your best Saville with your briefcase and your wallet full of credit cards. The police cruisers will pull up to you

55

and the officers will ask you what you're doing in the neighborhood. If there's been a robbery or a mugging within a twenty-block radius of where you're standing, you're automatically the prime suspect. You in your Saville and your years of higher education." He laughs harshly. "Of course that's never happened to me. And I have to admit that there's a good part of me that doesn't want anything to change. Just so Bradley Langford-Stewart can keep on living high and mighty . . . and white." He clasps her hand, leaving paint on her. "Sick, isn't it? Especially when it's so easy to be myself around you. You understand what I am. But out in the world, I can't. I don't. When somebody makes a racist remark I never say anything. Never."

She draws him closer. She knows that his parents, too impatient to wait all the many years it would take to adopt a white newborn, found him in New Orleans at the Basin Street Sacred Heart Orphanage, where they had gone looking for a biracial baby they could pass off as white. They changed the racial designation on Bradley's birth certificate, intending that neither he nor the rest of the world know the truth. But he found out at seventeen, when he stayed out all night with his girlfriend and his parents panicked, fearing present or future pregnancies and the scandal that might result. They told him the truth, told him callously. He took the commuter train to the city and wandered for weeks around Times Square, spending his days in the video arcades and two-dollar porno houses and his nights in the lower levels of the Port Authority Bus Terminal, sleeping in corners and stairwells until six in the morning, when the police rapped their nightsticks near his head. He eventually got a seasonal job on an upstate farm, where he met a recruiter who promised him a better one. In the jungles of Central America, he fought for people with whom his textbook Spanish barely helped him communicate. Several months later, he gave up and took refuge at the U.S. embassy in

San José and played prodigal son and his parents flew him home.

He shuts off the computers and they whine into silence while the Dow Jones and Reuters news wires continue their quiet clattering. He stares out the windows, hands in his jeans pockets. "I wanted you so much that day I saw you at the seaport. I admired you for standing up to that bastard."

"That's called survival, pure and simple," she says. But she should tell him how much she hates those men, how they talk down to her.

"It's more than I can do. Look at me, I still can't tell people, not even my friends. What would they think? Mackenzie, for example. He's from Arkansas, for God's sake; his grandparents still live on what was the family plantation back in the bad old days."

"Well, you know the old cliché. If these friends of yours are going to reject you, they were never your friends to begin with."

"Wanda, I'm forty years old," he says, sounding enraged. "I'm not some gangly, shy teenager who's trying to be popular at school."

She suddenly feels no more sympathy, no more desire to soothe and cajole him. His self-pity reminds her of how she used to be as a teenager, hiding in her room more often than not, afraid to see anyone, even her mother or father. She remembers being forced to see a psychiatrist, a light-complexioned, matronly woman with rhinestone-studded cat's-eye glasses and heavy perfume who told her to repeat silently to herself, "I am a proud member of my race," whenever someone called her names or teased her.

"That's right, you're no teenager," Wanda says, folding her arms and nodding impatiently. "You've spent the last twenty-three years of your life lying—and that's the word, lover man—*lying* about who and what you are. *That's* what you can't deal with."

57

"Stick to the facts, sister. Assumptions were made about me. I just never bothered to challenge them. But I *will.*"

"When? Tomorrow? Next week? Next year? More like *never.*"

"Don't do this to me, Wanda! Why can't you—"

"Why can't I *what?*" He stares at her, stunned. "I mean, look at you, Bradley. You've decided you want to be this dynamic and totally aware African-American man. Well, that's fine. But just because you forget to tell somebody where to go the next time they make a racist remark, don't pack a gun and try to shoot yourself in front of your girlfriend. The one who you think is supposed to save you."

"No, no, no, you don't understand." He paces the floor. "I was only going to tell you goodbye. I didn't mean to do anything else."

"Oh really? Then why did you stick a gun in your mouth?"

"I don't know why I did that. Look, I know you must be angry but—"

"Of course I am! You had no right to do that to me! You weren't really going to kill yourself, were you? You just wanted to scare the shit out of me and—"

"—Listen to me. Just listen." There is a tremor in his voice. "It will never ever happen again, I swear to you, sister. But we've got to stay together, you know." He lowers his voice and slips an arm around her. "It's a hard life for both of us."

"What's been so hard about your life? Tell me, Bradley, I want to hear this." She pulls away from him.

"Don't insult me, Wanda. You know the answer to that."

"No, I don't. Let's hear it."

"Stop it! You of all people know how rough I've had it with the divorce and—"

"You don't know what a hard life is!" She is so angry she can't look at him.

"It *was* a hard life till I met you."

"Bradley, listen to your maudlin self. I'm not stupid." Her

58

hand shakes as she runs it through her hair. "This sudden and desperate need to be African-American. It's not what you really want. I know what you're going to do. Just as soon as you can, you're going to disappear right back into your old life—your lily-white life—and settle down with suitable wife number two. You've probably found her already."

He grasps her hands again, rubbing more paint on them. She just stares at him. "You listen to me, will you?" he says. The look of desperate pleading on his face shocks her. *"You're* that suitable wife, Wanda Higgins Du Bois, and you know it. Why do you think I keep living here in this goddamn slum? I'm waiting for you, for when you decide to live with me in Greenwich. I've got all these house plans." He points to the stacks of architectural drawings beside the easel. "But we don't have to use Mackenzie's. I don't see why we couldn't build one of yours. Maybe one of the earth-sheltered houses. Maybe the one with the gables you designed a few months ago. You know which one I mean. If we can't find a twenty percent slope on the land, we'll make one, won't we? I know you'd rather live in a house you designed. Isn't that every architect's dream?" She's shaking her head as she listens to him. Now he turns away from her, rubbing his forehead. "It's what I thought you wanted me to do for you," he says, almost whispering.

"I don't want you to build me a house. You hear me? I don't want you to!" She heads for the door, but he plants himself in front of it and puts his hands firmly on her shoulders.

"Where are you going, sister? You belong here."

"I'm not your damn sister and I don't belong anywhere near you!" She tries to free herself from his grip but can't.

"Don't leave," he whispers. "Don't."

She looks away from him and down at her hands, at the paint drying powdery and taut on her skin. He tries to kiss her, but she turns her face away.

59

"Well, get out, then!" he shouts. They stare at each other. The strong river currents tossing the houseboat make it seem adrift.

●

She wakes up beside him on the sofa bed, late morning, shivering. Her black dress is crumpled on the floor, covered with grayish blue handprints, blurred, as if she'd been trying to run away from him. She failed at it, completely. She's not ready to face him, not this morning. He's still sleeping soundly through the noise of outboard motors, portable stereos blaring with rock music, and neighbors shouting their conversations across the marina. She showers quickly and puts on a pair of his Levi's and a crimson-and-white cotton rugby shirt. She has to be alone for a while.

She takes the Ninth Avenue El to Park Row. She could buy a bag full of whole grains and fresh, organically grown vegetables at the Korean greengrocer around the corner from her loft. Squash in yellows and greens that look lacquered, artichokes, corn, asparagus, and others whose names she doesn't know. Preparing elaborate vegetarian dishes is the closest she has to a hobby. But she decides instead to go to Festhaus on the corner of Greenwich and Murray Streets. The pub, a favorite after-work haunt of hers and colleagues at the Consortium, is quiet this early on a Saturday. She heads to the back room, where trails of cigarette smoke float toward the low ceiling of imitation-Michelangelo frescos. In the dim light of neon beer signs and hurricane-glass wall-mounted lamps, the frescos look more skillfully executed and mystical than they really are. The pub is decades old, with a history of famous bohemians who spent their evenings here; the walnut-paneled walls are covered with autographed black-and-white photographs of movie stars, swing bandleaders, and cabaret singers. Banister-back chairs and closely placed tables, each with a candle burning in a wine bottle. A handful of frankincense burns on a red clay censer at the edge of the bar. An old Marlene Dietrich recording is playing.

Wanda sits down underneath a neon Schultheiss-Patzen-hofer sign, washing her in blues and reds. She orders a shot of Absolut and listens to the three middle-aged businessmen at the next table speaking in German about refrigeration technology and how to circumvent the ozone treaty. The pub reminds her of the ones clustered around Harvard Square. She misses those days. It was enough to go to Harvard, say she was going to Harvard; studying and working toward her summa cum laude graduation, learning all she could about architecture and design. She felt free, dashing back to her room in Lowell Hall from the library late at night, past the traffic and intersecting streets of Harvard Square and the Out of Town Newsstand where she browsed through the wooden shelves of tightly rolled daily newspapers from all over the world.

She takes out a pad of Swiss tracing paper and looks through her bag for a marker pen, a pencil, anything. She's got an idea for the Abbott's Quay Center. She finds some graphite and a mechanical pencil, THE ANDOVER INSTITUTE etched in white; a Washington-based think tank Bradley belongs to. It feels like poison in her hands and she wants to throw it across the pub, at the telescreen above the bar, make it explode. The businessmen start talking about the Rhine, fondly, like an eccentric aunt long dead. It was a real river once, famous, sung about.

She sketches a sphere, partly earth-bermed, like a meteorite sunk in its crater. It will be constructed of white, textured concrete-porcelain. From a distance, the sphere will look impenetrable, solid, self-contained; the plaza entrance on the southeast side hidden by the sloping land around it. The interior will be monumental and expansive, sunlight pouring through hundreds of skylights; strong, directed beams constantly shifting patterns of light and shadow. The ceiling will resemble a planetarium's, only much larger. At night, quartz-halogen floods will make the structure glow as if it is made of light.

She works on the entrance, with its plaza of birch and willow trees, white quartz and granite benches, and sidewalks facing the harbor. So much fanfare and civic pride pouring into the Toronto Harbourfront, but the ocean will swallow all the buildings in a matter of decades or even years.

She sketches the main level's plan, indicates where moving walkways will traverse the floor. There will be three sublevels; the lowest will have a transparent Antraglas floor suspended several meters above the foundation, the quarry-like maze of rock and soil intact. It will be a permanent exhibition, and a geologist will give lectures, answer questions. The transparent floor might be considered a gimmick or at best impractical, but she won't get rid of it. She remembers the psychology experiments with kittens born and raised on transparent floors. They grew up psychotic, unable to walk. But people will manage splendidly, and regain lost curiosity about the natural world.

She keeps sketching. On the plans of the sublevels, she indicates that the art gallery walls will be constructed of transparent Antraglas. The library and lecture rooms will be furnished with Perspex tables and chairs. The recital halls will have rows of translucent Mattelite seating, surfaces gleaming richly as liquid. The entire structure will be an exploration of light as a dynamic, changeable force and a sustainer, a fulcrum. Daylight creates and defines the space. On cloudy days and at night, the absence of light will suggest alienation and deprivation, despite the mercury-vapor down-lights and white neon spiraling along the walls. She will call it a study in translucence and reflectivity, a visual meditation on the contradictions of public and private space, of a culture's fear of both openness and aloneness.

The Borderline

BROWNOUTS AGAIN and the Savings of America Tower's innovative integrated system is failing. She is too warm, even in her T-shirt, with a historical map of Africa and a red, green, and black banner cutting diagonally across the front. The laser plotter beside her silently turns out full-color presentation drawings of the seven-hundred-acre corporate park she and her colleagues cynically call Sandcastle, Inc., knowing the developers have intentionally ignored the rising sea level at the Connecticut waterfront site. A short-term investment that will displace hundreds of homeowners and threaten nearby wildlife sanctuaries. She's sorry to be a part of the destruction. On the elevations of the microelectronics laboratories she adds a shelter belt, staggered rows of poplar and Douglas fir trees to stop the soil erosion that northeast winds will cause. She wants to believe she's being custodial and reverent toward the land, but she knows better. She's helping a global corporation destroy it.

She glances at the remnants of a long, hectic workday: empty Coke and seltzer bottles, slices of cold Sicilian pizza, a deck of playing cards with Gemini and Apollo astronaut photographs on the backs scattered on the black-lacquered module table by her computer terminal. She's the last to leave tonight. The Sandcastle, Inc. workload is getting excessive and there are rumors that the New York office will go on a twenty-four-hour schedule. She will miss staying here by herself half the night, talking to colleagues in cities around the world. She's glad her diligence is accelerating her career at the Consortium, but she doesn't know how else she would live. She's long since given up on unreliable friends, lengthy, forgotten conversations with acquaintances, or even solitary hobbies and pastimes. She picks up the cards and shuffles through them, trying to remember how to play solitaire. When she returns to the computer screen, the gray and black lines of the Sandcastle elevations blur in her fatigue.

She picks up the phone headset, its small oval screen perched on a chromed-metal pedestal base, calls Reggie, her mother's youngest sister, and talks her into going out to O'Sullivan's on West Street for a drink. Family, some of the family at least, is all she can depend on. It's more of a principle than an emotional reassurance right now. Reggie's at work in her Franklin Street loft, putting the final touches on a series of print ads for a downtown winery whose warehouse is always flooding out; she's looking tired and ready for a break.

Wanda shuts down the computers and plotters, picks up her bag and coat, walks out the plate-glass doors to the elevator bank. The integrated system turns off all the lights and locks the doors for her. The elevator's voice drones on about how to get to the New York Stock Exchange, the Neil A. Armstrong Aerospace Center, the World Trade Center, Trinity Church. Outside, the reflective glass towers gleam like part of a monumental stage in the new high-power arc lights, fail-safe methane generators roaring. But the sidewalks and streets are ragged and deserted, a lost terrain.

●

She and Reggie sit in one of O'Sullivan's back rooms, surrounded by pool tables, in a booth made from a pair of vinyl-covered seats from an old Greyhound bus and a table of black Formica. Reggie resembles Francine except for a hook nose she proudly refuses to have fixed, or to speculate on its genealogy. She always wears purple and tonight is no different: faded purple denim jacket and jeans, and a jewel-neck sweater with photographically perfect purple roses. Her black shoulder-length hair in hundreds of microbraids, like the ones Wanda used to wear a long time ago, and on her wrists bracelets of antique telephone wire macraméed in intricate designs. The herbal cigarettes she's smoking smell like a sugary sweet incense.

"What I need is a career change," Wanda tells her, sipping ale from a pewter stein. "I should become a fashion designer." She picks up one of Reggie's cigarettes from the sleek gold pack, shreds it on the table. "Imagine the power to make millions of people throw out their entire wardrobes every year. Make them be ashamed to be seen in something they loved six months ago." She laughs and slides her stein back and forth on the slick table surface. "Or just imagine if every major architectural firm did a show twice a year, displaying scale models of the season's stylish new buildings."

"But then you'd have people destroying their houses and offices every year," Reggie says, lighting a cigarette with her Zippo. The bracelets clink together softly as she moves her hands.

"You mean like they do already? How many times has New York built Madison Square Garden and torn it down and started all over again? I've lost count." She breaks the cigarette in half, shakes out the yellowish-brown herbs onto the table.

"So what's bothering you, Wanda? Besides Madison Square Garden."

Environmental sickness, Wanda wants to say. Maybe the city's getting to her, literally. Tyler has told her there are at least seventy toxins in the water that the filtration systems can't handle. But the toxic ash from all the incinerators will kill everyone first. She's always been tempted to move upstate to a bioregionalist community, where people sometimes succeed in detoxifying their immediate environment. She really wants to believe her problems can be solved with changes in geography or career or, most of all, in the political climate. "The world's just too crazy," she says. "No wonder people want to go back to the past. But Jim Crow I can do without."

"And Jim Crow can do without you, honey. He wouldn't know where in the bus to put you."

Wanda frowns and sweeps aside the small mound of herbs from the cigarette. She wonders what more bad news Reggie might have for her. She knows Reggie lost her NYNEX account shortly after the marketing executives met with her and discovered that the woman who'd been doing their New York Viewphone Preferred Customer newsletter layouts was African-American. Not long ago, for a brief time in history, this would have been automatically illegal. Wanda's been following the story of a coalition of civil rights and other progressive organizations which is trying to have the concept of race declared unconstitutional. She's heard the arguments, most astonishingly that, statistically, the average black American is 25 percent white and the average white American is 6 percent black. Or, put another way, 95 percent of white Americans are 5 to 80 percent black. Her Aunt Tyler has told her stories about these whites researching their roots in the National Archives and finding they've got an African-American or two in the family, some becoming so hysterical they have to be carried out by paramedics. She thinks of Bradley and how he's been verging on the hysterical lately.

"Things are bad, sister," Wanda says. She doesn't say anything else for a while. Sinatra sings "Autumn in New York"; the sound is tinny on the Wurlitzer. The pub has gotten quieter, nearly everyone has left except for a group of aging longshoremen huddled at the bar, watching football solemnly. The dim blue holotorch lights strung up like party streamers from the low ceilings are starting to annoy her. She's tired. Always tired and unable to sleep.

"I keep saying you ought to go on the Freedom March with me," Reggie says.

Wanda can't imagine enduring the endless weeks it would take to march from Montgomery, Alabama, to Washington, D.C., singing "We Shall Overcome" like in the old days. She doesn't want to talk about civil rights anymore, so she starts telling Reggie about her Abbott's Quay design. How she and the Brothers Guam are having serious creative differences. They still want a tower. One hundred five stories; her sphere design, radically modified, would go on top. She tells Reggie who Wilson Ruffin Abbott was, surprised she doesn't already know. He was one of the first African-Canadian real-estate brokers way back when, as well as a philanthropist and political activist. He was so wealthy he purchased freedom for fugitive slaves.

Wanda isn't prepared when Reggie changes the subject abruptly. "I've been meaning to tell you about your father," she says.

Her father? What news could there be? She hasn't heard anything about him, or from him, for that matter, for years. "It's too late at night and I'm too goddamn tired to hear about my father," she says, trying to sound irritated, though she's actually afraid to know anything more about him.

Reggie puts a hand over Wanda's and says, "I was on my way to see a client at Armstrong Aerospace and there we were, waiting for the same elevator. So we chitchatted in the lobby a little while. Turns out he just got a job at Suntel and he's living here in the city now, on East Fifty-seventh Street. He asked about you. I think he really misses you."

Wanda shakes her head. "He puts on that old Generalissimo Charles Stoller charm and he can fool even you. Let's not talk about him anymore, all right?"

"You don't hate your father half as much as you think you do. Remember, I know you. I raised you, after all."

"You were ten years old when I was born," Wanda says. "You still needed somebody to raise *you*." Reggie laughs. Wanda takes her Zippo and lights the ragged scraps of the cigarette, letting them burn in the ashtray. "I know you already think I'm a mental case because of Bradley," she says. Reggie's never liked him; she told her months ago that he was really passing for white and not admitting it to her. How else could he have gotten so far at J. P. Morgan and at all the colleges where he's taught? The U.S. Constitution was written by and for white male property owners, Reggie's always reminding her.

"Well, Wanda, I've said what I have to say about that brother."

"You can't tell me anything about men. You gave them up for Lent, remember?"

"Gave them up for Mardi gras, honey, so as not to spoil my fun," Reggie says, laughing.

"You're lucky that way." When she thinks of Reggie's lover, Lizabeth, she sees her dancing in shimmery metallic leotards on a stage of fog and light. It must be a poetic sort of love Reggie and her Alvin Ailey star have, something Wanda can't even imagine. But what she has with Bradley has become painful and illusory. She realizes at that moment that somehow she and Bradley are inevitably doomed, either by a horrible moment or by their own mutual indifference. She starts to dread the future.

•

Later, as she says goodbye to Reggie at her doorstep and takes the freight elevator to her loft, she forgets the conversation and thinks about her sphere. The ponderously slow elevator makes its clatter and she imagines she's walking around the main floor of the structure. It is late at night and the rings of white neon along the walls illuminate the interior. The building is in Antarctica and there is nothing to relieve the night but the aurora australis—iridescent colors covering the skylights, seeping into the building. In the bitter cold, the walls have constricted, leaving spidery cracks. She knows she has been here much too long.

She walks in the door and finds Sterling lying on the sofa, asleep, white shirt and chinos contrasting starkly with the black sofa. He's left the telescreen and teletext on, tuned to an art auction in Tokyo. How many millions of dollars' worth of art has he bought or sold tonight, she wonders. It's just how he thinks of art, abstractly, as mere investment, like stocks and bonds. He spends his days buying and selling and talking to his financial advisers on his newly installed viewphone line. She thinks of taking a photograph while he sleeps, but doesn't, afraid that he's really a ghost or otherwise invisible everywhere but in her own thoughts. She remembers the first photograph she ever saw of Cronheim, taken by Moholy-Nagy's wife, Lucia Moholy. He was on a stage, in a white leotard with heavily padded shoulders, arms outstretched and hands completely covered by the small metal spheres he was clasping. Two large sheets of metal with horizontal accordion folds towered beside him. He was dancing the Metal Dance, one of Schlemmer's Bauhaus dances, and the photographer caught the dark hair and exuberant idealism of his youth. Cronheim really had wanted to be a dancer, had studied in Munich. He danced again, years later, at the Bauhaus, and the dances were about space, everyday space. Schlemmer filled his notebooks with grids, diagrams, and geometric forms, analyzing and describing the space Cronheim and the others danced in.

He starts to mumble in his sleep. When she stoops beside him, he jumps up suddenly.

"I didn't mean to wake you," she says.

"It wasn't you." He sits up slowly, stretches his arm across the sofa back. "Nightmares."

"Well, for heaven's sake, don't keep trying to sleep. Let's go see a movie at the D. W. Griffith."

•

She taps her foot to the syncopated rhythm of the end-title song, vaguely bossa nova. The houselights come up on the small movie theater, a converted Lispenard Street warehouse, its walls painted with scenes from *The Cabinet of Dr. Caligari.* She and Sterling walk down the narrow aisle out of the theater, through the crowded lobby. She hesitates at the exit doors, dreading what she can't name. They head downtown on Church Street, past the old cast-iron industrial warehouses and loft buildings; architects who loved the classics adorned them with columns, cornices, arches, porticos. Now they are all looted, façades rusting, stripped of their coats of pastel paint, gaping holes where the polished plate glass of show-rooms should be. Still, this is a historic district and none of these buildings can be demolished. Block after block is lighted only by smoldering street fires and the headlights of passing cars. Another brownout. The cobra-head street lamps are bent and sagging.

"These directors don't know how to light a scene," he says. She waits for him to continue, but there is only the sound of cars passing, like bursts of rain. She taps the sidewalk with her umbrella and the pavement sounds hollow.

"It's a new sensibility. If we manipulate the elements of light and shadow, it implies that we can manipulate and shape the world. That's a crock, of course. The truth is, they're not a tenth of the film director you were. I really mean that. People might not understand or like your art and your theories, but nobody could dislike *Night Without a Day.*" She has seen the film four times and remembers it frame by frame. Teresa Wright as the invalid young bride and Farley Granger as her naïve, small-town-lawyer husband. He goes off to Chicago on business, meets and falls for Joan Bennett, a cabaret singer. In true *film noir* tradition, he

70

becomes embroiled in deceit, adultery, embezzlement, and ultimately murder. The final scene gave her nightmares the first time she saw it: Farley Granger in a mannequin factory, trapped in a freight elevator shaft as thousands of mannequins fall on him and bury him alive.

He stops walking. "You can't be serious about that movie. It was a mediocre script and I had no say whatsoever in the final cut."

"It's better than you think." The original nitrates were intact, and Kino-Universal restored the cut scenes. A minor miracle, as half the movies ever made no longer exist. But he doesn't seem to care.

"I never think about that movie. You couldn't imagine what I went through trying to shoot it. I'd gone to Hollywood to be an art director, not to land in the middle of battles between producers and studio executives. Getting out of there and going east to Philadelphia, well, that was as good as going to heaven after suffering like the good Catholic I never was." It was true. He'd started to hate everything about Hollywood. Even the long, sunny days made him feel worse. It was never the reunion he'd hoped for, working with directors, writers, technicians he'd known back in Berlin during his first few years at UFA, before designing set after set became drudgery. But Wanda doesn't understand this, doesn't understand him anymore than anyone else has. She sees the films, the photographs, the paintings, but not him. He wants to tell her more, tell her all about himself, why he's been hiding all these years. Telling her, he could tell himself.

●

They don't say much to each other for a while. She puts on a black-and-red kimono, sits in bed, a red blanket draped around her, and reads issue after issue of *World Architect*, old ones she's borrowed from the Consortium's library. He sits on the Cesca chair by the window, looking through a

71

photographic-supplies catalogue, about to order more paper
and materials to make photograms. He's taken over a corner
of her studio space, with his stacks of high-contrast photographic paper, bottles of fixers and developers, and developing trays set out on a card table. A yellow-green Wratten
safelight, two fifteen-watt spotlights with foot switches strung
against the wall, black curtains and strips of blocking film
sealing off outside light so he can create his photograms.
Industrial weight Ziploc bags full of the common objects and
pieces of glass, plastic, and wood he places on the photographic paper, exposes to light, then develops just as he
would a photographic enlargement made from a negative.
Intricate compositions, images of shadow and light, unmis-
takably Cronheim. Clotheslines full of them strung up,
drying in the corner. Cameraless photography. Painting with
light. He and Moholy-Nagy spent years experimenting with
(or, as some say, inventing) photograms.

Later, they sit side by side on the bed, turn off the lights,
and listen to a big band playing Cole Porter and Duke
Ellington standards live from the Ritz-Carlton Hotel Ballroom. The vocalist is thirteen years old and blind. It's just
what Wanda would do if she couldn't see; she'd sing with
her own orchestra in nightclubs, dance halls, and hotel
ballrooms all over the country. The musicians would be like
family to her, she'd know them by touch.

"Do you want me to turn it off?"

"I'd rather stay awake and listen. Everything comes back
to me when I sleep."

She doesn't overlook the implication—that he would sleep
here in her bed, not his own. It's not innuendo, she decides,
it's how he lives, drifting from place to place, unconcerned
so long as no one knows who he really is. "Can't you tell me
what's on your mind?" she asks him, soothingly, she hopes.
He seems to treat it as a rhetorical question. She sits down
at the vanity, turns on the frosted glass and nickel lamp. She

brushes her hair slowly, like someone in a trance. But it's him she's watching in the mirror.

If he weren't Cronheim he wouldn't be living here with her. He's somehow mythical, not someone with whom she ever has to argue or divide household chores. Having him here, her life is changing and she can't say how or why. Better this way, not knowing, not having the words to explain it. She turns around to look at him and he is staring at her. The vocalist on the radio is singing "How High the Moon," embellishing the melody with coloratura runs. She hums along, an octave below.

"Drink?" He nods and she goes downstairs to the kitchen, pours him Chivas on the rocks and Absolut straight up for herself. Both bottles are nearly empty and it's well past midnight; the liquor stores will be closed until Monday morning, when the long lines of people are comical and sad. She can hardly believe they've both been drinking for most of the night, even during the movie, premixed cocktails concealed in paper bags.

She sits beside him on the bed and gives him the drink. He is toying with a burned-out photo-lamp bulb, shaking the loose filament.

"Why are you giving up architecture?" he asks her after a long silence, swirling the ice in his Scotch.

She hates both the question and the ice, which she hears acutely. "I'm not giving up architecture. What's with you? Do you hate the Consortium, too?"

"I'm talking about you, your work. You should be exploring your own ideas. They're quite good. But you're letting the Consortium swallow you whole."

"I'm using the Consortium to my advantage, not the other way around." She gets up, looks out the window. A motorcade of white limousines is speeding across Chambers Street. "You see, I've been designing an arts and cultural center on the Toronto waterfront. It's going to be as close to an actual sphere as I can put on a landfill site. Building codes are as insane there as they are here, but with a bunch of great engineers, lawyers, and one of those Papa Pentacostal voudou spells, who knows? Assuming I win the competition, of course." She closes the Venetian blinds. "Crönchen, I wasn't even going to tell you about it till I finished it." She knows from reading the biographies that his friends called him Crönchen, or sometimes Crön. She'd like to think he's becoming a friend. "I admit, it's tempting to give it all up." And she is tempted. The only people having any fun and turning a profit are a few notorious billionaire developers and, of course, the demolition companies who love it when the real-estate market is sluggish. It's all a total bastardization of Cronheim's generation's vision of affordable, high-rise housing and she hates being part of it.

"I'd like to see your sketches," he says, setting his drink on the nightstand.

"You will," she says, sipping the vodka. "I just have to finish them."

He can't help noticing how slurred her speech is becoming. "You've got to stop drinking so much," he says.

She tosses the glass from hand to hand. He recoils as if she is about to throw it at him. Instead, she throws it across the room and it shatters in the corner opposite the vanity. The vodka trickles along a tiny path perpendicular to the baseboard.

"I don't know why I did that." Nor does she know how she feels right now. She's simultaneously trying to draw him closer and push him away, that much she knows. She's uneasy now. She's noticed how he looks at her sometimes. Her hands are trembling.

"Do you want to be alone?" he asks.

She tugs at her kimono, rubs a hand against the textured antique silk. It is fragile and tears when she moves too suddenly. Sometimes she can't believe she's really talking to Cronheim. Cronheim, who everyone believes is dead. She sits down at the vanity and thinks of her arts and cultural center. On the walls are abstract murals commissioned especially for the subtly curving space. He has done the murals by himself, working day and night for months, and she hasn't had to see him or keep quiet about him. Everyone knows he's alive. There is solo piano music on the radio, a jazzy larghetto, but she imagines it is a grand piano, made of glass and silverized bronze, in the main level of the center. People listening to the music are folding their arms, complaining of chilly drafts. It's the building's monumental scale, she tells the slender microphones of eager reporters. The space represents caves, mandalas, the primordial imagery of Gaia, the Earth itself. Structures like New Orleans's Superdome or Toronto's SkyDome are kept at a constant room temperature, with an unnoticeable one kilometer per hour wind. But people still shiver.

My sphere has light, she is saying. Shifting patterns of sunlight streaming down from triple-glazed skylights. A visual metaphor of our planet. From space it's a blue sphere in the middle of cold, dark outer space. But to be on the earth, breathe the air, look up at the blue sky is an entirely different experience. The earth is vast and encompassing, not a fragile sphere of reflected light. I wanted to create the same contrast between the exterior and interior of this structure.

"I don't think it's possible anymore. To be alone," she says to Sterling's image in the mirror, speaking in the same coolly modulated voice of her daydream, as if he is one of the reporters.

He does leave her alone, going to his bedroom. She goes to the kitchen, washes vegetables, straining them in a large black-enameled colander. She runs the water hard, remembering that Tyler says washing is no use. There are toxins even in organically grown produce; the air, land, and water permanently and perhaps irreversibly poisoned.

She imagines this is occupied Paris and everyone she

75

knows is trying to save the country, whispering Dutch passwords with consonants the Germans can't pronounce without an accent. A simpler time is what the books call it. The present time must be too complicated to write about; everywhere there are pictures and images. Collage, the world is collage, she thinks. Torn images.

●

Sterling doesn't sleep for long. He thinks about Wanda, not romantically or fraternally, but as some expert might: wondering what makes her what she is. He's never seen such a mixture of confusion, cynicism, and competence in one person. She drinks too much, stopping just short of hospitalization and ruin. He wishes Lenore could have been like that, reckless, but saving herself just in time. His whole life would have been different.

She Was Reading
War and Peace

As a young painter I often had the feeling, when pasting my collages and painting my 'abstract' pictures, that I was throwing a message, sealed in a bottle, into the sea. It might take decades for someone to find and read it. I believed that abstract art not only registers contemporary problems, but projects a desirable future order, unhampered by any secondary meaning . . . Abstract art, I thought, creates new types of spatial relationships, new forms, new visual laws—basic and simple—as the visual counterpart to a more purposeful cooperative human society.

LÁSZLÓ MOHOLY-NAGY

HE IS TAKING THE TRAIN to Berlin, fleeing Bauhaus workshops, darkrooms, disputes, and conflicts, as he does every other month. Not yet sunrise, and the sprawling brick factories along the railroad tracks have powerful floodlights, steady light the color of pearls, shining on the buildings and their large, textured glass windows. In the train window, he watches his reflection sketch left-handed on fine-grid paper. The sketches are diagrams of where to place colors in a painting. They remind him of Moholy, who, hoping to save some time in his experiments in how changes in dimension and color affect a painting's compositional harmony, consulted with an enamel factory. He called the foreman and gave him instructions to manufacture a series of colored

enamel compositions on metal for him. His telephone paintings, he called them. The day the paintings were delivered
was like something out of a dream. Sterling wonders what
it will be like once Körting and Matthiesen manufacture two
of his ceiling light fixture designs and put them in hundreds
of homes. They are chromium-plated steel, holding the
opalescent glass-diffused light he worked with for months
and still sees at night before he sleeps.

It isn't a secret to anyone whom he's going to visit, but he
can say the exhibitions at Sturm and other galleries bring
him to Berlin. Klee's last month; now Feininger's spatial,
understated watercolors. He and Feininger, his fellow
German-American, walk along the cobblestone paths in the
Schillergarten for hours, speaking English and talking like
spies about the Germany around them.

Feininger also thinks art and technology can't be reconciled, and like Sterling, he keeps painting unapologetically.
They both know machines and technology can't take away a
tradition thousands of years old. Sterling believes a new kind
of painting will evolve, as different as cave paintings or
frescos are from easel painting. He's gathering up his ideas
for the book he's writing: *Form und Farbe* (*Form and Color*).
He will discuss the perception of color, the emotional and
subjective experience of color. How both color and form
reflect the dynamics of social, industrial, and cultural change.

Every day he reads Lenore's letters in the canteen at the
Bauhaus, with its high ceiling and brick walls, multiple rows
of steel refectory tables and chairs all contributing to the
terrible, echoing sound. He sits next to the picture windows
overlooking the pines of Wieland Platz, drinking cup after
cup of black coffee, reading. She writes on graph paper,
sometimes printing each letter in a separate square.

Both of them talk so much when they see each other. Art,
politics, culture. They smile at awkward moments. He suspects she's as confused and overwhelmed as he is. She adds
a closing paragraph of German in most of her letters. Wildly

effusive words, as if she's learned German from Schubert and Schumann *Lieder*. Missing him gives her *Sehnsucht*, she writes. But he wants to tell her *Sehnsucht* kills poets and painters who walk in the countryside talking about beauty and wondering if the war and the machines have taken it all away.

The train leaves him under the yellowish stone vaults and arched entryways of Anhalter railway station. He walks to the warehouse-like Romanische Café, its gray walls adorned with theater and art gallery posters. Crowded already in the late morning, as he plays chess for hours up in the balcony. With so much unemployment, more people have time to become proficient at chess. Game after game, he is slowly losing money. He is too distracted to concentrate. He thinks of stepping outside on the Kurfürstendamm, looking over the *Pupenjungen*, the young men out on the street and in the bars. For a few deutsche marks he can get exactly what he wants from them.

●

Hours later, he goes to meet Lenore at Philharmonic Hall, dropping off his bag at her house along the way. The Berlin Philharmonic is playing Mahler's Ninth Symphony tonight, a mournful work. Someone told him that in the first movement Mahler approximated the rhythm of his irregular heartbeat, but Sterling listens and hears telegraphic pauses, a code no one understands. He and Lenore sit ten rows away from the orchestra in the majestic concert hall, built in the Wilhelmian style, lavish with red velvet seating and damask walls. He notices how beautiful she really is, in her short maroon dropped-waist dress with sequins that shimmer like the straight-line garnet necklace and earrings she's wearing. Her platinum-blond hair is radiant and he wants to touch it, touch her. He thinks of clasping her hand as she sways slightly with the broad phrasing of the adagio finale. But he doesn't. He closes his eyes and listens to the music

ANOTHER PRESENT ERA

as grays and dark blues swirl in front of him. The colors are
sporadic; his synesthesia is different from that of Kandinsky,
who never sees darkness when he closes his eyes. Sterling
knows colors by touch. When the symphony ends, he's
astonished that people are clapping and cheering as if they
have just heard a rousing speech. He joins the standing
ovation and Lenore clasps both hands around his arm and
stands on her toes trying to see conductor Bruno Walter
take his bow.

"I don't want to die like Mahler," she says as they follow
along with the exiting crowd down the marble steps. She
clutches her silver fox stole and silk gloves. "In the middle
of my life, in a foreign country."

She sounds so contemplative, he doesn't know what to say
for a few moments. They walk silently, on Unter den Linden,
crowded with slowly moving cars, horns honking loudly in
the clear night.

"We're going to eradicate epidemics," she says, spiritedly
now, taking his arm. "No more untimely deaths."

He nods, thinking of how he barely comprehends these
changing moods that seem to cause her so much pain. He
and Lenore take a taxi back to her house in Charlottenburg,
and he talks about Mahler's Tenth Symphony. Alma Mahler
Gropius has told him it is unfinished and should never be
performed.

"No virus stories tonight. I promise," Lenore says when
they get to the house. But he admires her love of her work
and tells her so once again. She goes to the kitchen and sets
tea water to boil as he wanders the parlor and drawing room,
filled with the eclectic assortment of furniture she and Kally
have gleaned from bankruptcy auctions. A pair of Regency
sideboards and secretaire bookcases opposite the windows,
overflowing with stacks of scientific journals and manuscripts.
Biedermeier sofa, mahogany library armchairs, all with
nearly the same well-worn cerise upholstery. Walnut long-
case clock ticking softly in the corner, and her collection of

contemporary paintings on the powder-gray stenciled walls.

They sit facing each other in the kitchen next to the window, listening to a recording of "What Does It Take to Make a Berliner Happy?" on the gramophone. The slowly turning ceiling fan tosses shadows across the table, the dim light from a single incandescent bulb suspended above the porcelain sink. A large heater in the opposite corner clatters and hums. Lenore thinks of how she decided she loves him. She decided the night she met him. A real decision, not a feeling. For months, she's talked and written to him freely, told him things she's never told anyone but Kally. She's never tired of looking at him, but he pays no attention at all to his appearance. She's never even seen him look at himself in a mirror. His side-parted hair is the dark rich brown of coffee beans, a bit shaggy and long in the back, and his eyes are blue-gray. In twenty years he will be handsome, but now he is still boyish and too thin.

She knows his art and his theories as thoroughly as his colleagues and students. She's watched him sketch early in the morning, eagerly, like a man drunk and happy who knows he will awaken the next day remembering nothing. But no matter who he is, who he'll become (and she knows he will be truly great, in some way), she loves him, and loving him is a regimen, binding and consuming as any other. A regimen that has little to do with him; he's remote and minute as the microorganisms. She is certain he is afraid of her, as other men have been, lowering his head and barely glancing at her. She already suspects he will never know exactly what he wants from her, or that his wants will change dizzily, confusing them both. But he will have to understand she is a woman who has always lived her life exactly as she wants to.

"Kally?" she calls out loudly when she hears someone coming in the front door. She will never be without Kally. Sterling will understand this, too. It's not too much to ask of an artist, a fellow freethinker.

Kally walks in the kitchen, taking off her black Persian coat, laying it on the stove and laughing when Lenore frowns. "My dear, I'm just your absentminded friend who doesn't quite know up from down or a stove from a coat rack." She moves the coat to an empty chair and makes the gestures of someone old and feeble. But she's as young as Lenore. They look like sisters, both of them fashionably slender, with bobbed platinum hair.

Fine, Lenore thinks, let the world assume they are sisters. To love Sterling may be a discipline, but loving Kally is simply how she lives, how she might always live. The record ends and she gets up quickly to take it off the gramophone.

"I thought you two would be hobnobbing at the Romanische," Kally says in her soft, Boston-accented voice, shaking Sterling's hand, hugging Lenore and kissing her cheek. She and Lenore sit side by side at the table. Kally takes a cigarette from Lenore's case and lights it.

Kally has just taken a long walk and talks disdainfully of the Nationalsozialisten organizers she encountered at Leipziegerplatz. They were peddling their newspapers and talking about Zionist conspiracies to anyone who would listen.

"Where do they get those ideas?" Lenore says. There is a sudden, uncomfortable silence. "I'm so exhausted, *Liebchen*," she says to Kally to end the silence. She knows that more than the long hectic week has tired her out; being with both of them—her energies and loyalties so challenged—is sometimes too much for her.

Kally laughs. "My cue to entertain our esteemed Bauhäusler while you get some sleep?"

"If you will." She touches Kally's arm lightly. "We'll still go to the galleries tomorrow, won't we?" Lenore asks Sterling. "I just wish you didn't have to leave so soon. Or that the Bauhaus were in Berlin."

"The Bauhaus is lucky to be anywhere at all," he says, placing a hand on her shoulder. "You get your rest, my dear. Don't worry about me."

82

"Gute Nacht, Freunden." She kisses both Kally and Sterling and leaves the kitchen.

Kally gets up, refills the teakettle, lights the stove. She stands and listens as Lenore closes the bedroom door. "I'm worried about her," she whispers, sitting across from Sterling. "She doesn't sleep much these days."

"She doesn't know how to relax," he says, cradling his teacup. "It's her way, isn't it? Her ambition."

"No, that's not what it is." Kally picks up her cigarette, relights it with a stray kitchen match on the table. "When she's away from you, she spends a great deal of time thinking about you. She works harder than ever and whiles away the nights at Romanische. Always her forceful, charming self. I'm the only one who knows how she's really feeling."

He doesn't like her tone or her impertinence. He sits in silence, not quite knowing what to say. It's hard for him to imagine what Lenore feels, she never quite tells him. "I see her as often as I can. We've got separate lives in separate cities," he says finally, hoping this will end the discussion.

"No, no, no, Crönchen," Kally says, shaking her head. "Let's be on the level."

"She's a very dear friend, nothing more. She knows that."

"But she doesn't know *why*." Kally puts her cigarette in the ashtray and looks at him, steepling her chin. Not hostile or confrontational; he believes she's a true scientist, always observing, as if in bringing up the subject she only wants to monitor his reaction. She seems too calm to be as jealous as he knows she must be.

"I can't make myself feel for her what I don't." He looks away, stares at the ceiling-fan shadows crawling across his arms. He hears himself breathing uneasily.

"Then what do you want from her?" Kally raises her voice. He says nothing. "Don't you get what you want out on the Kurfürstendamm?"

The teakettle whistles, startling him. She gets up and takes it off the stove, staring at him all the while. "I don't know what you're talking about," he says shakily, wishing more than ever she would simply leave him alone.

Kally sits down again. "You're trying to lead a double life, aren't you? Well, I saw you out there last month. I wasn't spying, it's just that I walk through those districts all the time. My perverse fascination. I know the streetwalkers like to dress up like schoolchildren, but some of them really *are* children."

He's noticed all the children, too. There are so many of them lining the Kurfürstendamm the cars can hardly pass. The huge, dark cars of businessmen and government officials are backed up for blocks all along Weidendammbrucke, waiting in line to pick up children. He reaches for a cigarette, but his hands are shaking and he drops it quickly. "I leave the children alone, if that's what you're asking. And I don't want to talk about this anymore. You're trying to involve yourself in something that doesn't concern you."

"Lenore concerns me," she answers, stubbing her cigarette. "You can't begin to know how much. I won't stand by and let you make her part of your deception, your tawdry masquerade."

"There's no deception, Kally. No tawdry masquerade," he says. "At least not on *my* part."

"Don't get self-righteous, Cronheim. You don't accept what you are. Nor do you seem to care that Lenore is hurt in the process. I hate it that she's picked a man who hasn't got the decency to—" She stops herself. He imagines she will start to cry or run out of the room, but instead she stares at him again. Then her face reddens and she looks away suddenly.

"You hate it that she's picked a man, period."

She sits quietly, as if composing a damning retort. She lights another cigarette. "That's nothing new. She and I have both had our share of brilliant artists and writers."

"For sport, no doubt," he says, matching her scornfulness, almost forgetting his discomfort.

"You'd know more about that than she and I would," she says coldly, and leaves the kitchen.

He wants to pack and leave right now, as if in leaving he and Lenore would forget they ever knew each other. He would sit in the dark, drafty Anhalter station, feeling as indifferent as its remote, iron-girded vaults. Piece by piece, he would give everything he has to the beggars who wander the station. But he won't do this. He will go to the Kurfürstendamm.

•

Cabaret Dionysus is bright as the daytime, white marble walls and Doric columns, full-sized plaster casts of classic statues and caryatids. Replicas of Greek temple pediments hang like paintings on the walls. Crystal chandeliers and sconces with so much wattage he is truly afraid they will explode. He looks over the young men in their leather jackets, sailor's uniforms, spread-collar white shirts, and stovepipe pants. Painted faces, large Harlequin eyes. Well-tailored middle-aged men with goatees, monocles, watch chains, and top hats on the table grasp huge wads of deutsche marks.

On the small center stage, with its curving backdrop of the Parthenon painted in bright pinks and sky blues, two tall, muscular men wearing red cutaway coats and G-strings dance a minuet to an eight-piece band's jazzy rendition of a Mozart divertimento. The band members are emaciated teenagers, wearing nothing but white makeup and top hats. They and the whole cabaret are beginning to look like frantic, sad hallucinations. He sits alone, drinking too much Scotch, smoking too many Salem Aleikums. The strong Turkish tobacco is making him hoarse. But he doesn't intend to talk much. He lets the young men come up to him. No, he wants to tell Kally, they're not children. With their painted faces and tired smiles, they are truly much older than he, creeping along from one table to another, cigarettes perched in their mouths. He refuses them all, muttering some Hungarian he's learned from Moholy: an old proverb about God and the tillers of the earth, which they assume is a polite refusal.

But a young Hungarian smiles at the proverb and sits down beside him, takes one of his cigarettes. He's short and well built, wearing a tightly fitting white suit jacket, and a plaid beret that hides one of his darkly painted eyes.

"Are you a clergyman?" the young man asks in perfect German, leaning toward him. His cologne smells like a sharp, bitter spice.

Sterling shrugs. The performers finish their dance and nearly all the men stand up whistling and clapping.

"Hotel Casanova?" Sterling asks. He leaves a few deutsche marks on the table, puts his coat on, and wanders with the young man through the crowd. Outside, on the Kurfürstendamm, the *Pupenjungen* are everywhere, their clothing carnival-like in the bright light from the street lamps: impossible combinations of plaids and stripes, shoes and hats in vivid primary colors. They lean against dance-hall and hotel entrances, elaborate with terra cotta and stone façades from a dead era, and along the curbs where the cars pass by, picking them up.

The hotel is a few doors away, its faded canopy flapping loudly in the wind, sounding like the flocks of crows in the Tiergarten. He gets a room key from the desk clerk and he and the young man walk up three flights of narrow steps to the room. The window, right below the garishly flashy neon hotel sign, is larger than the bed. Or anything else in the mildewed and dismal room with its peeling yellow floral wallpaper, torn voile curtains, light bulb hanging from a wire over the dresser. The neon flashes its harsh pink light on and off, making him more uneasy. The young man stands against the door, hands on his hips, impatient or sneering—

Sterling can't tell which. He counts out a small stack of deutsche marks, lays it on the dresser. He walks over to the window and opens it wide; a wailing soprano saxophone, bass, and piano trio from Club Eldorado pours into the room, which seems to expand and contract with the pulsing neon.

"*Yats*," the young man says, dancing a fast, disjointed Charleston and ripping off his shirt. The buttons fly all over the room. "*Yats*," he says again and again.

"*Ist jazz*," Sterling says, and motions him over to the bed.

•

He struggles with the door latch. He has done this for months: sneaking out, walking all the way back here to Dorotheenstrasse, where street lamps are spaced too far apart. A dim light shines into the high-ceilinged foyer. The long-case clock begins to chime, startling him. He closes the door as quietly as he can and stands against it, his fingers tapping nervously on the door frame.

"Come sit down," Lenore says. He doesn't move, barely even breathes. "Well? Come on in here. Don't stand out there as if you don't understand your native language."

He walks into the living room, where she is sitting on the sofa in her paisley-print silk robe, smoking and leafing through a large book with gold-edged pages. He sits in the library armchair opposite her, wishing he were at Anhalter, waiting to leave.

"I couldn't sleep, so I'm rereading *War and Peace*. I'm on page 90." She closes the book and holds it in her lap. She looks away from him, keeps smoking. "Where do you go? Should I be angry? Should I be worried?" she asks, sounding as if she will cry.

He crosses his legs, runs his fingers on the beveled edge of the bookcase beside him. She knows the truth, she's challenging him to lie. He suspects she will throw him out for good no matter what he tells her. "It has nothing to do

87

with you," he says, clutching his Donegal wool coat around him, though he is too warm, perspiring.

"Tell me something I don't know." She exhales the smoke angrily and it lingers in front of her.

"*Spatzierengehen*," he says. He leans toward her, resting his chin on both hands. He tries to smile, but he can barely look her in the eye.

"It's not that you walk. It's *where* you walk." She throws the book onto the fragile-looking sofa table. The dishes in the china cabinet behind her rattle. "Kurfürstendamm." She makes it sound like profanity.

"Kally told you, didn't she?"

"She didn't have to. I overheard the conversation." She finishes her cigarette and lights another one with it. "Accidentally, of course. So like her, always looking out for me. But I've suspected this for a long time. I kept thinking, No, it couldn't be. Not the illustrious Sterling Cronheim, not the man I'm so crazy about." She shakes her head, looking wistfully sad.

"Listen to me, won't you?" He wants to comfort her, but what will he tell her? Maybe it's better that he leave her alone, find a man, live with him, be inseparably close, as she and Kally are. But instead, he's made everyone unhappy, not wanting to do without Lenore.

"Of course I'll listen. I'll listen to you tell me you don't need those strangers, that I'm the one you really want to be with." She takes out a handkerchief from her robe pocket, twists it tightly with both hands.

He wants to tell her that, word for word. But he doesn't know how to make it the truth. He gets up and sits beside her on the sofa, puts an arm around her shoulders. "Please, *Liebchen*, I—"

"Don't you dare call me that. Save it for the boys." She pushes him away, stands, pulling the robe around her tightly. "I'm going to bed. And I don't want to find you here in the

each other, bright, discordant, and more jarring than her dream.

She turns off the telescreen and hears cabinet doors opening and closing, a piano arrangement of "Mood Indigo" on the radio. She gets up and finds Sterling at the center island unit, making fresh orange juice. He's wearing a white Oxford shirt, sleeves rolled up, Levi's, his hair starkly silver under the fluorescent light. Looking rested, serene, like the great artist and teacher he once was.

"I know what you're thinking," she says, walking up to him, the shawl wrapped around her like a floor-length, strapless dress. She glides around the kitchen table, in tempo with the introspective piano solo. "The city never sleeps and neither does this woman."

He looks up from the juicer and the piles of oranges on the gleaming white counter. "You don't take care of yourself," he says, pouring a small glass of juice from a lead-crystal pitcher and handing it to her.

"Neither do you. You're too busy trying to take care of me." It's what she wanted, she thinks, someone with unswerving benevolence, the fairy-tale figure he's becoming for her as he hides from the rest of the world. Better him here with her than Bradley, who's too volatile these days, making her constantly anxious. She sits down at the table, which Sterling has set picturesquely, like a country inn's; red and turquoise plates she's hidden away and never used, red linen napkins, ogee bowl stemware. The kitchen window is full of light, the mobile of prisms and holoreflectors throwing sparkling, translucent colors on the black-and-white table. He squeezes the last of the oranges, pours a second glass of juice, gathers up the rinds.

"Save them. You dry the peels and carry them around with you to attract love. And God knows I need some love in my life."

He stacks the halved oranges like bowls and puts them on a red platter. He sits down across from her, not knowing

91

what to tell her. She is in a somber but unpredictable mood. He's afraid of her this morning. He was starting to feel good again, fearless, up early to go to the Metropolitan Museum before work. He plans to take his sketchbook with him and draw motifs from Japanese paintings, gather ideas for his photograms. Later, he will spend a six-hour graveyard shift developing C-prints of other people's negatives. His new job. Something to get him back into the world. That and the long walks he's been taking every day, ten kilometers, sometimes more, all over the city.

"Have dinner with me tonight," he says, with a bright, sudden smile.

●

Later that morning, after sitting through auctions broadcast from Sotheby's in London, and buying two of Klee's paintings, he walks to the Met. He wanders through the Asian Art galleries and sketches the Japanese motifs, just as he wanted to. He spends most of the day marveling at their sense of form, balance, and color. He knows the aesthetics of these works are completely different from his own, that there is no insurmountable separation between the artist and his art, or the artist and the world around him. He wishes for the unity he only knows of but never experiences, of the energies in the universe.

The galleries remind him of a lantern party a long time ago: It's late at night or even early in the morning by now, at a chalet just outside Weimar. Japanese paper lanterns hang everywhere, from the ceilings and chandeliers, around the door frames, outside, on the porch, strung from tree to tree, glowing festively with light. He is here with his friends, colleagues, and students, but he does little more than smile and joke lightly, as if they are all strangers. He wanders out to the flagstone terrace, bordered by ivy, overlooking a forest of pines. He is alone, sipping his Scotch, watching the people and their costumes, which consist mostly of layers and layers of brightly colored diaphanous fabric. They are to demonstrate a sculptural, plastic use of cloth, without sewn seams of any kind. He wears red across one shoulder as a sash. But where he's standing, under the lantern light, everything is black and white, like a film; the light altering the world, doing what his own eyes can't do. He wishes he had gone to Berlin for the weekend. But he stays away because of her and forgets that Berlin is an entire city. He sees only her house, and the drafty guest room where he tried to sleep.

He hasn't seen her for months. He keeps writing to her as if nothing has changed. But she doesn't write back. A few days ago, the post office returned all the letters he'd written in a wrapped bundle, ADRESSE UNBEKANNT stamped across them in red.

He leans against the stone railing and listens to the Bauhaus band—banjo and accordion players, percussionist, pianist, clarinetist—playing their peculiar blend of jazz and traditional German, Hungarian, and Slavic dance music. An earthquake-like rumble from the people dancing on tabletops. Someone fires a pistol over and over to the beat of the music. Three of his students gather around him to talk. They are learning English and saying simple things with long words and phrases he never hears people use in conversation. Two brothers and their cousin, all of them at least fifteen years younger than he is, wearing toga-like costumes over their white shirts and tweed pants. They drive around the countryside, taking photographs of farm families and their lands at night from unthinkable angles and heights, distances and proximities. He talks with them about how the camera sees differently from the eye. The camera doesn't have a memory to reconstruct the world when it sees. So does the camera see the world the way it really is? they ask him. Yes, he tells them, but we might not be able to see the photographs any more objectively than we see the world.

When they leave, he looks up at the sky, hazy, starless.

The band plays "Banana Shimmy." He closes his eyes, taps his foot, and swirls the ice in his glass in tempo. He tries to keep thinking about photography. He could go back indoors and look for Lucia Moholy; they've been talking lately about new darkroom techniques.

"I've just about finished *War and Peace*," Lenore says, walking up to him, startling him. He almost doesn't recognize her; she's wearing a hat with a black veil that covers most of her face and a cape, gray under the yellow light, over her dark velvet dress. He's extraordinarily glad to see her.

"But I don't want to read the rest of it tonight." She takes the cape off, drapes it on the railing, leans against it.

"Lenore," he says, putting his arms around her. She pulls away from him, coolly.

"Yes, I read all your letters before I sent them back, so spare me a rehash."

She's baiting him with her cold artifice and he can barely see her face through the veil. "You threw me out that night. Now what do you want from me?"

"The same thing you want."

"Then why didn't you come to see me?" he asks, ignoring her innuendo. "I know you've been here in Weimar. You'd never miss a Bauhaus evening unless you had to."

"And you missed all of them. Rudolf Serkin's wonderful concert, J. J. P. Oud's provocative lectures on architecture," she says in a mocking high-society voice.

"I meant to avoid you, and that's exactly what I did." He looks at her closely and he can see she's as angry as he is. "You had no right to pass judgment on me that night."

She lifts the veil from her face. "And you've still got no right to try to deceive me. You're doing a damn poor job of it. I know what you want from me."

He looks away from her and grips the railing with both hands. She steps closer to him and leans her head against his shoulder. The band's lively music fades in and out as people open and close the door. He's beginning to believe

94

he does want her. He can't keep ignoring the dreams he sometimes has, or the passing thoughts. Without thinking he slips his arm around her waist.

"Let's get out of here. Take me to your house," she whispers, stroking his arm. "I don't have a place to stay and the last train to Berlin is long gone."

He knows this isn't so much a lie as a plea; she has at least a dozen friends in Weimar who would put her up for the night at a moment's notice. "You expect everything in the world to go your way, all the time, don't you?"

"A simple 'yes' or 'no' will do, Crönchen."

"Come along," he says, taking her by the hand, leading her back into the house and the crowds and the bright paper lanterns.

•

She walks around his parlor as if she has never seen it before. Smoking, always smoking. He has virtually no furniture and he's painted murals in reds and blacks on the walls, abstract forms stretching up to the ceiling and dipping below the wainscotting. His painting studio is where the dining room should be, the large windows and connecting hallways are cold and empty in the nighttime. Not a place to live.

He notices how nervous she is, shaking nervous, as if she's never done this. But with other men there were distractions, she told him: too many glasses of gin or brandy, unnecessary conversations on literature, art, or politics. Unnecessary because all she could remember was straining to speak above a loud Victrola. Of course, those evenings didn't end with talking; he knows her, knows what she expected, what she expects from him now. He should be the nervous one, and he is; he can't mutter a diplomatic goodbye after this night and vanish from her life. He is about to turn on the hurricane-shaded lamp.

"Leave it off," she says, sitting on the serpentine sofa.

There is only the foyer light faintly shining into the room. She takes her hat and cape off. She's wearing elbow-length black gloves, no jewelry, and her cap-sleeved dress has an alluring V neck. Is she really so different from the *Pupenjungen*? He sits uneasily in the wing chair opposite her, its bristly upholstery scratching his arms. He should refuse her as gently as he can.

"I won't believe you're telling me no, Sterling Werner Cronheim, I won't believe it." She lights a cigarette. She knows exactly what he's been thinking. "It's not my habit to let someone tell me no. I know how to get what I want. I always succeed." She's calm now, smoking leisurely, waiting.

"Then I'm sorry to spoil your perfect record," he says. He can't predict how he feels from one moment to the next. He doesn't understand his feelings; how and why should he expect her to? "Listen to me, Lenore, I'm not the man that you deserve. You're a wonderful woman, beautiful, intelligent, but I—"

"Spare me the elegy. This is really about what happened to you right before the war, isn't it? That financier who helped you get to Europe. I don't fault you for what you had to do in exchange for that."

"I needed more than money from him." He's forgotten he told her any of the story, even his standard, watered-down account of this aging financier's wish to better the world with all his money in his later years. His "aging financier" was a youthful forty-six-year-old who set him up in a luxurious apartment on Fifth Avenue overlooking Central Park. He introduced Sterling to a vast and elegant underground society of richly paneled salons, private clubs, country estates of men just like him.

She puts out her cigarette, gets up, and sits on his chair arm. "What do you need from me?" she asks plainly. She touches him, drawing him closer, and he holds her tightly. Her satin gloves feel like a cool breeze on his face.

His hands shake badly and he releases her. "I can't do

this," he says, sounding frantic. "I can't. Don't you understand? I can't." She sits on his lap and puts her arms around
him. She helps him unbutton her dress and slip it off her
shoulders. He fingers the lacy edges and the smooth silk of
her camisole, slowly letting his hands ease it off her. He's
never felt so safe and so fearful at once, here in his own
house with a woman who knows him well, not wandering
desperately all over the Kurfürstendamm selecting young
men whose real names he will never know. She smiles at his
solemnity as she takes her gloves off. He kisses her, suddenly
and forcefully. When he lets go of her, she stands and helps
him up. She takes him to the bedroom, tugging him by the
hand.

Streetlight, fractured by the Venetian blinds, seeps into
the bedroom. He feels nothing but pain now, as if he will
never see her, never touch her like this again. She whispers
his name and he presses his face against her neck. He hears
his own breathing echoing back at him, jittery and loud. Her
hands feel like warm water running over him. He opens his
eyes wide and the shafts of light explode, hurting his eyes.
He is a blind man, touching, kissing her all over, trying to
make a picture of her in his mind.

This was for you, he whispers, much later. But she is
already sleeping, huddled against him.

●

Wanda finds herself waiting anxiously to see him at dinner.
She's dashed straight home after work, changed into a lacy
red-and-black draped-collar dress, taken the extra time and
care to make sure her hosiery seams are straight. Sitting at
the beveled vanity mirror, brushing her hair, wavier and
darker blond than ever from the humid, cloudy weather,
she remembers suddenly that the vanity was a gift from a
man. She doesn't even know his name anymore.

The phone rings. It's Francine in the middle of a departure
gate, crowds passing by her, bundled in raincoats and

ponchos. Wide-angle airport viewphones are overly flashy, or is it just that she misses her mother so much?

"My goodness, we are dressed to the nines," her mother says.

"Why aren't you back home yet?" Wanda asks, leaning against the vanity, holding the headset in her hands.

"I'm stranded in Montreal. The airport is shut down because of the flash floods. I didn't want you to think I'd become a statistic."

"Well, like they say, it's safer to go to the moon than to fly from one North American city to another," she says, shrugging. She doesn't know what else to say. Francine glances at her watch and talks about the terrible weather ruining her schedule. She's frightfully busy now with her new position as director of community mental health services at the Sara Josephine Baker Medical Center and these speaking engagements that take her all over the Northeast.

When the conversation is over, Wanda doesn't feel as if she's talked to her mother at all.

•

Her voice echoes in the brightly varnished pinewood-paneled restaurant with its high ceiling and rafters where colorful Navajo rugs hang. The restaurant is on the ground floor of a historic five-story brick structure just north of Fulton Market and the South Street Seaport. The Brooklyn Bridge is in view out the windows and Patsy Cline's "Seven Lonely Nights" is playing in rechanneled Surround. The walls of antlers, moose heads, pre-Columbian axes, beaded deerskin dresses take Wanda back to the Southwest and the pueblos she hasn't seen for several years. She'd spent most of her time at White Sands Missile Range, riding around in a jeep, her father telling her more about nuclear testing than she ever wanted to know. The land was already dead, treeless, with constant sandstorms that left all the buildings permanently encrusted with sand and debris. A terrible sulfur odor lingered everywhere.

She is telling Sterling about her sphere design: how she and the Brothers Guam have modified her original concept, made it suitable for the Abbott's Quay Arts and Cultural Center. As she describes it, she envisions the center newly built on the site of the old Hotel Admiral. She tells him about the active solar-heating system, showing him with her hands the convection path and how the moderately powered fans will circulate the solar-heated air throughout the center. He doesn't realize how much she needs to talk about her profession. It is a comfort that nothing and no one else is. Not Bradley, who teletexes her long, pleading letters, telling her he hardly sleeps and that he wants to see her more often. Sterling tells her the design is innovative and ecologically sound. He smiles, lifts his wine goblet toward hers, means what he says.

She shrugs. She should be talking about Bradley or talking *to* him. Instead, she's with Sterling having a glossy discourse on solar architecture. "We're trying. But it can't compare with the Chaco Canyon pueblos in New Mexico that the Anasazi built. Seeing those pueblos when I was growing up had something to do with my deciding to pursue architecture," she says, perpetuating her own myth.

"How so?" he asks. He likes to listen to her talk; her true, unshakable passion for architecture brings back his old days. She helps him forget the truth—that Modernism is long gone, part of the past. That Modernism failed. She's told him why Modernism failed. The books tell him, the art channels tell him, the critics tell him, everyone has a reason for Modernism's failure. But he can't believe Modernism is really gone or that his old life, and Lenore, are also gone. He's thought about Lenore more than ever today. She should be sitting with him here, wearing the appealing dress Wanda is wearing. She would be shocked to see how old he is, old and frightened of everything. Of course, he doesn't look it; in his close-fitting Levi's and starched white shirts, he looks decades younger than he is. He's still carrying himself with vigor and dignity, maintaining his health admirably. Waiting to die, she'd tell him. And she would shout at him for his charade. She would know how to help him. He realizes Wanda is talking to him.

"The more I learned, the more amazed I was," she is saying. "Some of those pueblos were four stories high and covered at least two or three acres. What's left of them is impressive to look at, the way they're nestled in the canyon. But that's not the half of it. The Anasazi knew more about thermal storage capacity and insulation and site-specific solar-energy design than most of the architects at the Consortium."

"Lost knowledge, I presume."

"Absolutely. Like the pyramids. Even the ancient Greeks admitted they learned about architecture and engineering, to say nothing of philosophy and mathematics, from the Egyptians. But the historians won't admit it. Just like they keep denying that ancient Egypt was a black, African civilization."

"Yes. No one wants to believe where and how Western civilization came about," he says absently, twirling his wine-glass. Doesn't Wanda understand how he feels, how lonely he is? Can't he let himself let her comfort him?

"Even the so-called Italian Renaissance didn't come close to the achievements of Egypt and the other civilizations of Africa," she says. She wishes the school textbooks had told her this and helped her have some pride in her heritage. She's glad she's learned the truth finally, and sees that what passes for advanced civilization now is in irrefutable decline, despite the Sony telescreens, L-5 space stations, and bold attempts to build two-hundred-story skyscrapers. She sips mineral water from the crystal tumbler, remembering that she used to have this conversation with Bradley. Better to talk and learn more about the glorious African past than slavery or colonialism. But now it's all gone wrong with Bradley. She's catching herself thinking of Sterling instead and wanting to see more of him, and he's developing C-prints at a Long Island City photo lab and is rarely home when she is. Dull work for meticulous advertising agency clients, but it gets him back out in the world, he says. He reminds her of the socialites who have paying jobs instead of hobbies. He's making a cozy routine for himself, taking over more and more of her studio space, with his stacks of photograms and inventory files of the paintings, sculptures, drawings, and photographs he owns, lists which get longer and more distinguished all the time. Lots of Kandinsky and Klee on loan in Zurich. His new life runs so smoothly she feels as if she can't ever know who he really is.

"You shouldn't lose hope," he says, seemingly out of nowhere.

She can't remember what she said that would precipitate such a remark. "*I* shouldn't lose hope? What about you, hiding from the world when you could—do I dare say it?—be doing something positive?"

"I'd like to think I'm already doing something positive . . . for you," Sterling says, gazing out the window at the crumbling asphalt and rotting wood of the loading docks and piers. Across the harbor, along the Brooklyn waterfront, are silos and red brick warehouses that remind him of the old days in Germany.

She leans back and sips her wine. The goblet throws tiny spectrums across the checkered tablecloth. She wants to laugh at their conversation, so veiled and platitudinous. What are they really trying to say to each other? She tsk-tsks. "You and I just can't stop telling each other how to live. We need a vacation, both of us, together. You'd like New Hope, Pennsylvania. My Aunt Reggie and I used to go there all the time to check out the antique shops."

He can't believe she's saying this. She has to know the story. How can she talk about it, about him, the way everyone else does? New Hope was a short distance from William's summer home. The secluded four-story Victorian house with its fifteen acres and private road is still there, still belongs to his family, who are everywhere, buying up what's left of the North American aluminum and steel industries and active in Toronto politics, where nearly every elected official is black. He wishes William were alive to see it.

But William was a casualty back then, just as he himself could have been. The House Un-American Activities Committee all but chased Sterling from Hollywood just days before he was about to direct *Sorry, Wrong Number*. He fled to the University of Pennsylvania the moment he was offered the position. Dean of the School of Fine Arts. HUAC had already swept through Temple University and the Jefferson Medical School; now they lingered around Penn. He knew he wasn't safe there, either. He and Lenore had been anti-Fascists back in Europe. He'd done more than enough for HUAC to try to label him a Communist.

At Penn was William Thompson, assistant professor in the architecture department and, with him, still more dangers. The trustees could dismiss them both. So they took no chances. They drove to New Hope for their tense and increasingly passionless weekends in separate cars, several hours apart. Sterling provided elaborate and excessive explanations for these trips to colleagues and friends: photography shoots of Lancaster County Amish houses and lands or visits with distant cousins and former students. Still, he always thought no one really believed him, and the occasional well-wishing phone call from a trustee would leave him suspicious and unable to sleep or eat for days.

"I won't be going to New Hope with you. And since you've been such a careful reader of my biographies, I don't believe I need to explain why," he says, raising his voice above the harmonies of Patsy Cline's backup singers.

"I'm sorry," she tells him. They sit silently for a long while. He stares out the window, looking fragile, like someone who could set himself on fire on the steps of a public building in desperation. "Can't we talk about something else?" she says, touching his elbow. He pours the last of the wine from the carafe, drinks it quickly, as if he's swallowing pills with it.

She was planning to ask him why he didn't turn to architecture sooner. It was unorthodox, establishing an architectural firm so late in life, mostly on his reputation as an artist and a teacher. She thinks of the unfinished drawings of the Philadelphia Civic Center, how innovative the design was. But his associates reworked it and turned it into third-rate Frank Lloyd Wright. Maybe he's never seen the building, never been back to Philadelphia since those days. Maybe he was happy then. He had influence, resources, money, a graduate school, and his own architectural firm. The biographies say he was considering retiring from Penn and building a country house and devoting himself to painting. Or going back to Paramount, where directors were getting more respect and more clout. She wishes he would talk to her.

"William was brilliant," he says quietly, setting his empty wine goblet down. He's talking for his own benefit and he knows it. He needs to say something about William, acknowledge him. He can't help but blame himself for William's suicide, for not knowing how to help him. William was so devoted to him in those years. They would sit for hours, drafting in the studio, far apart from each other, as if people were nearby, suspicious, watching them.

The waiter brings the check in a slender leather folder. Sterling takes out his wallet, counts out the amount in crisp twenty-dollar bills, their authenticity holograms of pyramids and sunrises glowing reddish-blue.

"I like the feel of real money. Not numbers on a screen," he says cheerfully, as if he has forgotten the conversation and this is a new one between strangers.

He sends Wanda home in a taxi and he takes the elevated to Long Island City. It's the kind of compact, low-ceilinged train from Japan people always complain about, revealing their bigotry. The train stalls between stations, power failing. In the dark, people are exchanging subway and El horror stories. He closes his eyes and sees rain outside the windows of William's New Hope house. Rain hitting the windows hard, as if someone is throwing tubfuls of it. He remembers how he made it rain in the studio-created Chicago in *Night Without a Day*. With low-angle shots and a clever manipulation of parallax, he made the rainstorm large and engulfing. Joan Bennett and Farley Granger stepped out of the neon-lighted Tahiti Sunset Club and rushed down the streets, black and shining from the rain. Now it's William standing outside, his suit, his hair drenched and black as the streets. Or William is in the train, the passenger standing by one of the doors staring out at the dark tracks, staring as if he really sees something.

•

Later that night she visits Bradley. The outside lights on his houseboat are off and she knocks for what seems like hours. She looks for her key, but she doesn't want to think he's unable to answer the door. When he finally lets her in, everything is the same. She puts her arms around him, and his skin is hot and slick with perspiration. He doesn't kiss her, but turns away and picks up the Zippo from the terminal table and lights it over and over; the flame throws flickering light and deep shadows across his face. He looks withered and weak. It must be the two-day-old beard, the uncombed hair clumped in tufts, the half-unbuttoned, wrinkled white shirt. He sits down at the terminal table and leans back against the computer, the green light from the screen covering him with a mortuary glow. A Bruckner symphony is playing on the radio, loud and morose.

She crouches beside him. "Bradley, what's wrong?"

"Why are you living with that white man?" he asks, with a calmness that frightens her. He turns on the task lamp beside him and picks up his pipe.

"Don't get upset, lover man," she says, placing a hand on his arm. "He's only a friend."

"Cut it out, Wanda. Just cut it out." He shakes his pipe at her and squints as if he's in sudden pain. "I know who he is, thanks to my hacker friends. He's Werner Schmidt and he's loaded. Big-time art speculator. Any one of his Klees would bring twice my net worth. You know how to pick them, sister. Rich, white, and old."

She's amazed that Bradley has found out so much about Sterling's assumed identity. A while ago, in the hopes of avoiding this confrontation, she'd casually told him that a Mr. Schmidt was renting studio space during the day. Maybe it's best to let Bradley know the real story, she thinks as she sits on the sofa, directly across from him. "I'm going to tell you the truth. You won't believe me, but I'll tell you anyway. Werner Schmidt isn't his real name. He's Sterling Cronheim. The artist."

"Cronheim who disappeared?" She nods. He slumps back in the chair, snickering. "You live with Cronheim. And on the weekends both of you visit Amelia Earhart."

"Bradley—"

"Come on, sister, listen to yourself. It sounds like the Saturday-morning cartoons," he says, "the superhero and his secret identity. Now tell me this is your idea of a bad joke." Bradley gives her a look of impatient contempt.

"It's the truth." She doesn't understand why he won't believe her. Or why more people haven't figured out who Cronheim is, not even his financial advisers or his coworkers. After all, he looks just like his photographs. Bradley keeps watching her, an odd but unreadable expression on his face.

"I almost feel sorry for you," he says finally.

"Stop it! You know I hate this Waspy restraint of yours."

"Well, you'll have to go tell Cronheim and Earhart about your terrible boyfriend and his Waspy restraint." He gets up suddenly, puts down the pipe, takes out a pack of unfiltered Lucky Strikes from the terminal table drawer, and lights one. He paces as he puffs, looking out the windows. She's never seen him smoke a cigarette.

She swats the clouds of smoke with her hands, reaches over to open a window. A Coast Guard cutter speeds by, throwing red light into the cabin. "Just say what's on your mind, Bradley."

He sits down on the far end of the sofa. "Get rid of that man. You have no idea what you're getting yourself into. Cronheim, indeed. When we get rich enough and old enough we can be whoever we want." He starts to laugh. "He's probably been Picasso and Matisse; Van Gogh on his off days. Rembrandt when he's feeling daring. And you're his artist's model, his sole inspiration, right?" He laughs some more, waving the cigarette around.

She lets him sit there and laugh. She should have known he would react like this. She takes off her coat and self-consciously looks down at her party dress.

He looks her up and down coldly. "That's exactly what I'm talking about. Look how he's got you dressed. It's pathetic."

She leans against the sofa arm and mocks his up-and-down until he frowns at her. "You know me, I would have dressed this way anyhow."

"No, you wouldn't," Bradley says, shaking his head. "He took you to dinner tonight, didn't he?" She shrugs. "I know he did. I can smell the wine on your breath. You never drink wine unless it's a good vintage and somebody else is paying."

"That's a rotten thing to say to me."

"What you're *doing* is rotten." He lights another cigarette. "You must think I'm some kind of idiot. You were supposed to come see me hours ago. Now it's eleven-thirty. You've had your dinner and put the old bastard to bed and tucked him in."

She tugs at her dress hem, suddenly feeling transparent. She hasn't worn this dress for ages, or spent so much time getting ready for dinner at a casual restaurant. But she

106

refuses to consider any of his harsh insinuations and she can't stand the way he's staring at her. She stares back. "I'm not his whore, Bradley."

"What else am I supposed to think!" He gets up, shoving the keyboard to the floor. The system beeps wildly. "Goddamn you, Wanda, get rid of him!"

"No! You get rid of your goddamn paranoia!"

"What paranoia? The man lives with you, doesn't he? He's got to have one hell of a good reason to pick Chambers Street over Park Avenue." He keeps staring at her. "Just give it up, Wanda."

She doesn't say anything for a few moments, hoping he will calm down, perhaps even apologize. He doesn't. He paces, smoking and staring at her so much she can't look at him. She wishes she hadn't said anything at all to him about Sterling. A mistake, telling first her mother, now him. "Bradley, we'll talk about this later," she says at last, using her mother's best professional manner.

"Oh no, we won't!" He kicks his chair and it rolls across the floor, slams into the bookshelf. "We're talking about it now!"

"There's nothing more to talk about. Cronheim is staying at my loft and he's going to keep on staying there."

"You listen to me, sister. Can't you understand I'm trying to help you? I want you to—"

"Bullshit. You're jealous and you've got no reason to be."

"Most other men would just dump you. But I don't want to see you doing this to yourself."

"Your benevolence knows no end," she says, forcing herself to laugh.

"You think this is funny? Well, it's not."

"It's my life and it's my loft and what I do is none of your goddamn business!"

He takes a step back, stumbling and knocking over one of his easels. "Is that so?" he says, laughing. "Is that so?" He starts imitating her in a shrill falsetto.

"Bradley!"

But he goes to the bathroom, cursing as he slams the door shut. She won't forget this conversation. He's never been so condescending. She opens more windows, trying to get rid of the smoke. The wall sconce next to the hatch flickers and burns out, leaving the diode-green glow of the Tokyo and Sydney stock market Quotrons. She sits on the wicker chair beside the starboard windows. Out on the piers teenagers are dancing to heavy metal, covering and uncovering a portable mercury-vapor searchlight, flashing the marina into night and day. She closes the windows and begins to feel the same dread she felt the night she saw Reggie at O'Sullivan's— that she and Bradley are doomed. She thinks about leaving him for good.

She does leave, not considering whether she will see him again or not, and takes the trolley home. A long, slow ride downtown, but she's in no hurry. She's about to take out her sketchbook when she suddenly remembers a dream from last night. She's walking through a deserted warehouse that overlooks a gray and gutted city with holes and slabs of wood where windows and lights should be. Steam is pouring through the warehouse rooms. She's looking for Bradley, but can't find him. Instead, it's Sterling she finds. His hands are in a dye vat and they are turning purple from the steaming remains of thousands of murices. Icicles are form-ing on the ceiling, water and ice falling from nowhere. She and Sterling are deaf, and they speak to each other with their hands and faces. The dripping water makes the dye vat overflow and fill up the room, fast. She and Sterling are trapped, reaching toward each other. They are the color of the murices, watching themselves slowly dissolve in the water like powder.

Mirrors

WANDA STANDS IN THE LOBBY of One World Trade Center waiting for her Aunt Tyler. She hates the World Trade Center towers, arrogantly bland, and this high-ceilinged lobby, with its banks of chromium-plated elevators, royal-purple carpeting, and clutter of airline and spaceline ticket counters along the walls, corporate logos and colors clashing. Tyler walks up to her, slender and tall in her coat-dress ensemble with a Mondrian-inspired motif. Even in the harsh downlights she looks no older than thirty, though she's almost fifty, her own best advertisement for vegetarianism, good nutrition, and toxin-free living. Her curly, shoulder-length hair seems brighter red than usual. She carries a burgundy briefcase and a carry-on bag which Wanda knows are both stuffed with nothing but books and files.

"Well, hello, my fellow sleepless wonder," she says in her Texas drawl, dropping her bags and hugging Wanda. Her voice is gravelly, as if she's smoked and drunk herself nearly to death, though she's done little of either. Wanda is still amazed that Tyler gets by with two hours of sleep every night. As much as she studies the decaying worldwide environment, Wanda can't imagine how she sleeps at all. But Tyler never looks burdened, she's as pridefully cheery as the rich heroines of the nighttime soaps. Wanda carries her bag and they ride the express elevator two-fifths of a kilometer into the sky. No view today, so the restaurant is virtually empty. The large convex windows look out on layers and layers of gray clouds. Without the view, the restaurant is cage-like and confining, even with its austere elegance: shoji screens and palm trees in brass-rimmed black laminate pots interspersed among tables draped with white antique-lace tablecloths. Outside, the city looks as if it will float away, the buildings insubstantial and gray as the clouds.

They sit next to the windows and order mineral water and lunch. A young blond woman in a red velvet dress plays Art Tatum piano solos on a baby grand. Wanda tells Tyler about the building design she's about to submit to the Abbott's Quay Foundation. She describes the active solar-heating system—difficult to keep it cost efficient in overcast Toronto. Next to tall structures like the CN Tower, the cultural center will add needed contrast to the skyline. It will be respectful of its context, unlike environmentally irresponsible and overscaled Toronto structures like the SkyDome.

"Let me make a toast to the shape of things to come," Tyler says, lifting her glass and smiling. "Sweetheart, your aesthetics are all right by me. There are scientific studies that say non-angular spaces have a spiritual, tranquillizing effect. Believe me when I tell you the only reason we haven't been blown to the highroad in the heavens is that the President's got that Oval Office."

Tyler starts talking about the men she's met in Washington lately; they're usually neoconservatives, all wrong for her. Most of them work in the Departments of Technology, the Environment, or the Interior. Frivolous and shortsighted, she calls them. She's already been married and divorced four times, and both her daughters are off in law school. Today, she talks mostly about the ozone layer; the Semiannual International Ozone Symposium is about to take place in Venice. The last time Wanda saw her, Tyler was enraged that her friends on the Hill were still looking the other way as nuclear weapons were being transported all over the country's interstate highways in Winnebagos, under questionable safety precautions.

The waiter brings out the appetizers and Tyler starts to toy with a plate of stuffed mushrooms, separating the stems from the tops. "There's something I've got to tell you, sweetheart," Tyler says.

Wanda sips her water. The air-conditioned air feels stale and ruined, and she puts her white angora sweater back on. "Reggie already told me about Charles," she says.

Tyler picks up her glass and swirls the mineral water. "I thought the move back East would do him some good. But it hasn't. He's a depressed man these days."

Wanda tries to imagine her father depressed. He went about his life in such a tense frenzy, she wondered for years if he ever thought—about anything. "Maybe it's guilt. Not that his guilt does my mother and me any good now. Whatever it is, he doesn't need my sympathy. God protects fools and babies and fascists."

"And their daughters," Tyler says solemnly.

"That's the difference between us," Wanda says. She's got no patience for Tyler's grief. "You won't admit who and what *your* father was."

Tyler drops her fork, her green eyes open too wide, and she takes in a breath of air that sounds like a whistle. "I have to know the truth before I point any fingers, Wanda. It won't be easy, not now, with my father many years dead and buried," she says in a tiny voice, both frightened and astonished. She reaches for her glass and nearly drops it. And besides—" Tyler stops talking when the waiter brings large oval plates of pasta primavera. She looks down at the food, unable to say anything more.

Wanda remembers those days. Tyler's father (she has trouble thinking of him as her grandfather; he never spoke to her), Ernst Stoller, was in the last stages of Alzheimer's disease and he would walk up and down the halls of the

Bethesda nursing home where he was staying. He would peek into the rooms, calling his associates by name. He had forgotten the last several decades and he was living and working in the Dachau of his memory, trying to push the sick, dying, crutch- and wheelchair-bound residents out of their rooms. He would shake his head from side to side as he walked, speaking German in a shrill voice and stretching out his arms like a scarecrow in front of the full-length mirror in the lounge. He had scraggly white hair that hung down to his shoulders and he combed the balding top of his head, leaving red marks that swelled. She was afraid of him, vampire-pale, with eyes so dark they looked painted. He would spit into his hand and rub it into his white terry-cloth robe. *Der Glanz, der Glanz,* he'd say over and over. He thought he had to polish the robe like shoes.

It was years after his death that Wanda found out about the reporters who hung around in the nursing home lobby and the halls with tape recorders and sometimes even television cameras. Only Ernst Stoller's poor health saved him from extradition. He'd been one of the founders of the U.S. space program, though not someone whose name most people would recognize. The State Department, the Defense Department, the Air Force, NASA—they all had to have known and covered up the truth for the sake of the space program, that Ernst Stoller had killed countless Dachau prisoners in atmospheric-pressure experiments. There would hardly be a space program without Stoller and the rest of the Germans and their knowledge of aviation medicine and rocketry. The country of her birth has its priorities.

Tyler takes out a handkerchief and dabs at the tears about to fall. "You know I didn't mean to upset you," Wanda says to her. Outside the windows there are flashes of lightning and the sound of thunder, muffled and low.

"It's not your fault, my darling. I've been trying to find some answers, anyway."

"The National Archives again?"

Tyler nods. "I'm sifting through Dachau meeting rosters, immigration papers, you name it. Digging through our nation's closet." She laughs, painfully. "In about two hours, I have to forget all this and meet with the Adirondacks Environmental Impact Commission and talk about landfills leaking toxic chemicals into the ground water in the Wood- ward Lake region. A metaphor of our rotten lives. Not yours, my dear Du Bois. Mine and the rest of the Stollers', as you'd be quick to agree."

Wanda sits silently, trying to finish lunch. The delicate scents of whole-grain breads and Continental cuisine are revolting now. The fog glows with bright, distant sunlight, making the entire restaurant look artificial, like a wax museum exhibit.

She remembers a recurring dream from a few years ago, of being among thousands of corpses, brittle as porcelain, about to be bulldozed into a mass grave. She was alive, but couldn't move or scream. She started having the dream after her Austrian lover, a tall, red-bearded United Nations trans- lator in his early forties, told her he had lost a hundred and twenty-two relatives in the death camps. One night she described her dream to him. He sat still for what seemed hours, not saying anything at all, staring at the floor. She sat beside him, called his name, but he didn't seem to hear her. Then he started shouting at her, mostly in German, and he threw her out of his apartment into the freezing rain on East Forty-ninth Street. She never saw him again. Later, she imagined he thought she was being disingenuous, like the whites who tell her they want to play jazz, play basketball, eat chitterlings, live in Harlem.

Tyler gets the check from the waiter. Flustered, she first hands him one of her key cards instead of her American Express card. She runs her fork through the pasta primavera.

"A shame to waste food, isn't it?" she says.

•

"You're mighty pensive today, young lady," Francine says, putting an arm around Wanda's shoulders.

Wanda shrugs. She's with her mother, on the upper deck of the festively painted, red, white, and blue ferry. It was her idea, the Circle Line tour. Neither of them has ever taken the ride. Southeasterly winds gust around them. The Manhattan skyline disappears in the bright sunlight, shadows, and painful white reflections. Charcoal-gray factory smoke pours across the sky from a quartet of incinerator smokestacks on the New Jersey shore. What do they see, what do they want to see, she wonders, looking at the tourists around her. They all seem to be from Middle America or Asia, shivering in their colorful shirtsleeves, trying to hold on to their cameras and maps and children in the heavy winds. Except for the proud references to new landfills in lower Manhattan, the tour guide's amplified voice says nothing about the rising sea level and New York's inevitable destruction.

She thought she'd tell her mother about her conversation with Tyler, as she always does, any time she learns something new about the Stollers. But as usual, Francine sees right through her, expecting real answers, not speculations and gripes. Wanda hasn't talked to Bradley since the night he confronted her about Sterling. He's writing her letters again, over the teletex, backlogs of them, more than she has time to read. She doesn't know what to do for him and his self-loathing. She doesn't want to tell him to be proud of who he is. Being lectured to never helped her. Lately, she's been too busy at the Consortium to look after him. She and Mackenzie and a few others stay at the office until midnight or later, absorbed with life and work in cities where it's the middle of the next day.

"I'm just tired. My glamorous career and all," Wanda says. She dodges the group of young children running with their colorful Japanese kites. A passing motorboat startles her. The tour guide is talking about the history of New York Harbor. Wanda thinks of all the floods in her neighborhood and elsewhere, of how toxic the water is. She folds her arms and leans against the railing. It feels prickly against her back. She should have worn sneakers. It's hard to move around on the corrugated-steel deck in the stiletto heels of her ankle boots.

Francine clutches her steamer coat; the strong wind tries to rip it away. "Here's something else for you to mull over. Your father's been calling me. He calls me at home when he knows I'm not there and leaves long, rambling messages. How he is, what he's doing. As if we're friends or something and nothing's happened between us. He always looks nervous and rushed. And unkempt. If you could just imagine the impeccable major general unkempt and wearing colors he used to hate. Something's not right with him. But I'm not finding it within my heart to give him a shoulder or whatever it is he wants from me," she says in a soothing voice of apology and regret. She takes out an unopened pack of Salems from her black eelskin purse.

"Well, in case you're getting sentimental," Wanda tells her, "you just come and hang out with Tyler and me sometime."

"If it's what I think it is, I know the gist of it. But Tyler's got her own conflicts. I've heard some not so pretty stories about the way her father used to punish her. It's a wonder she's doing as well as she is."

"No, the wonder is how Ernst Stoller and all the other Nazis got away with everything," Wanda says.

"We really don't know what your grandfather was. He said all kinds of things no one's been able to prove or disprove." She reaches a hand toward her daughter, but Wanda pulls away.

"Don't you think you're getting a bit too sympathetic to these Stollers? Next thing I know you'll be talking to Charles and—"

"That's enough, young lady," Francine says. "Now I've got a thing or two to tell you. You've been spending more and more time these days worrying about your father and his ancestors, about your color, about Bradley's color. But you don't understand what's really going down."

"Oh yes, I do. I can hear it coming. If I want to worry about something, why don't I worry about colonialism in Africa, segregation in the South, civil-rights legislation getting overturned by the Supreme Court, and so forth and so on," Wanda says, making sweeping oratorical gestures. She's been having variations of this conversation with her mother for years; she's been tired of it for years.

Francine frowns. "Well, as Reggie would say, if we all spent more time *doing* something about these problems, there would be less time to worry about them."

"Yes, indeed, that's just what Regina Mae Du Bois would say. Good old Reggie and her braided hair and West African art collection and visibly African-American lover and—"

"What is wrong with you, girl? Are you drunk?"

Wanda shakes her head. "No, not drunk, just unenlightened. After all, I bitch about my dead Nazi relatives and my poor little rich boyfriend, who everybody thinks is white. I'm just the picture of self-indulgence, aren't I?"

"What do you think?" Francine says in a stinging tone. They stare at each other and Francine opens her pack of cigarettes and lights one. She's getting more angry with Wanda than she can stand. She's thinking of her own disappointments, and there are many. Her naïve love for Charles and their disaster of a marriage. She can't forget him, can't make him stop calling her. Out in the world there are bitter and constant injustices. She wanted to be Chief of Staff at St. Vincent's and she knows exactly why she wasn't chosen. Just as she knows why Reggie lost her NYNEX account and why her youngest sister, an obstetrician, got sued for malpractice in Louisiana. These are real problems, she thinks, and she can't help but compare her life and her

116

sisters' lives to her daughter's: a vice president of the Consortium, an associate project manager on what she likes to call Sandcastle all before her thirtieth birthday. Francine hates to think she's envious.

"Just say what's on your mind," Wanda tells her.

Francine doesn't say anything at all. She tries to, but she can't. She doesn't even want to look at Wanda right now.

Wanda walks away, to the aft deck, purposefully pushing aside as many of the tourists as she can. She leans against the corroded railing and stares out at the dead harbor. The wind is blowing, the mid-afternoon sun scalding. She knows exactly what her mother is thinking. She senses her mother condemning her just like everyone else does. Wanda can't stand it anymore, her mother turning away from her, even hating her. It takes awhile before she realizes she's gripping the railing so hard her palms are bruised and bleeding. The tourists are rushing past her to the foredeck to look at the Statue of Liberty. She doesn't ever want to talk to her mother again, she thinks, wiping sparse tears with a corner of her handkerchief.

●

Later that night, she sits in the living room, in the dark, watching her telescreen, eating raw cauliflower she has soaked in red wine vinegar. The Socrates Channel is having a satellite failure, so they are showing an old *Nightline* broadcast on Chernobyl. The videocamera floats through the ruins of Pripyat, through the streets and houses people have fled. Everything is a cold blue, an electronic wash of color, she presumes. The camera crew must have been in environmental suits, creeping around slowly as if they could avoid the radiation, like in mine fields. But it's everywhere, drifting around the world from Chernobyl, Three Mile Island, Stanhope, Lexington-Addison, and from all the secret accidents (more than five thousand worldwide, some say) kept out of the news. The wind howls on the sound track, blowing window shutters, leaves, and newspapers in the unnatural blue city. A grade-school teacher once told her that no one could live in an environment completely devoid of the restful properties of the color green.

Nuclear power station number four at Chernobyl erupted like a vengeful volcano . . . took ten days to control.

She reaches for more cauliflower from the teak salad bowl. The vinegar stings the bruises and lacerations on her hands. She watches a computer graphics simulation of the exploding reactor: the grainy, colorful stills look like landscapes Kokoschka might have painted. They are beautiful and sharply edited. But nuclear power is consistently beautiful. She thinks of the mushroom clouds rising gracefully from the land and into the sky, the glowing, mystical white filling a fiery red sky. Even the ash is beautiful, finer than sand or snow, and so light it flies.

She feels a kinship with blue Pripyat and the howling winds blowing all the lifeless air around. She picks up the small packages of industrial clay from the end table and hurls them across the room. The sound isn't as loud as she wants it to be. Her mother seems ready to disown her and Wanda doesn't know when she'll ever talk to her again. She doesn't know what she is to Sterling, beyond an image of Lenore. Bradley's true feelings are a mystery; all he talks about are his own failures. Secretly, they might all be deciding her effect upon them is like radiation, and wondering how much they can withstand. Maybe they will abandon her. Like Pripyat.

The phone rings, the shrill flutter a cross between a teakettle whistling and wind chimes. She knows it's Bradley even before she looks at the call-origin indicator. She answers it and lets him do the talking. He's wearing a paint smock and standing out on the upper deck with his cellular viewphone, its wallet-photo-sized screen reducing her anguish to crude pixels. The lulling voices of experts on the telescreen

118

citing nuclear power plant safety statistics distract her as he talks.

"We need a vacation together, don't you think?" he says with a cheeriness she believes is genuine. But it makes her laugh. She watches him watching her laugh. She keeps laughing and leans back on the sofa, cradling the headset on her shoulder. He looks at her, puzzled and disturbed, the streak of blue paint across his forehead like a sacred symbol. She hangs up the phone, forgetting to ask him when they will leave and where they will go.

•

She peers out the trapezoidal plate-glass windows as a water taxi speeds by, its lights distant and tiny like aircraft lights. The nighttime is uncomfortably dark and quiet here in Point O'Woods at Bradley's beach house of plate glass and cedar. Mackenzie's design, with its sharp interplay of angles, looks more like sculpture than a house.

"Bradley," she calls, still gazing out the window overlooking the beach and the open sea on Fire Island. She fingers the floral-patterned silk kimono he's given her, along with the long weekend at this house, which he usually rents out to acquaintances. She turns off the hi-intensity lamp beside the wicker armchair where she's been working for hours with her sketchbooks and architect's scales, waiting for him to return from his visit with old college friends a few doors away. He keeps telling her to stop working, to relax. She can't. He walks into the living room carrying lighted purple candles in a large Victorian silver candelabrum. His shadow curves up above him and across the slanted, beamed ceiling, swallowing the light.

She stands and walks up to him slowly, kissing him warily, as if she's never kissed him before. He seems to find it amusing. She undoes each button of his white shirt, more slowly than she has to, and slips it off. The scar stretches from the tip of his right collarbone laterally across his chest, like a jagged beam of light beneath his skin. Standing behind him, she puts her hand on his chest, feeling the scar and the ridged, pliable skin around it. Weeks and months will go by when she doesn't notice it. All he's told her is that he received the injury as he was avoiding capture by the rebels. She walks back to the window, leans her forehead against the plate glass, and puts both hands against it as if it's an invisible force field.

He sits down on the olive-green chintz sofa, crossing and uncrossing his legs. "Last night I dreamt about the war. The rebels were about to assassinate me," he says, picking up his pipe and lighting it.

"You never talk about the war."

"I don't think about it." He purposefully drops the lighter on the end table.

The way he says that, so coldly and angrily, leads her to believe he does think about the war, and often. The room crawls with odd shadows from the sloped ceiling and the protruding octagonal tower in the corner. She turns and can't see Bradley's face anymore in the dim candlelight. The mantel clock chimes the Westminster.

"I'll tell you what I *do* think about," he says. "Your drinking's out of control."

"What about *yours*? You've already gone through a fifth of—"

"—and you won't get rid of that old man. I can't believe it sometimes, you and he in a building that ought to be condemned when you and I could be living together in Connecticut. But no, you'd rather have Herr Schmidt."

She turns to face him. "Haven't we gone over this enough? I'd still be living there, with or without Cronheim," she says. She knows she shouldn't be talking about Sterling at all, that he'd hate it. But he lives safely, protected, exactly the way he wants to. Why can't she?

Bradley looks at her with pity and disgust. "You couldn't

go and have an ordinary affair. You had to make yourself believe he's somebody famous and great from the past. Delusions, sister." He goes to the liquor cabinet and pours himself Scotch into a highball glass, making more noise than he needs to. She turns back to the window and the dark ocean she can barely hear through the walls. "No retort? I'm shocked." He puts the glass down, walks up behind her, and slips his hands inside her kimono.

She turns to face him, touches the scar lightly, and quickly pulls her hand away. She's not even paying attention to this banter about Cronheim. She's confused about Bradley and his increasingly erratic behavior. She doesn't want to leave him. "I didn't come all the way out here to have this same old tired argument. So go find something else to talk about."

"Or *not* talk about," he says as he slips her kimono off. She kisses him and tries to forget.

They tumble across the chilly parquet floor and he makes love to her. She can't move, can't get involved. She reaches up to touch his face and he kisses her fingers. He is so large, moving so swiftly, she believes she must be just as large, sprawling all over the room. She feels trapped below, in the sand beneath the house, listening to two people gasp and moan on the creaking floor. Her favorite poet tried to die like this, drugged and crawling underneath her house.

●

"Tell me something," he says the next morning, getting up to open the raw silk drapes next to the vanity. The daylight is faint and gray in the bedroom, its sloping, truncated ceiling attic-like and confining. "How would they build a two-hundred-story building? And keep it from swaying too much in the wind?" He lies back down in bed beside her.

"Why do you want to know?" She yawns as she glances at the wall clock. "At six-thirty in the morning, no less."

He leans toward her, kisses her lips. "I just woke up from a nightmare. I was on the observation deck of one of the

Armstrong Aerospace towers and it was swaying like crazy."

She sits up. For no reason at all, she's extraordinarily happy. "In your next dream you be sure to fall in love with the structural engineer of your dreams and let her worry about it."

"What's wrong with the *architect* of my dreams? I already have *her*."

"She won't do windows or the towers to put them in." Wanda sits up, gathering the pine-green sheets around her knees. She expects him to say something, but he doesn't. She leans away from him. "Maybe your dream is about our relationship. We've built too high and the structure isn't sound and we've got to go back to ground level and start all over." She is about to get up when he pulls her down on top of him, kisses her.

"Damn you, child of the shrink. I don't want to start over, I want to marry you. You know that." He kisses her again. "But deep down you're scared to death of social trappings. So you build the buildings where other people live and work . . . and die."

"I'll find my own conflicts, thank you," she says, slipping away from him and getting up. "Just as you found your special talent for melodrama." She puts on her kimono and opens the drapes wider. The early morning WPA crews are bulldozing away the debris that washed ashore overnight. No, she doesn't want to marry him. Not now and maybe not ever. The overcast morning, getting up too early, trying to contend with Bradley—already she feels worn down.

"There you go, gazing out the window like some Gothic heroine waiting for her soldier," he says, getting out of bed and walking up to her. He catches her in a clumsy embrace.

She pushes him away and sits down at the vanity in the corner of the room, watching him in the large oval mirror as he puts his robe on. She's tired of his intrusiveness. He's looking at her, astonished and hurt, waiting for her to say something. "We need to be apart for a while, I think," she says, looking at herself, haggard, sad, whiter than ever. "A little while at least. You see how we're picking on each other all the time." She fingers the sculptured roses on her hairbrush. "Bradley?" He's disappeared from the mirror. She turns around and faces him. "Bradley? We can be adults about this, can't we?"

"It's that so-called Cronheim, isn't it?"

"At least you got the name right this time. He's a friend. A dear friend. You don't mind if I have friends, do you?" She wants to do whatever it takes to stop these constant disputes over Cronheim. It seems as if he is all they talk about now. She turns and looks up at Bradley. He pretends to suppress an outburst of laughter. She brushes her hair, wavy, unruly, and full of static.

"Wanda, you know men like that are never your friend. They just—"

"Shut up and listen to me for once!" She puts her hairbrush down and looks at him closely. He's folded his arms, but he's a comical bully. "You're getting to be less and less worth my while. I still haven't gotten over you sticking a gun in your mouth. What were you trying to tell me—that I was to blame for your troubles?"

"I wish you'd quit bringing that up. We don't need to talk about it anymore," he says.

"*I* do. I still think about that night, it gives me nightmares."

"There's nothing I can do about that."

"Oh yes, there is. For starters, you could apologize—really apologize. And as I was saying, let's think about spending some time apart."

"No! I don't want to!" he shouts, grabbing her by the shoulders.

"Don't be so goddamn theatrical." She pulls away from him. "I'm trying to have a serious talk with you."

"When are you going to get rid of that man?"

"Stop asking me that."

"I'm *demanding*, sister. I'm demanding that you get rid of him, or I will!" he shouts, shaking a finger at her.

She starts to laugh. She doesn't know what else to do. Everything is so unreal now: this argument over Cronheim, Cronheim himself, Bradley, who can't or won't understand how angry she is because of that night. "You're going to get rid of him? This I've got to see. What are you going to do, threaten him? Send a couple of hoodlums over to beat him? Or are you going to do it yourself?" Now she's laughing so hard she puts her head down on the vanity.

He yanks her out of the chair and slaps her. She screams and tries to cover her face and turn away. He knocks down the vanity mirror trying to get to her and it shatters. He slaps her again and again, until she falls to the hardwood floor, her face stinging from pain. She struggles to her feet. He's gone.

She wants to cry, but she can't. She steps carefully across the room, avoiding the broken mirror pieces, and goes to the bathroom. In the hazy fluorescent light, she tends to her face expertly, like a paramedic, thinking she should be more upset than she is. He's never hit her before. She wants something terrible and fatal to happen to him.

She puts on her trench coat and goes out on the porch, holding an ice pack over her eye. There will be terrible swelling within minutes or hours. She doesn't know how she will hide it. Bradley is gone and the beach is full of strangers, setting out their beach umbrellas and blankets a safe distance from the water. Killing themselves with ultraviolet rays, she thinks. She doesn't belong in this place, she doesn't belong with Bradley. A talk-radio station is blaring loudly, a discussion on surface-to-surface missiles. Teenage gangs are using them in the streets of Midwestern and Southern cities.

She dresses, packs her garment bag quickly, and takes the ferry back to Bay Shore. She sits on the upper deck of the ferry, wearing large tortoiseshell sunglasses, a red scarf covering her hair and part of her face. The bruises aren't noticeable, she tells herself, and no one cares or wants to know. The sky is an antique and fragile pinkish violet, streaked with gray from the incinerators that ring the shoreline. The waters of Great South Bay are full of soda cans, garbage bags, rags, gasoline and motor oil slicks. She's used to the debris; it isn't horrifying.

•

At home she tries to forget the weekend. She's afraid Bradley will pay her a visit within days or even hours. By then, she may be sorrowful enough to let him in the door. He might bring two or three dozen roses, and maybe an exquisite piece of Native American or African jewelry. She's never known him to cry; still, she imagines he will fall to the floor and sob, clutching her knees until she starts to cry with him. She sits at the drafting table in her studio and tries to forget him as she leafs through the portfolio of black-and-white photographs she's checked out from the public library. Inexpensive reproductions of Cronheim's famous photographs of Lenore Hayden. She knows Cronheim spent hours setting up the distinctive chiaroscuro lighting as Hayden worked, absorbed in the microbiological world she could peer at only through electron microscopes. Wanda doesn't consider the damage Hayden and other microbiologists have caused; mutating, deadly viruses unleashed, failed vaccines. She was doing the best she could. In the photographs, the laboratory is like a meticulously crafted stage set: black counters and tables full of hundreds of glass beakers and flasks, filtering equipment, and centrifuges, a row of industrial sinks, white cabinets, checkerboard tile floors, shadows cast by Venetian blinds.

Sterling appears unexpectedly, peering over her shoulder. She swivels around to face him. "I used to check out these photographs every now and then," she says.

She adjusts the architect's lamp above the photographs,

125

making a bright spotlight in the otherwise dark loft. He leans his elbows against the brushed-aluminum table edge and watches her study one of the photographs. Five Erlenmeyer flasks in the foreground, at the corner of a table, sparkling in the strong light, warping the space around them, like the air around strong blasts of heat. Behind the flasks, at a counter in the middle ground, is Lenore. She is concentrating on the several petri dishes in front of her, tweezers in hand, a large notebook beside her. Her light hair is pulled back, her white lab coat partly unbuttoned, a dark, lacy collar showing.

It is as if the shutter had been open for hours, soaking up light, saturating the negative with the memory of place and time. Sterling and Lenore were living the kind of bohemian life Wanda's only read about. He had a few classes to teach at Beaux-Arts and hours to spend at Le Dôme and the other cafés. She wishes there were still a bohemia, but the creative artists have all scattered, suspicious, competitive, and afraid of each other.

"What's happened to you?" he asks, looking at her closely and touching her chin.

"Just a little accident on the beach," she says, looking away from him. She knows he doesn't believe her. She reaches for his hand, kisses it. He puts an arm around her shoulders. "I missed you, Crönchen." He walks away, into the dark corner of her studio. She follows him.

"It's the photographs, isn't it?" He doesn't answer. "I'm sorry."

He leans forward into the light, resting his chin on his hands. He looks like a giant, sitting on a footstool with her scale models of skyscrapers scattered around him on the floor. "Don't be sorry. During the war I thought these photographs were lost. I don't know what I would have done if they had been." It's all he can say. He's closer to tears than he's been in ages. No thoughts or memories of Lenore come to him now. There is only a dull but painful sorrow that forms a bright yellow as he closes his eyes.

"I know it's difficult for you." Her voice is breaking and she is nearly in tears. The feelings are sudden and frightening. She feels terrible, for him now, not for herself.

Sterling closes the portfolio and embraces her. He watches her begin to cry and he thinks of the grieving he has never finished. For years he couldn't believe Lenore had really died. There are only the photographs, the short films he shot of her, the newsreel of her research team at Pasteur when the cure for Singapore influenza seemed imminent, and countless letters he's locked away in a safe-deposit box in Berlin. He will never allow them to be published. They can't comfort him, not any more than these reproductions, passed around the city, the brown portfolio accumulating red-stamped return dates that go far into the past.

"It's late. You need to sleep," he says emphatically, as if that is all she truly needs. But she doesn't sleep; she watches various experts debate each other on the Socrates Channel while she works on the detailing of scale models. The designs aren't hers; they are towers full of cornices, trusses, grille-work, and other direct quotations from the architecture of the past. Trendy, unfocused, inferior architecture, they both agree.

She wipes her tears with the back of her hand. "I need a drink badly," she says, getting up and pouring herself some vodka from the bottle in the living room, left on the floor she can't remember from when. She sits alone on the sofa, in the dark, drinking. The vodka tastes like poison. Her face is still hurting.

"What happened to you out on the island?" Sterling asks from across the loft, his voice almost echoing. She doesn't answer. "Isn't there anything I can do?"

"The camphor lotion. In the bathroom," she mumbles. He goes to get it for her.

"I'll be all right. I just need to be alone," she says, taking the bottle from him. She pours the lotion into her hands and covers her face with it. It dries smooth and tight, like a mask. She isn't thinking of anything but the color of the lotion, like ancient pyramids and temples decaying in the sun.

"Don't you stay up here all night drinking." He leans down, kisses her forehead. She puts her arms around him.

"And don't you ever run off and leave me," she says, embracing him again. She hates how she's sounding, clinging and desperate. Sterling, sensing her displeasure, clasps her hand and kisses her forehead. He makes his way up the narrow steps to the bedroom, going slowly in the dark.

He lies down on the bed, this time not forcing himself to stop thinking of Lenore. He knows he can't. His bedroom, so familiar now, feels constricting, small. He's thinking of the places where he lived with Lenore. They were all designed for the perfect and grand living he and Lenore always dreamed of. But no one is happy; no one lives perfectly and grandly, he decides.

Transients

The new architecture on its highest plane will be called upon to remove the old conflict between organic and artificial, between open and closed, between country and city. We are accustomed to neglecting questions of architectonic creation in the dwelling because the emphasis is upon use, the house as a place of relaxation and recuperation. The future conception of architecture must consider and realize the whole. Individuals who are a part of a rational biological whole should find in the home not only relaxation and recuperation, but also a heightening and harmonious development of their powers.

LÁSZLÓ MOHOLY-NAGY

THIS WAS STERLING'S NEW HOME on rue Jacob, Lenore's fourth-floor apartment in an old, elegant building, its huge, rounded entryway topped with a mascaron looking down sinisterly at passersby. Lenore had lived here for months with Kally, who'd taken a new apartment one flight below, both of them working at Pasteur while he was still in Berlin teaching a photography course at the university and designing sets for Universum Film, AG, or UFA, as it was called. It took months, but he finally landed himself a teaching job in Paris, at École Nationale des Beaux-Arts. He left Berlin and the long shadows of tall stone and ironwork gates that hid the sunlight. Riots, uprisings, assassinations. Little wars, constant, everywhere. Berlin had become treacherous and cold, leaving him with nothing but grueling hours

129

at UFA and the solemn decadence of the Kurfürstendamm. Now the National Socialists were stepping in, taking over, saying violence, poverty, economic depression would end. But he knew Germany was changing for the worse.

He had left the Bauhaus a few years earlier, along with Moholy and a few other colleagues, all of them tired of constant disputes with the new director, who, Sterling believed, wanted to force upon everyone a purer application of technology and his own political views. Most of all, Sterling had wanted to be with Lenore, in Berlin. It wasn't enough anymore visiting once or twice a month, writing to her, thinking about her. Over the years, he had become a different person because of her. Different, not better or worse. He was always trying to avoid Kurfürstendamm and his old life, his old habits; sometimes succeeding.

He remembered the day he moved in with Lenore in Paris. He could tell it would be a problematic apartment; the building was more than a hundred years old, with antiquated plumbing and poor insulation. Cracks in the gray stenciled walls, which had been papered over and repainted so much the corners were rounded. The parquet floors were gray from water damage and neglect. But this was home and would be for some time, he decided. He unpacked his oils, easels, and canvases in the new studio, one of the bedrooms. Scrubbing the walls and the floors, organizing and storing his materials on steel racks. Later that afternoon Lenore walked in, tossing her pumps aside, puffing on a cigarette, twirling her shoulder-length hair. She stooped beside him as he sorted his oils, put her arms around him, and kissed him.

"The paint," he mumbled. Specks of titanium white and ultramarine blue on her dark gray dress.

"It doesn't matter. I'm just glad you're here, finally." She clasped both of his hands, rubbing the paint on them as if it were something rare and magical.

"I've been in Germany so long it feels as if I was born

130

there," he said, unpacking his brushes and oils from the old brown leather suitcases he'd had since his early days in New York. Pensively, he ran his finger along the gut stitching of the handles, as if what he needed, what he lacked, was within these suitcases.

She lit another cigarette. "We expatriates always want to pretend we can't remember America." She went to the window, pulled apart the Venetian blinds carefully, and looked out.

He stood and walked up beside her, put his arms around her, kissed her. Her perfume smelled like lilacs; it cut through the pervasive odor of linseed oil. He had missed her those months, missed her unrelentingly. There was no reason to go to the Kurfürstendamm; it was Lenore he needed. He kissed her again. "Do you regret leaving America?" he asked.

She raised the blinds and bright sunlight covered them both, her emerald necklace throwing sparkles onto the opposite wall. It was an heirloom from her great-grandmother, one of the first women doctors in Connecticut. She turned and leaned against the windowsill, smiling her distant smile. "No, my darling, I don't have any regrets. I told you years ago, I get exactly what I want. And whom I want. I should have, the way I chased you so shamelessly." She walked away from the window. "Let's go outside while there's still some daylight," she said, taking him by the hand and carefully dodging his piles of oils and canvases. Walking down the wide stone stairway with him, she suddenly gripped the carved banister, almost falling.

"What's wrong?" he asked her, helping her sit down. The stairway was dark, cave-like, chilly, a breeze floating from nowhere. He went down the last flight of stairs to turn on the *minuterie* light.

She took a cigarette from the case. "Light it, please," she said when he came back and sat with her. Her hand shook. "Maybe the paint fumes got to me." She took a deep drag and leaned against the banister. "Who am I fooling? I'm just plain worried about us. Paris is full of attractive young men."

"So was Berlin," he said, more rhetorically than truthfully. The *Pupenjungen*, overpainted, garishly dressed, were never attractive to him.

She stood and slowly walked down the stairs to the front door. "I was afraid you'd stay there."

"You know everything's changed now." He walked up to her and put his arms around her. He believed what he was telling her. He never considered that his exhilaration and desire for her would still be as sporadic as it was in Berlin. "Everything's changed," he said.

"Everything's changed but you," she said, opening the door, tossing out her cigarette. She took another cigarette from her case, let him light it for her. "On the level, Crön, I'm afraid for you. I don't want you to become one of those pathetic old men leering at young boys in the park."

He let go of her, turned away. He hated to be reminded of growing older, of how he'd drifted for so many years, meeting strangers, leaving them. His past was blurry and he couldn't sort out the years or the men. It was like what he imagined looking out of an airplane window might be like: static, unreal countryside too far away to touch. Remembering too much might bring him down, crashing. "I don't want to talk about this anymore," he said, raising his voice louder than he'd intended.

"Darling, don't fight me. I want to help you," she said, tugging at his arm.

"Then don't talk to me, just leave me alone." He wanted to shout at her, but he couldn't. He'd gone years without talking about his needs with anyone. He didn't want to start now. She gathered up her things and rushed off to the institute, whispering goodbye and leaving him there in the dark lobby.

He felt better then, as if he'd walked out of a stuffy,

crowded room. She had brought in the crowds with her pleading and prying. He didn't understand what he needed to explain to her. What made him so different, so deplorable? He knew Lenore was going out to the Deux Magots, Le Dôme, and the other cafés, to the cinema and the revues with men those months he was in Berlin. They were her friends, she would tell him, these intellectuals, artists, writers, some of them a generation older than she. But among them she had a few lovers. He was sure of it.

He went back upstairs, lowered the blinds, and lined up all the tubes of paint on the steel racks according to the logic of the color wheel. He sat on the X-frame stool in the middle of the room and watched the sunshine streaming in through the blinds; the shafts of shadow and light were growing wider and longer. Someone in the world must have been curious enough to translate these patterns of light into mathematical formulas. He took several large sheets of paper and quickly sketched the shadows. Sterling was still trying to content himself with formulating an absolute science of line and form, like Kandinsky. Or was Kandinsky really content? He couldn't imagine what he and Lenore talked about when they saw each other every week at Le Dôme. They were both scientifically rational and erudite in a way he didn't understand. Or remember. He had once written a passable book on form and color, back at the Bauhaus. He wanted to demonstrate indisputable laws of form and color. Back then, he saw the laws clearly in dreams. He tore up the sketches and sat with his eyes closed, doing contour drawings of Lenore; feeling nothing but the soft lead pencil wearing down as he drew.

It was dark outside; he had fallen asleep. He put the drawings down. He would discard them later. He never kept his drawings of Lenore. He stood at the window and raised the blinds. Lights in the shops and apartments along rue Jacob were coming on in the nighttime. He was certain a man was standing at an open window across the street, looking out, looking at him. The man was a silhouette, blocking the light, swaying as if he were listening to jazz. Sterling lowered the blinds and turned away from him.

There's no light in this room, he remembers thinking that evening. He can't see me.

•

Even with the windows wide open and all the ceiling fans running, it is much too warm in the cluttered laboratory. Moisture from the Erlenmeyer flasks collects on her hands as she works. She keeps rubbing them against her white lab coat. The coat makes her look like a medical doctor and she moves around the lab with an omniscience she doesn't feel. The work takes years, injecting viruses into animal tissue, extracting and filtering the virus cultures, spinning them in centrifuges. With the electron microscope, a brand-new invention from Germany, column-like and as tall as the ceiling, she can finally see the viruses.

From a radio one flight below, BBC news broadcasts echo loudly through the corridors. In the adjacent room, monkeys and rabbits are jumping around in their cages, creating an eerie chatter through the thick walls. Outside the windows, fog dulls the city. But this is home, where she is with Kally all day long. The apartment has a contrived hominess: shelves of books she doesn't have time to read, walls of paintings she walks by without seeing. And Sterling, whom she can't picture clearly. They are together only at night, touching, talking, never bothering with lights. It isn't enough for her.

She sits down by the open window, trying to remember a time when she wasn't so overwhelmed with work and confusion. She thinks of a particular spring afternoon in Berlin years ago when she and Kally were still bleaching their hair and wearing dresses slightly above their knees. They had carried their picnic basket and gramophone to the Tiergarten and sat back to back on the sprawling green meadow, knees pulled up to their chests, swaying and singing along with

"Falling in Love Again." A short man with a salt-and-pepper beard, wearing a heavy gray coat, had stopped a few paces away. He photographed her and dashed away like a phantom. That night she couldn't stop thinking that somewhere across the city a photograph of her was drying in a darkroom and she was all the shades between black and white, Kally in the background, only the shimmering outline of her hair and the tips of her shoes showing.

Now she wants no one but Sterling to photograph her. Right in the laboratory while she works, concentrating so fiercely she ignores the photoflood lamps clustered around her and forgets he's present. She always wants too much, she knows, from Sterling, from Kally, from everyone. So she is always too busy, and there are always too many parties and nights at cafés. And other men.

She thinks of her quiet liaison with Kandinsky. Of long, engaging conversations with him about music, of lying side by side listening to symphony concerts on the radio. He believes music, like art, has underlying laws, discernible and objective. He would have been an excellent musician, she often tells him. He tells her she would have been a brilliant physicist. It's what both she and Kally wanted to be, years ago. Columbia denied them the opportunity to pursue doctorate work in physics. Only the tiny world of microorganisms was a woman's domain, they seemed to say, not the physical universe. A tiny world to suit a woman's tiny, delicate mind. She thinks of all the viruses present in the laboratory, volatile and dangerous like passions.

Kally walks in with sandwiches from the commissary, sets them down next to the flasks and a stack of leather-bound notebooks on a shelf below the window.

"Dr. Hayden, are you moping again? Are you having your female trouble?" Kally says in a mock-French accent as she walks with the stoop-shouldered limp of their research supervisor, Dr. Passy, a large, white-haired man who squints behind his pince-nez and mutters to himself all day. He often rummages through their desks, looking for and sometimes stealing their papers.

Lenore puts her arm across her forehead and sighs. "Alas, I am the weaker sex. My delicate brain and nervous system were never meant for all this learning. I'll expire now, a fallen woman, unchaste and overeducated." She slumps slowly to the floor in imitation of a dying opera heroine.

"Passy really thinks that's what's going to happen to us," Kally says, laughing. Her black skirt is so narrow she nearly rips its kick pleat and falls herself as she stoops to help Lenore to her feet.

"That wasn't entirely an act. I almost fainted from hunger," Lenore says, clasping Kally's arm and making her way to the dark wood counter beside the windows. "But if hunger were my only problem, I'd be happy." She switches on the radio and finds *Le Jazz Hot* on Radio Paris. A trio is playing "Memories of You" and something about it makes her want to cry.

"You're nostalgic for your old life, aren't you?"

"*Our* old life, you mean," Lenore says, attempting a flirtatious smile. She looks away from Kally. Remembering is too painful right now. Kally seems to understand this and puts an arm around her waist. They sit in silence, eating the sandwiches.

"I used to think about you all the time," Kally says.

Lenore laughs and clasps Kally's hand. "I *still* think about you all the time. I can't believe you're keeping company with that dreary Irish writer."

"You're jealous, aren't you?" Kally says.

"Can't help it, my dearest," Lenore says in a breathy voice.

"Neither can I," Kally says, no longer cheery and smiling. They are making terrible mistakes, Lenore thinks, talking to each other about their respective lovers, describing them in excruciating detail, as if all they really need now is to be each other's confidante. It's puzzled her for years that she's wanted Sterling and received so little from him for her trouble. Worst of all is that she's drifted from Kally.

Kally pulls her closer, strokes her hair. "Let's go someplace and cheer you up."

•

They are at Le Dôme, sipping coffee as the warm, heavy night air blows across them. They have both let their bobbed hair grow long, slightly past their shoulders, but always pulled back primly. In their matching black dressmaker suit jackets, beige gloves, long white linen scarves, they look like film actresses meeting clandestinely, shunning admirers in the dim street lighting of the outdoor café. It is crowded, as usual. Some people have been here most of the day and evening, the café doubling as office, study, and salon. Lenore has tried the café life but it doesn't quite suit her anymore. She used to come here in the mornings with Sterling, spread out her ledger-sized notebooks, and analyze the virus cultures. But this was some time ago, when she was translating for Sterling, who was still learning French, baffled by the local idioms and elisions of words. There was little she could do outside the laboratory, but he would sketch for hours with charcoal and pencils. She watched him closely and began to believe in the underlying scientific, even mathematical, language of drawing he and Kandinsky talked about.

Her own mood drifts like the cigarette smoke in the café. Friends and acquaintances of hers and Kally's and fellow artist friends of Sterling's drop by their table. One of Sterling's colleagues from Beaux-Arts, a tall, sandy-haired British man in a brown tweed cape passes around a tin can, collecting money for the leftists in Spain. She and Kally slip several francs through the narrow slit and they all talk in English about the trouble in the world. A few self-proclaimed Surrealists are out tonight, carrying Gothic-lettered red-and-black cue cards of Latin phrases from *Principia Mathematica*, as are the collagists, as she calls them, scrawny young men hardly past their teens who collect newspapers, empty cigarette boxes, wine bottle labels, and whatever else they can find in the cafés and around the city.

Her companions notice she is quieter than usual. They hold up palms to her forehead or tell her to eat more liver or drink more table wine. She watches Kally talk with her hands, her gestures as carefully considered as those of a mime. When they are sitting by themselves again, smoking Gitanes, perfectly sober with their cups of black coffee, Lenore begins to ramble. English is effortless and her thoughts pour out, unlike Kally, who has learned to think in French and sometimes confuses English word order. Mostly she is complaining.

"Lenny, there must be something I can do," Kally says, lighting a cigarette for her.

Lenore laughs. "Are you being sympathetic now or salacious?"

"I've always gotten the two mixed up where you're concerned," Kally says, sounding humorless, almost bitter. She's picking at her hair, running her fingers from the roots to the ends.

"Kallischen," Lenore whispers, looking out at the boulevard. Long rows of shiny black Lagondas and Hillmans parked on either side. No one on the sidewalks except for an old man with a long gray beard, carrying a large trunk on his back. He stops and begins to skip around it.

"What are you thinking about?" Kally asks her.

"That we're both still here in the world of the senses," Lenore says, placing both hands on Kally's. "Waiting for something extraordinary to happen."

I've Got My Love
to Keep Me Warm

STERLING PUTS UP THE LAST of his photograms on the walls of both bedrooms. He's covered the walls completely, at Wanda's insistence. The shadowy, tonal explorations of light and form overpower the small rooms. There is no logic of chronology or a lifetime of stylistic development and refinement, nothing to assist the viewer in understanding the work. He remembers the afternoon his last retrospective exhibition opened at the Guggenheim Museum. The clamor, the pressures of being well known were beginning to drive him away. He thought about the Guggenheim's wasted space. Frank Lloyd Wright believed in liberating people from the stifling rectangles and right angles so prevalent in Western architecture; destructing the box. The space within was the reality of the building, Wright told him. But Sterling believed the space here was something to look at, not inhabit, though Wright meant it to be the other way around. Sterling thought of this museum as the destruction of the art as he stood on the ground floor looking up at the spiral ramps and skylights high above him. The walls were covered with his paintings and drawings. There were even old letters of his to Gropius, Kandinsky, Schlemmer, Moholy-Nagy, and Feininger in glass display cases, the type badly faded. He hadn't meant for any of his works to be strung along a curving wall. A museum assistant told him that hanging the paintings and drawings threw his back out of alignment. All those hours on the spirals, tilting the works ever so slightly, giving the illusion of straightness.

The ramps were too narrow. One couldn't step back far enough to look at his large-scale works, like the *Density* series. Eight paintings, with bold colors and mosaic-like forms, reminiscent of stained-glass windows, anticipating Pop Art's vivid colors, the curator's essay told him. He disagreed emphatically; he always shunned images from the mass media in his art.

Crowds gathered around him, filling the space, clustering near the artworks. Beside him was Adele Marinbach, noted professor of archaeology, Penn colleague. Since William's death she had become his closest friend, his social escort and confidante. She was wearing a double-breasted wool suit in a brooding Rembrandt color, her white hair a faint pink under the halogen lights. Her voice was as strong and clear as ever as she leaned against her bronze-tipped mahogany cane, swaying from one direction to another for emphasis. She talked about her excavations of the Citadel at Hasanlu in northwest Iran, which had been going on for years. She took the dozen or so listeners gathered around her through ancient Persia from the sixth through the first millennium B.C., describing the iron and ceramic artifacts as if she herself had made them and used them all her life. She managed to deflect attention from him for a while, exactly what he hoped her effervescent presence would do.

A tall, pinstripe-suited reporter and her camera operator approached him. The portable floodlight reminded him of how he used to endure the tedium of live broadcasts, technical failings, and rambling, unconfident questioning. Back then he was certain that television would become another artistic medium. The reporter asked him to comment on the trends in the art world of the past twenty years. Of course the question needed a book-length answer.

"I don't believe in summations," he said, glancing at Adele, who smiled conspiratorially. "Look around you. There's

140

more than fifty years of my work. Show it to your viewers." He turned away and took Adele by the arm. Other reporters and photographers gathered around him, shouting their questions.

"Don't look so damn irritated," Adele said, pulling him aside. "It's a miracle to be appreciated while you've still got breath in you, my dear living legend."

"You and I both know this has nothing to do with appreciation," he whispered. "They're just waiting for me to drop dead. And when I do, the value of my art will quadruple."

He and Adele walked slowly along the ramps, stopping to greet old friends and colleagues he hadn't seen for years. People he didn't recognize began to crowd around them. Men of indeterminate age and nationality, in dark suits with carnations in their buttonholes; women in pastels, with matching handbags and shoes. A large group of art students in refreshingly iconoclastic clothing. Sterling could hardly see the artwork with so many people trying to talk to him at once. It was like attending his own funeral, everyone so cautiously kind, discussing his work with effusive, vague language. He was getting old, but not looking as old as people expected. He didn't intend to retire from Penn. He still rode his bicycle and walked several kilometers a day, got up at five in the morning to paint and work on his new book. He had tentatively titled it *A Modernist Looks at Post-modernism*. But everything he wrote pulled him further back into the past.

He tried to imagine what Lenore would have thought of this, what it would be like to have her here with him now. He still dreamed of her. They were together in the dreams, in Paris those terrible months before he lost her forever. Her face unbelievably young, her hair ragged and old, the way the rest of her wasn't. The older he became, the more vivid she was. He often drew her from memory in charcoal and solemnly destroyed the drawings at night. No one ever knew about them. He managed to slip away from the crowds for a few moments to find the photographs of her, new gelatin silver prints. In the glare of their protective glass, he saw himself next to her, shadowy and pale like his own hallucinations.

A young woman is standing by a display case of first editions of his books. She is too thin, a teenager who's grown several inches in one summer or starves herself. She wears a long tie-dyed T-shirt and a cotton madras skirt. Her wavy blond hair is pulled back into a ponytail and thick bangs fall nearly to her eyebrows. A small portfolio beside her as she stands, writing in a spiral-bound sketchbook.

He walks up closer and she turns and smiles at him. She shakes his hand enthusiastically, speaks a few praising words, for which he thanks her. Adele is nearby, leaning on her cane, frowning at him. Later, she will tell him to stop taking advantage of young people. But he craves them, what they give him. He can forget all his misery in those small, private moments. He smiles at her without meaning to. He doesn't see her smile back. He is full of regret and loneliness, and it turns the white walls of the Guggenheim into the color of a storm.

His viewphone awakens him with its shrill ringing. He hopes it's Sotheby's confirming his purchase of three of Moholy's paintings. He shuts off the visual.

"This is Charles Stoller, I'm Wanda's father. Who is this?"

Sterling's number is identical to Wanda's except for the last digit. Still, after all he's heard, Stoller is the last person he expected to call. He gives him his alias. "She's at work. You might want to call back after—"

But Stoller says he's in the neighborhood and insists on coming up to wait for her. Sterling agrees. Better this way than to cause suspicion, he decides.

A few minutes later, he lets Charles in the door. He's a fairly short, thin man with a fringe of white hair. Trench coat, fedora, and briefcase in his hand, his gray tweed suit jacket wrinkled and smelling faintly of mothballs. He looks professorial, and too old to be Wanda's father. The men stare awkwardly at each other and shake hands.

"I've been trying to get in touch with her for weeks."

"She works long hours."

"She doesn't want to see me."

Sterling nods. He takes Charles's coat, hangs it up in the closet by the front door. They sit in the living room on the sofa. Charles picks up the copy of *Die Weltbühne* that Sterling has left on the coffee table.

"Hers?"

"Mine." Sterling tells Charles a few details of Werner Schmidt's life story. That he's visiting New York for a few months before returning home to Berlin.

"You met my daughter at an art gallery," Charles says, lighting his pipe. Sterling goes to the kitchen and gets a porcelain ashtray for him.

"I can't tell you how surprised I am to see someone like you here. I'd never have thought she'd pick herself a father figure," Charles says in a slight drawl.

"It's not what it looks like," he says reassuringly, he hopes. He's been expecting a fatherly interrogation all along.

"There's no need to cover for her. You seem like a decent-enough man and I haven't got my shotgun with me." Charles smiles quickly and looks away, tensely quiet for a moment. "I just moved to New York. Seized an opportunity to work for Suntel. I'm an engineer, aerothermodynamics. I just wanted to be near my . . . family." His hand trembles slightly as he sets the pipe down on the ashtray. He gets up, walks around, admiring the bookshelves, the scale models in the studio, every detail of the loft.

"My sister told me Wanda designed and renovated this place all by herself. That there wasn't even plumbing when she moved in."

"She's very good at what she does."

"Yes, a fine architect, isn't she?" he says in German. "So

she won't be back for a while, you say. Let's you and I go to Festhaus. That is, if I'm not keeping you from something."

•

"This design is a cross between a nursery school and a federal prison. I'd hate to be committed here," Wanda says, sitting on a green sofa and tapping its palm-leaf-shaped sofa arm. Francine sits down beside her, putting her briefcase and gray suit jacket on the mushroom-shaped table. Three women nearby watch a Mexican soap opera on the telescreen, a yellow plastic tea set on the table in front of them. With their gray robes and black hair curlers they are lost in this Technicolor lounge cluttered with molded fiberglass furniture in playhouse shapes.

Wanda smooths the wide pleats of her black skirt. It's not just the interior design that's making her feel uncomfortable, or even the women with the tea set who are playing like children, huffing at each other, hands on their hips, giggling. Wanda decided to visit her mother here at the medical center on a whim after her office closed for the afternoon because of bomb threats. Unknown extremists are determined to wipe out a small, Oglala Sioux–owned securities firm one flight below the Architects Consortium. The world is as shaky and uncertain as ever, and the hatred and bigotry is killing everyone—a terrible time to become estranged from her mother. Wanda had to talk to her, pretend that her mother understands, that everything is all right.

Francine lights a cigarette and pushes back stray strands of her upswept hair. The air is already hazy gray and full of cigar smoke drifting down from faulty ceiling vents. "Wanda?" Francine looks at her closely. She rubs her hand against the heavy layers of foundation makeup and powder on Wanda's cheek. "You've got some bad bruises and some swelling. I want to know why."

"I don't want to talk about it," she mumbles, trying to absorb herself in the barrage of songs and glitzy concert

144

performance clips advertising a Tony Bennett album. What her mother will say she doesn't want to hear.

"This was Bradley's doing, wasn't it?"

Wanda has been trying not to think about that weekend or about him at all. She believes he still cares in his peculiar, troubled way. "It was just a misunderstanding," she tells her mother.

"I doubt that. I'd say it's high time you let this one go. What is it going to take before you realize that?"

"He's not usually like this," Wanda says, grasping the arm of the sofa and digging her nails into the vinyl upholstery. She doesn't think of it as violence. That means police sirens and trips to the emergency room and telling lies. Most of all, it means desperate, unknowing people, which she and Bradley are not.

"I'd say he's become 'like this,' wouldn't you?"

Wanda turns away. What does her mother really know about any of this? It's her mother who's made the worst mistakes and won't admit it. "You ought to leave me alone and examine your own life," Wanda tells her. "If Charles hadn't left you, you'd still be with him, still hoping. All you can say for him is he never beat you. And you know why? He was too busy beating me."

"Wanda, you listen to me. I never said I didn't believe you. But there was never any physical evidence, so I couldn't get a court order. Even when I—"

"Don't you hear how lame that sounds? You've got no goddamn business trying to run a mental health center if you can't even stop abuse when it's going on in your own family!" She is shouting now and all the women have turned around to look.

Francine holds a finger up to her lips. "Hush! How many times do we have to go over this? Charles is out of our lives."

•

Wanda spends most of the next day putting finishing touches on the Abbott's Quay designs. Her injuries are hardly noticeable now and she manages to preoccupy herself with the drawings, which have been videotexed between New York and Guam for days. Compromises, compromises; but the structure still has the illusion of a sphere. And an extensive underground concourse and exhibition space that one of the brothers designed. He'd spent years designing underground tunnels and silos on a few of Micronesia's hundreds of islands. Some kind of nuclear testing, she surmises, but three years after leaving the Army, he's still keeping secrets. She's fought for and kept the Antraglas floor and geological observatory intact in the design.

All day she was trying to think of reasons not to see Bradley, not to go to the Association of Global Economists party at the U.S.S. *Intrepid*, aircraft carrier *cum* museum permanently moored where West Forty-sixth Street dead-ends at the Hudson. She hates these parties: they are overpublicized, overphotographed, populated with quasi-celebrities hoping to be quoted.

At the end of the day, Mackenzie, dapper in his gray sharkskin suit and as frightfully energetic as ever, practically dragged her here. Bradley was waiting for her, tears in his eyes. She sat with him under the murky, aquatic lighting of the Undersea Frontier exhibit and they held hands while video monitors beside them showed tape loops of recovery dives of the *Titanic*. He'd never hit anyone before, he told her, crying, and swore he'd never let it happen again. Now he is cheery and she is telling herself that she should be glad to be with him instead of at home alone. Sterling is working. Her mother is away, attending a symposium in Boston. There are flash floods in New Jersey and the storms are moving north. Air-quality alerts all over the city. Nothing in the world is ever ordinary.

"This place is great," Bradley says as they walk past several large monitors and holodisplays. Fighter jets swoop in the

146

magnificently blue computer-generated sky. Muted light, neon, theatrical spotlights, and a big band playing swing, near the fantail, on a stage that seems to float in silver-gray fog. Dimly lighted glass cases of battle dioramas, grainy poster-sized reproductions of newspaper front pages and photographs, deteriorating weapons. The entire carrier is decaying, chilly and haunted. She runs a hand across Bradley's back, feeling the cool wool of his charcoal-gray chalk-stripe suit.

"Feeling guilty for leaving the old man at home all by himself?" he asks, kissing her forehead. His cologne is a woodsy Scandinavian musk, overpowering.

"All you need to know is you're here and he's not."

"I'll make you forget you ever met him." He kisses her forcefully, slipping a hand underneath her silver-beaded lambswool sweater. They sway in half-tempo to the fast music that echoes throughout the deck. But she isn't forgetting about Sterling. She closes her eyes and imagines it's him she's dancing with now. She knows he likes to ballroom dance and hasn't for years.

"I'm sorry. For being such an awful bastard," Bradley whispers against her ear. He sounds as if he's about to cry again. She touches his face and it feels smooth as candle wax. Why not take Sterling to Manhattan Starlight Ballroom, she thinks. Tomorrow night.

She clasps her hands behind Bradley's neck and lets him kiss her again. "We're just a couple of misfits that the world doesn't want to know about," she tells him, imitating a pouting movie *señorita*. "And if we hadn't found each other, there'd be four miserable people instead of two. How's that for the truth?" She laughs louder than she'd intended to. Laughs till he joins in.

"Sister, the truth will set you free," he says, kissing her again until she pushes him away.

"Later, brother, later," she says.

They walk across the crowded hangar deck to the brass-

and-marble bar set up underneath suspended Mercury and
Apollo capsules, stopping as Bradley chats with people he
knows, all dressed as conservatively as he. Reporters and
their camera crews move around the deck with bright
spotlights and microphones. Bradley introduces her to everyone as the Screen Goddess. She sips her vodka and tries to
smile as they tell her she looks like Rita Hayworth.

She and Bradley go up to the flight deck, wander around
the landing section, where fighter planes from past wars are
floodlighted in cotton-candy colors. Cole Porter songs, in
tepid big-band arrangements, are playing over speakers
placed along the deck's railing. Her glass of vodka is lukewarm and almost empty, but she walks slowly, as if to keep
from spilling it. She stands along the railing, facing the
Hudson and the hundreds of lights on the Jersey shore,
while Bradley and Mackenzie talk with mutual friends
from the Century Club. They all seem so old to her, with
their dyed hair and inability to conceal their excess weight
with the right clothing. A woman in a forest-green suit, old
enough to be Bradley's grandmother, is falling all over
him, doing a grind to "Don't Fence Me In." Wanda doesn't
ever want to be that foolish. She turns toward the river
again. Thunder rumbles from far away and sheet lightning
flashes. She counts thirty-five seconds between the lightning
and the thunder. Later, Bradley walks up to her, leans his
arm against her shoulder. He's as drunk as she is, stag-
gering, his red tie stuffed like a handkerchief in his jacket
pocket. Mackenzie tap-dances his way to them, trying to
sing a melody against a languidly played "All Through the
Night."

"It's impossible to dance here. That fabulous swing band's
packed up and headed off to the Waldorf-Astoria," he says.

"Take a lesson from your friend, Lang-Stew. Bad music
didn't deter him one bit."

"Don't tell me you're actually jealous." Bradley leans

against her, laughing. "I should dance with my former professors more often. But, baby, you and I can go to the Waldorf and—"

"If you want to dance, take Kenzie."

Mackenzie laughs. "I knew being a Joffrey Ballet School dropout would come in handy sometime."

"Not tonight," Bradley deadpans, lighting his pipe.

Mackenzie makes some sweeping Fred Astaire gestures, pirouettes, and throws his empty glass into the river.

"And we wonder why the Hudson's so polluted," Wanda says, leaning against the railing.

"At least glass decomposes. Not much does these days, besides love, of course," Mackenzie says. He starts dancing again.

"I wouldn't know anything at all about love," Wanda says.

"Look out, Lang-Stew. The lady's sharpening her claws."

She looks at Mackenzie sternly. He pretends to be suddenly bashful. "Is that how it goes? Men have disagreements and debates and women have claws?"

"Please, kiddies. The *Intrepid* is a *retired* battleship," Bradley says.

"What's the matter, old buddy? Don't you and your lady friend fight anymore?"

"You know me better than that." He puts an arm around Wanda and puffs ostentatiously on his pipe. "I'm not happy unless a woman's giving me brain damage with her skillful left hook. Every morning I pledge allegiance to Leopold von Sacher-Masoch, patron saint of masochists everywhere. One nation, one man under a woman's sexy heel. No liberty. No justice."

Wanda pulls away from him, wanting more than ever to leave. Mackenzie always brings out Bradley's most irritating and juvenile qualities.

"Old buddy, you need a mail-order bride from the Far East, one who doesn't know a word of English," Mackenzie says. "But be careful, it's still illegal in twenty-three states. We white men aren't supposed to step out of our own gene pool."

"I hear you, Kenzie," Wanda says. He revolts her with his posturing, his exaggerated Arkansas drawl. Why is she surprised that Bradley still hasn't told Mackenzie the truth about himself? "I bet it's true what they're saying at the Consortium—that *you're* the one who's been putting those ads in the *Voice*, looking for 'black beauty.' "

Mackenzie's laughter is forced. "The good Lord knows I love a headstrong woman." He steps closer to Wanda, rubs her forearm. "And white chocolate is my favorite—"

"Hey! This is my woman you're talking about. Keep your perversions to yourself," Bradley says, stepping between them, putting an arm around Wanda. He starts to laugh.

"Leave me alone, both of you!" She runs to the ship's island, climbs up to the bridge. There are people all over the bridge, stooping around dime-store Parsons tables, cutting and snorting coke lines. The bridge is dark except for the penlights some are shining on the coke. She's drunk, too drunk to take care of herself. Why doesn't she leave, hail a cab and go home? She sits down on the dusty floor beside the navigation center and takes out her handkerchief. But there are no tears. No one here tries to bother her. She falls asleep.

●

"Sweetheart, where've you been?" Bradley asks in a heavy whisper. "We've been looking for you." He and Mackenzie sit on the floor on either side of her. She lowers her head to her knees.

"I thought you two were off somewhere fighting over me," she mumbles. They ignore her irony and laugh. She doesn't want to talk to them, but they apologize profusely to her and help her back down to the flight deck, both of them grasping her arms. She's too drunk and indifferent to resist.

She only knows she'd rather go anywhere at all than home, where she'd sit up for hours waiting for Sterling. She wants to forget him tonight.

They take the Ninth Avenue El uptown. Mackenzie tells Bradley the plots of zombie movies and the two giggle like schoolchildren as the train speeds along. Bradley holds her tightly as she stares out the window, at the city lights, blurred to white streaks.

At the marina, Bradley and Mackenzie walk along the ledges of the stone terrace that overlooks the Hudson. They two-step and heartily sing "Don't Get Around Much Anymore." She sits down on the steps, shivering in her black velvet coat, waiting for them to finish. She tries not to think about how drunk they are and how high the ledge is. They have walked on the catwalks along the West Side Highway and walked the balcony railings of Mackenzie's eighty-second-floor apartment. It is a ritual by now.

She wonders how she will make it home tonight. She looks around and can't quite remember how to get out of the park. Not far away, in the rotunda, are the whispering voices of vagrants and drug dealers.

"Bradley," she calls weakly.

●

It is a gray, early morning. She has a terrible headache. She remembers lying on a park bench, on one of the hundreds stretching along the river promenade. Quieter than she could imagine the city to be. The bishop's-crook street lamps were off and it was almost dark enough to see the stars. A dusty cloud above, the shape of a rainbow. Some might mistake it for the Milky Way, but it was the floating debris of the city.

Now she is lying on the sofa in Bradley's houseboat, the drone of *CBS World News Roundup* on the radio rouses her. She's wearing all her clothes, wrinkles spiraling all over her red silk skirt. She sits up and leans against the starboard porthole. The Jersey shore looks like the frontier coast of another planet: tall buildings rising above the trees, the same alien shade of dark purple as the incinerator smoke in the morning light. She tries not to be as upset as she should be that she can't remember most of last night. A blackout. She gets up slowly from the sofa, puts her coat around her shoulders. She goes to the bathroom and looks at herself in the mirror. Her hair needs combing, she has dried mascara tears, and the bruises show through what's left of her makeup. She washes her face and makes her way to the upper deck, where Bradley and Mackenzie are playing chess with a pewter Civil War chess set.

"Chess masters of the universe," she says in her ragged morning voice. Bradley extends a hand to help her as she steps across stacks of economic journals covered with a plastic drop cloth. Unsteadily, she sits on the white chaise longue beside the table.

"Good morning, my love," Bradley says, kissing both her cheeks.

"What happened last night? All I remember is something about a park bench."

Bradley and Mackenzie look at each other and break out laughing. "Dear Lord, if all she remembers is the park bench, what does that say about us?" Mackenzie says.

"What the hell are you talking about?" She sits up on the edge of the chair, clutching her coat around her.

"Sweetheart, it's what you wanted last night. Right out there in the park. Well, Kenzie and I, we thought maybe it wasn't such a good idea. But wouldn't you know, you talked us into it."

"You're making this up."

"Yeah? Then you tell us what happened," Mackenzie says.

"I don't remember. I must have been—"

"Drunk. You'd better watch out, sister. You may wake up a thousand light-years from home with an opportunistic man. Lucky for you we're perfect gentlemen." Bradley picks up his pipe and lights it.

"Perfect liars," she says, drawing her coat around her shoulders. "Especially you, lover man. Ever told your dear friend what you really are? He'd be glad to know."

"You'd better calm down, Wanda," Bradley says. "We're just indulging in a little good humor."

"Oh, this is supposed to be a joke? Well, you two jokers can go fuck each *other*! You'll really love it, Kenzie, 'cause Bradley's more like me than you know." She dashes off the boat and onto the pier. A westerly wind at her back blowing the white petals of tree blossoms into the river. Hundreds of petals, thick as confetti. She keeps running, out of the marina and through Riverside Park, feeling sicker than she's ever felt; but she doesn't stop. Can't. She hates Bradley for certain now, and maybe even herself. The grass is slick with dew, morning joggers passing her on all sides.

The Wrong Men

STERLING SITS DOWN in a phone booth and the overhead light and exhaust fan switch on. He doesn't want to leave First Quality Photo Lab tonight. He can't let himself do what he usually does at the end of his shift, go back to Wanda's loft, sit up the rest of the night with the Sydney and Tokyo art auctions. He's tired of buying and selling art, but it's all he has right now. His financial advisers urge him to diversify, to transfer some assets to the upsurging Tokyo stock market and the Chicago commodities market. But they don't understand he plans to invest solely in art; he wouldn't know how to explain it to them. He can't tell them these artists were his friends, and how much he misses them. Owning their works sustains him somehow, and he feels a responsibility to lend them to museums and galleries.

He's telling Wanda all of this, talking to her answering console, saying he'll be home late, saying that he doesn't know if he'll ever be home. He asks her to come here to the lab to see him if she can, telling her exactly where he'll be waiting for her. He hangs up the phone wishing he could erase the message. She's done more than enough for him already and he thinks of her far more than he should.

He goes to the lavatory and washes the chemicals from his hands. From a stall, a coworker talks to him about the flash floods in his Brooklyn Heights neighborhood. A young man from London, living perilously on an expired visa, he's been telling Sterling that the floods sweeping through London nearly every week are far worse than New York's. They speculate about the situation: how does an entire city relocate and where will everyone go? They can't decide if Londoners are spirited, determined survivors or not. The conditions in the world keep posing these unanswerable questions.

The man steps out of the stall, pulling off his T-shirt and draping it across his shoulders. He leans against the wall beside Sterling, smiling and trying to prolong the conversation. Sterling, disarmed by both the man's tanned, body builder's physique and his idle remarks on their common European heritage, almost forgets he's told him, as he's told his other coworkers, that he's an immigrant from Berlin. The man toys with his shoulder-length blond hair and keeps smiling as he looks Sterling over. Sterling suspects the man will invite him home, so he says good night hurriedly and leaves the lavatory.

He heads downstairs to the weaving studios in the basement to wait for Wanda. He hardly recognizes the world anymore, it's so gutted and inhospitable. People are now as terrified of all kinds of weather, even rainstorms, as they are of tornados and hurricanes. He remembers a bitterly cold rainy night in Paris years ago. Late at night, a cold winter, and he's sitting up in bed alone, trying to read the latest issue of *L'Illustration*, waiting for Lenore. Lightning sweeps into the room.

Finally, he hears her walk in the door. She will be exhausted from her long day at Pasteur, but wide awake, agitated. He will help her relax. She will sit on the bed and slowly remove her clothing down to her camisole and stockings. She will talk about the centrifuges, their rpm's improving with months of development, testing, and redesign. When he and Lenore stop talking they will make love, sluggishly, dreamily; they are always too tired.

By seven he will be preparing for the morning painting

class he teaches at Beaux-Arts; she will sleep till nine, be at Pasteur by eleven, return home about fourteen hours later. He watches the phosphorescent clock hands and twenty minutes pass. She should be here by now, lying beside him, telling him about her day. He gets out of bed, puts on his white chenille robe, and finds her in the kitchen. The lights are off and she's sitting at the table, hunched over, still wearing her raincoat. The windows are open, curtains flying in the wind.

"Lenny, what's wrong?" He pulls up one of the bentwood chairs beside her, embraces her tightly. She looks at him, her eyes red and unblinking. He has rarely seen her cry. The veil on her hat is torn. He removes the hat and loosens her hair.

"When I came in, I was thinking of you upstairs waiting for me," she says, her voice thin and wavering. He can barely hear her. "What am I to you but a crazy woman who works all the time?"

"You *are* a crazy woman who works all the time," he says, kissing her. He puts both hands on her face and her tears cover them. "Right now, you need to sleep."

"Can't." She gets up from the table abruptly. She turns on the overhead light and takes a cast-iron saucepan from the butcher's rack above the sink, fills it with water. She lights the gas stove and sets the water to boil. "Got a craving for hard-boiled eggs all of a sudden. I've got too many cravings, haven't I?" She takes off her raincoat and suit jacket, lays them on the table. She goes to the icebox and looks for eggs. There is little of anything else there: bits of pâté and preserves, half a roast. The melting ice drips loudly. "You know what I think, Crön? I should have been that sweet and gracious lady in Connecticut everyone expected me to be. My children would be old enough to take care of me by now."

"What's happened to you, Lenny?" he asks. She is standing with the icebox door open, ignoring him, not maliciously, it

156

seems; he's never seen her so aimless. He gets up and puts his arms around her, but she doesn't acknowledge his presence or even seem to realize he's here beside her. She takes out two eggs and slams the door. She brushes by him and carefully places the eggs in the empty ashtray on the table. She looks up at him as she might look at a stranger, glancing back and forth between him and the stove. She sits down and takes a cigarette from her handbag, taps it furiously against the case. Everything she's doing heightens his alarm.

"I study viruses every day, viruses so small I could fit millions and millions of them on my fingertips," she says, not with wonder or whimsy as he would expect, but with disgust. "I understand them better than my own life, or my life with you, which I understand even less."

This seems to come from nowhere. He isn't even sure what she's talking about. Hasn't he always done everything she's asked him to do? He's even given up his old life entirely for her. After all these years his life with her *is* his life, he wants to tell her. But instead he asks, "What's to understand? I married you last month, didn't I?" He lights a cigarette and sits down.

"You made an honest woman out of me—finally. And a dishonest man of yourself." She picks up a box of kitchen matches and starts to crush it.

He moves his chair closer and puts his hand on her arm, fingering the smooth silk of her pink blouse. "You don't mean that," he says.

"God, that's so typical of you," she says. She pulls her arm away from him and the matches spill into her lap. "You think that all you have to do is sit beside me and talk to me as if I were a child." She knocks the matches to the floor and goes to the window. "That's the problem, Crönchen, you don't know how to talk to me and you don't know how to listen to me. It's always been like this, for the whole sixteen years we've known each other. Sixteen years and I can't take another day of it. At the lab I start crying all of a sudden and I can't stop. I have to hide in a supply closet or go out on the roof, or talk to Kally, who'd rather not hear about it." She clutches the curtains, winds them like a bandage around her hand, so tightly they fall to the floor.

"Why don't you just talk to me right now instead of talking about *not* talking?" he says gently.

"You wouldn't want me to. You wouldn't want me to tell you I wish I'd bought your paintings and never bothered to meet you. Much less marry you." She remains at the window, looking out and tracing a finger on the panes.

He's astounded. What started this tirade, he wonders. He doesn't even understand her vague complaints or what they have to do with him. And why is he the villain? Does she really believe he doesn't know what still goes on, her inexplicably numerous affairs and her halfhearted attempts to hide them, pass them off as nights out at the cafés. "I already know how little you think of me and this marriage," he says.

"What are you talking about? I come home to you every night, don't I?" she shouts at him, in the horrible mid-Atlantic accent she's been slipping in and out of lately.

"Then what about Kandinsky?"

"What about him?" She turns away from him and takes her shoes off, leaning against the wall.

She's lying, badly, and her casual gestures are too studied. He thinks of Kandinsky, his old friend whom he hardly sees anymore, thinks of the fluidity of his paintings, changing color and form by the day. They are more changeable than Kandinsky himself, who, tireless and ageless, dressed in suit and tie, paints in his book-filled studio. But he doesn't want to think of him with Lenore. He shudders and forces the images out of his mind. It's not Kandinsky he blames, it's Lenore. "I know what's been going on. Those evenings at Le Dôme just weren't enough for you. No, you pushed and pushed till you got exactly what you wanted from Wassily. Does he know he's just one of many? Does he know what a challenge he was to you? The poor, honorable man doesn't know the likes of you exist."

"I don't know what you're talking about. What do you do, rehearse these speeches while you're waiting for me to come home?" She takes a step toward him and smiles, briefly and seductively. She lowers her voice as she continues: "For heaven's sake, Crön, we're talking about an old friend of ours. A great and dignified man who hasn't seen his home-land for decades and probably never will."

The grating accent again, and the condescension behind it. He can't stand her attempt to charm away his concerns. "Let it rest, Lenny. I know what he is to you."

She turns back to the stove, to the water that is beginning to boil. "No, I don't believe you do. I'm going to tell you just what he is to me. He listens to me, he respects me, he—"

"Don't do this. You hear me? Don't do this!" Sterling shouts, hurting his hand as he slaps it against the table.

"I haven't finished telling you about Wassily," she says, facing Sterling, smiling angrily. "He's twenty-five years your senior and he's a better lover than you've ever been."

"If you're so happy with Kandinsky, then go to him. Don't stand there and insult me. You've known all along who I am." He feels all the shame and guilt she wants him to feel. He looks away and drops his cigarette on the table, where it starts to singe a linen napkin. He's too shaken to pick it up. She puts it out.

"At least Wassily means something to me." She sighs forcefully and stares at him combatively. "I know I mean something to him. Now, that's the irony. Everyone thinks of him as a cold, pedantic sort. While you're supposed to be the warm and generous one."

"What's the point of this?" he asks, reaching for another cigarette and lighting it. He drags too deeply and coughs uncontrollably for a few seconds. She stares at him all the while. She'd like to see him die right now, he can feel it. "Answer me, Len. Answer me!"

"I come home crying and all you can do is get at me because of Wassily. Don't you—" She stops herself and turns to the stove, fingering the saucepan handle. "What can I expect of you? If it weren't for me, you'd still be out there in the streets picking up little boys. That's just what you are, a little boy looking for other little boys. You don't know anything about love and caring."

"God help you if that's what you believe about me," he says, shaking his head. He doesn't feel ashamed anymore; he knows how wrong she is, railing at him for what she thinks he did years ago, and what she thinks that makes him now. "Look at you, Lenore Hayden, crying because you're so unhappy. *You've* made yourself unhappy and you can't blame me for it." He says it so harshly he surprises himself. She acts as if she isn't listening. "You had some romantic notion that women like you could live carefree lives."

"Women like me? What in hell are you talking about?" she says, glancing at him over her shoulder and turning away before he can respond.

"I'm talking about your indiscretions."

"Oh, please! I can't believe what I'm hearing!" She laughs at him.

"It's nothing to joke about," he says, his voice shaky. "I should do Kandinsky a favor and let him in on the secret. There's no reason he shouldn't know the truth about his illustrious companion and what she does on the nights she's not with him."

"Can't you leave me alone, Crönchen?" she says wearily, her back still to him.

She might have been crying again, but he didn't care. He kept at her, speculating about who her other lovers were and when she saw them and what she did with them. He shouted at her, calling her the worst names he could think of. Then she turned to face him and the hand that gripped the long, slender handle of the saucepan came toward him and the boiling water flew at him in a single arc. He threw

160

up his arms to shield his face. He heard the pan drop to the floor and Lenore run out of the room. He wanted to chase her, shout at her, slap her, kill her. But he lost his balance and fell, arms and hands still covering his face.

It took a long moment to feel the pain, dense, traveling sluggishly into his arms. He was afraid to take them from his face, afraid he wouldn't be able to see. He kept his eyes closed and didn't realize at first—the pain was so overwhelming—that she was helping him up, guiding him to the sink, running cold water over his arms.

She was crying. He was trying to breathe, trying to make himself open his eyes. He didn't feel the wet rags she dabbed gently on his arms and hands because everything around him was already cold. Through the pain, he reached for her. She embraced him and he kissed her wet cheeks, stroked her hair.

"I'm so sorry," he heard her whisper over and over.

I didn't mean what I said, he wanted to tell her. But he didn't. He says it now, loudly, forgetting where he is, forgetting that Lenore is long gone.

●

An old train, graffiti on the walls, beer bottles rolling across the gritty floors, a strong smell of ammonia and the air conditioning is turned up way too high. Wanda pulls her black sweater coat around her tightly, shivers. She knows better than to ride the elevated alone this late at night, but all she can think of is the audio message Sterling left her. She hears it over and over now, his voice strained and tired, talking about his friends and colleagues long dead, and how much he misses them. Nothing and no one left for him.

She pretends to read *The New York Times* as a dark-haired man in a plaid flannel shirt and overalls sitting across from her tries to get her attention, saying he's seen her on *Days of Our Lives*. She looks through the "Weekend" section, at the dance and theater company advertisements, and she imagines Sterling as he was a long time ago, performing one of Schlemmer's Bauhaus dances. He's wearing a heavily padded blue leotard and a painted gold mask with schematic black eyes and a smiling mouth. He stands in the center of the black stage, a dancer on either side of him, one dressed in red, the other in yellow. They step with playful exuberance along a large painted white X on the floor, while two percussionists perform a sparse accompaniment on drums and xylophone. She is in the audience, as if she belongs here in the past. Behind his mask, she knows he is glancing at her, smiling even. After the performance he will take her to a party, one of the famous Bauhaus parties she's tried to get him to talk about.

The train stops with a terrible screech at Queensboro Plaza. She dashes away from the station, and down the narrow, deserted streets. The photo lab is in an old two-story red brick warehouse at the edge of a dead-end street, a floodlight at each corner shining down on the crumbling asphalt parking lot full of abandoned cars. She's feeling frenzied, worried about Sterling and hoping she will find him here. The stocky, red-haired security guard, watching a boxing match on a portable television, lets her in the steel-girded doors with little fuss. Nearly burned-out fluorescent lights flicker in the steep stairwell, and she can barely find her way to the basement weaving studios. She walks down the corridor, shining her flashlight, to a large, dungeon-like room full of weaving looms and vertical racks of hundreds of wool spools. She finds Sterling here, sitting on a bench by a wall of narrow windows.

"I didn't think you'd really come," he says, lowering his head when she sits next to him. He is wearing a gray industrial apron, which he clutches absently.

She puts a hand on his knee and he grips it tightly. When she thinks of him, she sometimes visualizes an old man muttering to himself, stoop-shouldered, barely able to move. But he's sitting here, tall and lanky as the dancer of

162

her imagination, in the faint light from the hallway. He's like someone who has already lived a thousand years and is too old and too proud to die. "What's happened to you, Crönchen?"

He gets up, paces. The corner of the room is very dark; he looks down and can't see his hands. He touches the cinder-block wall and feels nothing. He wanted to see her last night, but she never came home. He sat up all night waiting for her, never once turning on the telescreen. Maybe he would have talked to her then, told her all about himself. After all this time, she hardly knows him. He hasn't let her. He keeps thinking about the blond Londoner who would have gladly let him spend the night. He pushes the fleeting desire out of his mind. "Where were you last night?" he asks Wanda.

She shrugs, thinking about the *Intrepid* party and Bradley, who keeps leaving phone messages and teletexes, apologizing for his and Mackenzie's behavior. He insists that he stopped Mackenzie from assaulting her out in the park that night and he berates himself for going along with the joking about it the next morning. Why didn't you throw him out, why are you still his friend? she wants to ask Bradley. But she doesn't intend to respond to his messages or to ever see him again. She tells Sterling the entire story.

"He's the wrong man for you," he says sternly.

She nods. "I know it." She turns away from him and runs her fingers along the threaded loom beside her. "Seems as if all he's good for these days is keeping me from thinking about you." She wishes she hadn't said that. This isn't what she wants, not this desperate, cloying seduction. If seducing him is really what she's trying to do now.

"You don't mean that," he mumbles as he leans against the loom, strokes the splintery, unfinished wood. He doesn't want to believe what she's saying. What can he tell her, what can he do? He would only make her as tearfully unhappy as Lenore was. He doesn't know how to console her, not

163

her, not anyone. Consoling is what she needs. He turns around, but he can barely see her. She seems to be gripping the loom. Her silence unnerves him. He walks up to her, places his hands on her shoulders. He moves closer to her and they sway back and forth in silence. He slips her coat off and caresses her shoulders. It feels too pleasurable and he stops. He walks behind the metal racks of spools, fingering each of them. The colors feel like heat.

"We both know why you were afraid to come home, Sterling. It has nothing to do with the art auctions or missing your friends." She reaches out a hand to him and he sits with her. She takes his apron from him and tosses it to the floor. It isn't passion she feels at first, as she strokes his face, or if it is, the passion is dreamlike, vanishing, reappearing. "You thought you'd forgotten what you want." She has, too. She thinks of her own isolation and loneliness, unbearable now that she no longer has Bradley.

He clasps her hand tightly. He can't stop looking at her. She isn't wearing a trace of makeup and her half-combed hair falls in random waves to her shoulders. She must have gotten out of bed to come see him; she couldn't have been at the Consortium this late. He doesn't want to let go of her, to be left here alone. He pulls her closer, runs his fingers through her hair, feeling the color, stronger, warmer than any color has ever felt. He presses his lips against hers, timidly at first.

●

It was over before she knew it. She feels pain now, and the cold concrete beneath her back. A remote, lethargic memory; another woman made love to Sterling, not her. She gets up and buttons her dress, leaving him on the floor weakly trying to grope for her. She's perspiring and shivering all at once, feeling lightheaded and vaguely depressed. Her stockings are torn. She takes them off, stuffs them in her bag. She doesn't know what to say to him.

He is aware of having been lying on the floor with her for what seems like hours, holding her, stroking her hair, feeling an unsatisfied exhaustion. He wanted her, wanted to feel close to her. But he didn't want to treat her like one of the strangers, like someone he will never see again. Now he feels sickened, afraid he's hurt her. "We should forget this happened," he says. He gets up from the floor and sits down on the bench.

"Don't say that." She pulls her coat around her shoulders and takes his hand. She knows this is what they've both wanted all along. Now why is he trying to turn away from her? "Let's go home, Sterling," she says. She stoops to kiss his forehead.

"Go on without me." His disgust with himself, with his whole unhappy life, makes him stare at her, angrily, unblinkingly.

She rushes from the building. She holds a hand over her mouth, afraid she will scream, hurrying along the deserted streets, trying to forget the hateful look he gave her. She climbs the rusting cast-iron stairway to the elevated and paces the platform. Wholesome people with peach-colored skin and white smiles peer at her from war-bond posters. There are high-school boys in leather bomber jackets all around her, whistling and jeering at her in Spanish. She shouts the only curse she knows in Spanish and keeps pacing. She wishes she knew what to say to Sterling, to make him go away for good right now. Or what to say to herself, in a few moments or hours, when she's no longer angry with him, when she starts wishing for him all over again.

The streamlined train is new. It moves with a hollow rumble that almost lulls her to sleep. She gets off at Rector Street and walks over to O'Sullivan's, where the Friday-night crowd is the typical odd mixture of people at a Lower Manhattan waterfront bar: longshoremen; Coast Guard officers in full dress uniform; Merchant Marines from the nearby Water Street hiring halls, duffle bags slung over their shoulders; Wall Street executives in their pinstripes. Too many people who, like her, don't know when to go home. She knows she shouldn't be here, blending in, looking as white as the rest of them as she makes her way to the bar and orders a triple shot of vodka.

The pub recedes endlessly like a railroad flat, room after room of dark walnut paneling, flashy neon beer signs and tinfoil shamrocks, sweeping theatrical spotlights throwing carnival colors over the crowd. A recording of Glenn Miller's "PEnnsylvania 6-5000" is playing and people are dancing, though the makeshift dance floor is much too crowded. She stands along the railing, drinking the vodka too quickly and watching people move vaguely to the swing beat. If the room were empty it could be a dance rehearsal hall, like the ones she spent childhood Saturdays in, hating ballet classes. She felt awkward, blond, fussed over. Not much has changed. She sneers at the other blondes around her. Pale colors are in vogue and her vivid kingfisher-blue dress causes some to take a second look. A man walks up to her. He has strawberry-blond hair, skin a pale salmon color under the pink spotlights. His features are plain and soothing, like the ethnically neutral drawings of humankind on interstellar probes. Tall and stout, probably a Merchant Marine, judging from his faded gray coveralls and assorted microtools in the top pockets. His scholarly-looking, rimless, round glasses seem out of place. He comments in a subdued Southern drawl about how crowded the pub is.

"Name's Jake," he says, extending a hand. She shakes it reluctantly.

"You don't look like a Jake. Jake is the bad guy in the soaps who everybody thinks died in a car accident when he really went to Central America, had plastic surgery on his face, and then went back home to plan his revenge," she says, smiling at his puzzled expression.

"Well, ain't you the living end. You ought to be a gossip

columnist or something," he says, winking and batting the cigarette smoke about with his hand. "What do you do, anyway?" She points upward with her index finger. "You're a preacher?"

"No. Not heaven, buildings. I'm an architect."

"Well, I'll be," he says, disbelieving or awed, she can't tell which. She's relieved that he doesn't ask her to elaborate. Most people complain to her about buildings she didn't design and wasn't responsible for in any way.

"I'm studying mechanical engineering at the College of Staten Island. Do electrical work on Coast Guard ships in the meantime. Want to step outside?" he asks as he puts down his beer.

She sips the last of her drink and follows him. It is drizzling, and a cold harbor fog drifts across the city, its sooty industrial pinks and grays like the renderings of a Mannerist painter. She doesn't consider which will do her more harm, standing out in the cold on West Street or sitting with Jake in his Volkswagen in the nearly deserted parking lot of the Battery Park City Heliport. She simply finds herself sitting next to him while he plays a CD of Glenn Gould performing Bach's Goldberg Variations. The car has a suffocating, factory-new smell. Jake says he was one of Bach's sons in a previous life, Wilhelm Friedemann Bach, and that he was a prolific composer who sometimes threw away his old manuscripts like worthless rags. He tells the story with no enthusiasm. He is quiet for a while, whistling along with Gould's atonal humming, tapping the steering wheel.

"Gets you to wonder, don't it? Composing in one life, killing for a living in the next," he says, smiling.

She looks away, to keep herself from laughing. Sterling, Bradley, and now this man—it's how it should be, she thinks—men have become unnecessary and interchangeable for her. This one's professed violence is completely forgivable. Will he tell her anecdotes of the killings? Does he consider himself an American hero? "Mercenary, assassin, or—what is it you folks call yourselves these days—contract players?"

"U.S. Marines. Sergeant Major Dickerson, VFW," he barks in a mock-military voice. "If you care to know. But hell, you might be into Only One World or some such pigwash."

"So, Jake Dickerson, you've kept ruthless right-wing dictators in power so we could all sleep at night and have our pleasant Only One World dreams," she says. "Is it true what they say about the Marines? I've heard that in basic training the enlistees are fed a diet of white sugar and stew meat and they're allowed only two hours of sleep."

"Now where did you get an idea like that?" he says, as if she's a child. He strokes her cheek. "You're very pretty. You must be Scottish. Am I right?" She shrugs. When he opens the car door, slams it, and gets into the back seat, she flinches, wondering if she's blacked out an interval of time, wondering what she might have told him. She leans her head against the window, wanting to leave but unable to. She thinks of Sterling. She's afraid he's left her, that he's long gone.

Jake reaches over the front seat and rubs a hand against her neck. The music ends and now there is frightful silence, only the car engine idling away. Barbed-wire fences around the small parking lot and icy white beams from a mercury vapor searchlight stream from the roof of a nearby hangar. Her loft is only a few blocks away, but she feels completely lost. The hand on her cheek is like the hand of a child. She steps out of the car and into the back seat, where Jake's hand finds its way between her legs. He kisses her eagerly. It's too warm in the car and the windows steam up, intensifying the smell of his after-shave, spicy and too sweet. His whole body is as wet as his tongue. He mutters the names of saints and God, but mostly he is breathing loudly. She clings to him tightly.

"You like to be held," he whispers in her ear. He sounds alarmed.

A Rainy Sunday

THE TRINITY CHURCH BELLS RING, her Bakelite clock radio, the color of half-ripe tomatoes, wakes her up to the sound of Fats Waller's "I Ain't Got Nobody." She's slept twenty hours, on top of the blankets and sheets, in a red silk slip clinging to her with perspiration. A whole week of working until midnight, going to O'Sullivan's, staying out most of the night. And yesterday's visit to the women's health center at the edge of Chinatown. Numbing, exhausting. On her way out, the receptionist gave her a stack of pamphlets and a pink and lavender holodecal that said *Chlamydia is not a flower*. She went to a nearby boutique, bought a silver-and-green Chinese silk dress and some puzzle boxes to cheer herself up. A long, slow walk back home, across Canal Street, the medications making her drowsy as she pushed her way through the crowds on the sidewalks and around produce markets. Bins of freshly caught fish, crabs, lobster at the edge of the sidewalks; some still alive, trying to crawl away.

She could be killing herself, trusting fallible strangers. She shuts the radio off and crawls out of bed. Her hair is getting too long again, touching her shoulders. In the bathroom mirror, she stares at the indentations it has left on one side of her face, reddish crosshatching. She showers, puts on a black cotton circle skirt and a short-sleeve monogrammed white blouse.

With the Venetian blinds wide open and the London

Symphony Orchestra playing Schubert's Unfinished Symphony live on the radio, she starts to work on a scale model: a group of three ninety-five-story office towers, inspired by the Eiffel Tower and the futuristic cities in Buck Rogers comic books. The architect from the Consortium's Baltimore office evokes the Modern era with the austere glass and steel of these towers. She wonders what it's like to turn away from tradition so completely, the way the Modernists did, shocking the world. Did they ever draw people or landscapes secretly, dutifully rendering the external world, burning the work at the end of the day? But what she's really wondering about is what happened during the past four nights; she's had blackouts.

Sterling walks in the door as she is putting tiny wire pedestrians near the buildings' entrances. The steel door opening and shutting sounds heavy and sharp, like a prison gate.

"I keep thinking you won't come back," she says, without looking up at him.

"I wouldn't leave you, my dear," he says. He takes off his trench coat and fedora, puts them across her drafting chair.

"Don't be romantic. Don't say things you don't mean." She tosses the wire figure aside and turns toward him.

"I do mean it." He walks up to her, sits with her and the scale models on the floor. He puts an arm around her and she places a hand on his knee, leaving a perfect plaster-of-Paris print on his dark trousers.

"Then you'll be glad to know that Bradley and I are history. I don't even think about him anymore. All that's left to do is have the locks changed." She knows it could take weeks; locksmiths are always backlogged as the burglary rate keeps rising. She's placed her name on three waiting lists and tries to resist the urge to barricade the door with furniture. "FTD didn't deliver those flowers," she says, pointing to the red roses in a slender Argy-Rousseau vase with sculpted figurines on her drafting table. "If I hocked that vase I could pay my rent for a year. But I'm not going to let him buy his way back." She looks back down at the wire figures she has spent so much time detailing: businessmen and businesswomen with briefcases and copies of the *Financial Times*, and a trio of mimes in black-and-white jumpsuits. All dwarfed by the scale of the building, whose glass-enclosed atrium is ten times their height.

"You can't," he says. "You're an extraordinary woman, but you've got to stop throwing yourself at undeserving men."

"Like you." She crushes one of the wire businessmen.

"Yes."

"Well, you're warning me too late." He turns away. She stands up, away from the maze of industrial clay, plaster, fiberboard, and bundles of wire. She's furious at him now. He pretends not to notice or care how strongly she feels. She takes her black raincoat and an umbrella from the closet.

"You can't go outside," he says, reaching a hand toward her. "There's an air quality alert."

"It's the quality of my life I'm worried about, old man." She slams the door. The elevator screeches as if it has a soul.

The streets are deserted, saturated with the falling acid rain. She wanders down Greenwich Street, dodging the muddy pools of water where the sidewalk has crumbled completely. The klaxons wail loudly, another flood warning. Two long blasts. Silence. One blast. Coast Guard vans cruise slowly down the street, their bullhorns warning pedestrians and motorists away. But hardly anyone is around.

She walks across the plaza of the World Trade Center towers, feeling as dwarfed as her wire figurines. She keeps turning around, but the plaza is deserted. The skywalk spanning West Street to Battery Park City has its usual assortment of panhandling war veterans waving their disability papers and mutilated bodies at her. She throws a handful of change to the corrugated-steel floor and lets them fight for it. Cruel, but she's feeling cruel. Sterling falls

171

asleep with her and lets her wake up alone. She thought it would be different now that he's quit his job at the photo lab. To spend more time with her, he said. Maybe he meant it; if she hadn't been out drinking these past few nights she would know. Maybe all he can do is help her to bed and let her sleep. She's too angry to sort it out. She merely shifts the blame, seesaw fashion, from him back to herself.

She reaches the promenade that separates the Hudson River and Battery Park City's dilapidated high-rises, most of the windows boarded up, the once colorful granite façades faded to a watery gray. The two incinerators could be mistaken for sacred obelisks. Rows of green park benches, broken gas lamps glowing unsteadily, wrought-iron railing almost hidden under piles of garbage bags, and the water-front stench is overwhelming today. It's an utterly depressing place, depressing and dangerous. It matches her mood. She sits down, thinking she will cry. But she doesn't; huddled under her umbrella, she watches some vagrant children playing jump rope in the shallow, muddy water. The wind turns her umbrella inside out and the rain pours on her, making her shiver.

She walks uptown on Church Street, slowly, ignoring the Coast Guard vans. She wants to see Sterling again, wants to embrace him, talk to him, stop shouting, stop hoping. At her doorstep, she tosses her broken umbrella into a pile of garbage bags, abandoned mattresses, and furniture, remem-bering the night she went to see him in Long Island City. But she can't distinguish the night from her dreams of it. She steps in the building. The lights in the lobby are burned out, the circular fluorescent tube flickering a weak bluish-yellow in the elevator. In the dreams, she and Sterling begin to sink through the floor and they fall rapidly, gravity pulling them apart.

Laughter, voices speaking German, a shaft of light coming from the kitchen as the elevator door opens. She hoped she'd never hear one of the voices again. She throws her coat on the sofa and walks toward the kitchen. Her throat is dry and hurting, as if she's already done the shouting she expects to do.

Charles and Sterling are sitting across from each other at the kitchen table, a six-pack of Beck's and a plate of rice cakes between them. They are swaying back and forth, laughing. They seem absolutely joyful, as if they will sing drinking songs any moment. So absorbed they don't notice her until she pounds the floor with her heel. Charles stands up; his white button-down shirt has rings of perspiration. His face is far paler and thinner than she remembers, as if he's been bedridden. He looks at her sternly, though she knows he's trying to smile. When she was a child, she thought this was what growing up meant—learning to stop smiling, frowning, laughing, or crying at will.

"Why are you here?"

"To see you, of course." He finally smiles slightly, a flat-line smile. "You're looking well. Getting prettier all the time."

"No, just older, like everybody else."

"Wanda, it's been such a long time." He stretches out his hand and walks toward her, but she pounds her heel again and he stops.

"I wonder whose fault that is." He's acting as if war, international intrigue, or something equally prodigious is what kept her from seeing him. As if this is a jubilant, hoped-for reunion. She glares at him and his smile turns into a painful smirk. She turns to Sterling, who sits with his hands folded awkwardly. "I'm sorry about this," she says to him, remembering not to call him by name. He gets up and shakes Charles's hand, telling him in German to call sometime, he'd like to go out again. He takes his coat and umbrella from the hall closet and heads for the door. She follows him.

"Don't leave me here alone with him," she whispers, tugging at his arm. She can hardly believe how well he seems to know Charles. It seems so unlikely.

"You'll be all right. He's not the man you remember." For

173

weeks Charles has been stopping by and visiting with him, waiting for Wanda to show up, and Sterling has never mentioned these visits. Charles always said he wanted to surprise her like this, though Sterling tried to discourage him. Sterling slips his coat on, hoping to return to the loft shortly and find the two of them reconciled. He thinks of his own father, whom he never spoke to or saw for most of his life. Even his closest friends weren't certain that his father was still living.

"You hurry back," she says, as the elevator door opens.

He puts an arm around her, kisses her forehead, and leaves. She walks slowly back to the kitchen, already wishing Sterling were still here; he'd help her get rid of Charles.

"He's a charming man, that Werner Schmidt," Charles says, forcing a smile. "I thought he was a bit old for you at first, but now I heartily approve."

She stands at the table and sighs heavily, folding her arms, tired of Charles's attempts at lightheartedness. "I really wish you'd just leave. Right now," she says, without a trace of intensity.

Charles doesn't say anything for a long while. He turns away from her and stares out the window. Thunder rumbles and there are tremendous bursts of white light. The fluorescent tubes around the center island unit flicker out and the kitchen turns grayishly dim. A brownout. Civil Defense klaxons wail faintly in the rain. "I just wanted to—"

"You don't get it, do you? I don't want you here."

"Damnit, Wanda, just hear me out, can't you?" he says, turning toward her. His eyes are a bright blue that makes her think of acid. "This isn't years ago when I made you repeat my words to make sure you'd really listened. You're an adult now, you have a choice."

"I've made my choice."

"Yes, you have." He sits down at the table and lights the pipe. "And it's my fault. All of it."

174

"My choices are *your* fault?"

He shakes his head. "I mean I never wanted this to happen."

"Don't tell me you're going to get tears in your eyes and say how sorry you are for breaking up our family."

"Yes, Wanda, I'm sorry."

She wants to laugh at him, sitting there, expecting her to be exhilarated by this opportunity to forgive him. She steps closer to the table, leans against the back of the chair opposite him. He must be lying. He's always lied. He lied to her mother, told her he didn't care if his family or anyone else disapproved of their marriage. But he cared about what everyone thought, family, friends, and colleagues alike. Everyone, even his military superiors with their medals pasted across their chests, the strategists and arms negotiators from Europe who couldn't go to the bathroom without their interpreters, and the twenty-year-olds from California and Japan who designed and maintained the computer systems.

"What are you thinking about?" Charles asks her.

She sits down at the table. "You don't want to know what I'm thinking. That was the whole point of walking out on my mother and me."

He folds his hands and looks at her intently. She stares back at him, noting the perspiration forming on his forehead. "I shouldn't have left you, God knows I shouldn't have," he says, his voice breaking.

"But you don't believe in God, remember? Except God as in 'God bless America.' And we're not your family anymore, so leave my mother and me alone." He neither looks nor acts like the obsessive and arrogant Charles who got down on his hands and knees to smooth the carpet pile every day. Still, she doesn't know what to do, how to make him leave. Calling the police is too drastic, but she considers it for a moment. Or worse, calling her mother and getting her to talk Charles into leaving. She won't do either.

"Wanda, I can't leave you alone. Not anymore. You're still my daughter. I know things can't be the way they used to be, but—"

"What exactly do you miss about the old days?" He looks away from her. "Do you miss the cross burnings? Do you miss the rocks thrown through the windows in the middle of the night? Do you miss the dead rats on the porch? Do you miss your fellow Air Force personnel and all their friends in the local KKK?"

He shakes his head. "I worried about you. That was no life for a young child. So I tried to do all I could for you. That's why I took you places, let you meet my colleagues on the base. I wanted you to know there were good people in the world, of all colors. We had fun. Don't you remember?" He attempts a smile. "We'd go to Mission Control, Space Command Center, everywhere I could possibly take you. When I went to restricted areas you'd sit in the waiting room, pacing the floors and talking to your imaginary friends. People were always taken by your candor. But a child isn't trying to be candid; she's just being herself."

"She wasn't allowed to be herself," Wanda says, barely keeping herself from shouting at him. "That's the part you don't remember. She was supposed to be a cute little blond girl. A *white* girl."

"That was *your* wish, Wanda, not mine. You were my daughter and I loved you; that was all that mattered to me. But you hated your mother for years simply because she didn't look like you. You couldn't believe she was really your mother. You didn't care much for Reggie, either, for the same reason. You'd lock yourself in your room for hours and not so much as speak to Reggie when she used to baby-sit for you."

"You're lying and you know it!" she shouts, pounding the table.

"No one told lies, except you. But I'm not blaming you,"

176

Charles says softly. "This isn't a country that does much for minorities."

"Stop patronizing me." She turns away and sits on the windowsill, looking out, the rain blowing all over her. The street is gray from the rain and the clogged gutters are flooded. She shivers in the cold air. It will take a lot to get Charles to leave. She knows she will have to go through the whole long, painful scene she has always tried to avoid.

"If you want to know the truth, I didn't want to be white *or* black," she says. "The white kids would call me a Clorox coon baby and all kinds of names I don't want to repeat. And the black kids hated me. 'Look at her,' they'd say. 'She think she white. She think she cute.' I guess you forgot I spent half my childhood hiding in my room and the other half beating up everyone who teased me. Mom and Reggie drove me crazy with those 'be yourself' lectures. *That's* what I hated about them. You, at least, in your heavy-duty state of denial, didn't talk about race."

He is still shaking his head, cradling his pipe in his hands. "That doesn't begin to explain what was going on with you back then, Wanda."

"Well, it so happens I don't feel a need to explain myself to you or anybody else. Not that I'm not paying the price for it. But you don't hear me." She knocks a small jar of sun tea from the windowsill to the floor and it shatters. She remembers how much he hated to see her break dishes and glasses. She'd do it right now to watch him turn red and shout at her. She stands up from the window. Her blouse is soaked. She brushes the damp edges of her skirt and walks toward the table.

Charles takes out a handkerchief and wipes his forehead. He's acting as if it's too strenuous for him to even listen to her. "If you won't tell me what you feel, how can I?" he says.

"I'm telling you now. I didn't ask to be born like this," she says, sitting down directly across from him at the table. "I used to have dreams that I peeled my white skin off and underneath I was black, just like I wanted to be. Dreams don't lie, Charles." He doesn't say anything to that, just keeps puffing on his pipe. A few moments go by. She knows he could sit there an hour, expecting her to wait, intimidated, for his response. "I'm talking to you. Why aren't you listening?"

He looks up at her. "I *am* listening. I know it was painful for you, growing up. I wish I could have done more. I feel guilty now. For all the good my guilt is doing you."

"You've got a lot to feel guilty about," she says. It isn't enough to recount her childhood and listen to his remorseful talk. She wants to make him angry now, as angry as she's been all these years. "You know what I'm talking about. That late father of yours."

"You're way out of line now!" Charles shouts, shaking his index finger at her.

"*He* was out of line. He loved *Deutschland Über Alles* more than his own life."

"You sound just like Tyler." He frowns as he lights his Zippo over and over. "There's no way you can know the innermost beliefs and feelings of a man just by studying a few old documents. My father's ethics and morality were beyond reproach. Space exploration was his dream for the world and that's what he devoted the rest of his life to. He was obsessed with the future, not the past."

She shakes her head. "The only thing your father was obsessed with was obliterating the past. Just like you are."

"My father had nothing to obliterate and neither do I. I only regret that he never accepted you and Francine." Charles reaches into his back pocket, pulls out his wallet, slides it across the table to her. "As for my obsessions, go ahead and look." She turns away. "No, Wanda, don't turn your back. Look at it."

She picks up the wallet reluctantly and begins to thumb through the plastic insets. There is a group photograph of

Charles's mother, Tyler, and his younger sister, Karin, whom Wanda hasn't seen in twenty years. A publicity shot of Karin's son, a stage actor, and graduation pictures of Tyler's daughters. She finds two photos of herself: high-school graduation and a glamour photo that makes her resemblance to Rita Hayworth unmistakable. One of Charles and Francine cutting the four-tier wedding cake with its interracial bride and groom. The same black-and-white portrait of her mother that Wanda has in the living room and a video still of Francine from a recent appearance on a community affairs program.

"You don't quite know what to say, do you?" he says sadly.

"There's nothing to say." She's surprised only that he expected these photographs to win her over. Of course he carries them: they are part of his dream of a perfect family.

"I've made mistakes in my life. Terrible ones." He puffs on his pipe and lowers his head. "Leaving Francine and you, that was the worst."

"I hear you, Charles. You want to moan about what could have been. It's easier that way. But stay away from my mother. Quit trying to call her all the time."

"We've been talking on the phone lately." She's about to say something but he waves her silent. "I know you're wondering why she didn't tell you," he says, looking down at his pipe, speaking so softly she can barely hear him. "Neither of us has told anyone. We haven't met face to face yet, but we will, soon. I'm divorcing Unah, and Francine isn't seeing the judge anymore, so—"

"What?" She can't believe what she's hearing, and that her mother hasn't told her. When was she planning to tell her? She stares at Charles; he looks up and nods wearily. "You're getting back together?" Wanda asks, almost whispering.

"I hope we do. I don't want to waste any more time. She feels the same way. I'd like to think she does."

There is a sound in his voice Wanda has never heard before: worn out, lonely. His stoop-shouldered posture

179

matches it. A downpour suddenly, thunder, lightning. She gets up and shuts the window partway, runs a finger through the water on the sill. The rain pounds on air conditioners and fire escapes, making them rattle like broken china. She sits back down at the table across from him. Something is unbelievably wrong. She's never seen him like this, puffing on his pipe hopelessly, as if he has nowhere to go. Tyler and Sterling are right: this isn't the Charles she remembers. It's not the Charles who never questioned his life, who thought all the trouble was in other people, not in himself.

"I can't believe my mother never told me any of this. Maybe she thought I'd disapprove or something. Which I do. It's not fair, Charles. You run off with your twenty-year-old and when you're tired of her you think you can come back and act as if nothing happened."

He puts his pipe in the ashtray and looks up at her. "I know better than that, Wanda. Believe me, I know. I'm fifty-seven years old. I'm not the same man I was ten years ago, when I woke up one day and realized my life was more than half over. It sounds like a terrible cliché. It *was* a cliché, running off with Unah. I'm ashamed of that now."

"I don't doubt that. But you can't use my mother to get on with your life," she says, trying to soften the harshness of what she's feeling. Surprising herself that she's concerned about him at all.

He nods as he picks up his pipe. "I'm having a lot of trouble getting by these days with or without Francine. I've started worrying. Not about anything specific, I just worry. I walk down the street and images flash in my mind. Knives and bullets flying at me. Or everything suddenly goes dark. I don't sleep much, either. Francine thinks it has something to do with my work. There have been problems at Suntel. Mostly cost overruns and management shuffles—it's always the same. I've lived with it all my life, and now I'm tired of it. But there's nothing I can do about the system, it's unshakable." He pauses and rubs his forehead

180

self-mockingly. "Listen to me; I'm becoming a fatalist about everything. A hell of a way to live."

Someone is unlocking the front door, slamming it, whistling. "Werner? Werner?" She's remembering to preserve his identity, but she knows it isn't Sterling. "Who is it?" she calls, about to get up from the table.

Someone's shadow creeps past the living room and the bookshelves that separate it from the kitchen. Bradley. He stands at the center island unit, trying to twirl his umbrella in the palm of his hand. He drops the umbrella and knocks over a stack of tin cake pans, the clatter startling him. He hums to himself, unbuttons his trench coat. His gray tie is loosened, his white shirttail hanging out. He looks as if he's been in a fistfight.

"Bradley, I think you'd better go home," Wanda says, frowning at him. He is drunker than she's ever seen him. She's not feeling anything at all for him now, not even contempt. He's simply intruding, and maybe he always has.

He leans against the center island unit, stretches out his arms on either side, lets out a loud, amorous sigh. "I'll bet you'd like that. You and your friend." He tips his fedora at Charles, takes it off, lays it on the counter.

"He's my father, not my friend."

Bradley laughs. "Strange company you keep, sister. Cronheim, who's dead, and your father, whom you hate."

"Wanda, who is this man?" Charles asks.

"You mean you don't know who I am?" he says, posturing and laughing obtrusively. "I'm surprised my reputation hasn't preceded me. Just call me your worst nightmare. Pillsbury Dough Boy on the outside and raging black buck on the inside." Bradley laughs even louder.

"You're really disgusting. You know that? Just get the hell out of here!" Wanda shouts. She picks up an empty beer bottle and throws it at him, missing. It shatters loudly against a cabinet. She reaches for another bottle.

"Wait a minute," Charles says, leaning toward her. "Wanda,

181

put the bottle down. We've asked him to leave. If he doesn't—"

"Then what, old man?" Bradley leans across the table, knocking the beer bottles and the plate of rice cakes aside, his face within millimeters of Charles. "Come on, pale face, I'm all ears." He stands up, stumbles, purposefully, across the floor.

"I don't know who you are or what you are, but I've had just about enough of this," Charles says, standing and moving toward him.

"It's getting good now, sister. This old prick wants to defend your honor."

"Get out of here!" Charles shouts. Bradley takes a few steps back, until he's up against the refrigerator, pretending to be afraid. "I don't want you talking like that in front of my daughter."

They start to shove each other. Bradley sends Charles stumbling across the floor, landing in front of the window, against the radiator. Wanda watches them, not knowing what to do. They push at each other ineptly, tug at each other's shirt collar. Bradley wrests himself from Charles and takes a few steps back. He pulls out a revolver from his coat pocket and aims it at Charles.

"Bradley, are you crazy? Put the gun away!" Wanda screams. She rushes toward her father, stands in front of him. "I told you, this is my father!"

"Stop insulting me, sister. And for God's sake stop demeaning yourself with these old men." Bradley shoves her forcefully and she falls against a chair. He stalks around Charles, holding the gun shakily with both hands. "So what's your line, little man? Oil? Real estate? Old money or new? She doesn't care, just so you've got plenty of it. But you've had your fun with her. Now get out. She doesn't need you white men messing up her life. It's me she wants, not you."

"You'd better put the gun down. I'm not who you seem to think I am," Charles says. Bradley stumbles over an empty beer bottle. Charles lunges at him, at the gun. Two shots are fired. The gun falls from Bradley's hand. Charles collapses against the radiator and falls to the floor, a pile of clothing and dark, oozing blood.

Wanda stoops beside him. She knows without touching him that he's dead. She looks up at Bradley. He picks up the gun and aims it at her, moving around her slowly, his hand shaking. I'm going to die, she thinks, and she starts trembling. He keeps aiming, for what seems like forever going by.

•

Sterling wonders if she's right, that he shouldn't have left her with her father. But Charles Stoller wasn't what he'd expected. This was a man who loved the intricacy of bridges, aqueducts, dams; who understood the terrible, inhuman force of jet propulsion, nuclear fission, and directed energy and didn't want to unleash the power whimsically upon the world. He wasn't a harsh man, he wasn't a fascist, and certainly not a man Wanda should be afraid of.

Sterling knows the trouble isn't with her father. He's trying to understand what's happening to her and why. He doesn't want to consider that he's hurting her more than Charles and Bradley and all the men she keeps meeting in bars and clubs. He worries about her making it back home each night, to her arsenal of medications, and collapsing in bed beside him for an hour or two before she gets up and goes to work.

He sits down on a bench along the Battery Park City promenade, the gray harbor in front of him, mystically beautiful in its lifelessness. He thinks of Lenore suddenly. What did she look like when she died, he wonders. He has to keep imagining her death, even as he has to stop thinking he could have prevented it.

He cringes, closes his eyes. Alone, in an alien city.

PART TWO

AN INTERLUDE:
NIGHT PASSING
(ALL CLEAR)

The past is not dead. It's not even past.

WILLIAM FAULKNER

Drôle de Guerre

HE CALLS HER FROM the Beaux-Arts after teaching his afternoon drawing class, just as always. She isn't used to the curfew, to being home from Pasteur well before midnight. Now it shuts promptly every weekday at six o'clock Greater Reich Time; the heating oil shortage, the German officials say. Their soldiers patrol the grounds, whispering and turning their backs to the scientists, as if conspiring.

He knows she is with Kally at the kitchen table, wrapped in blankets, shivering, as they translate into English reports received by Cohors, a Resistance organization they belong to. The phone rings and rings. When she answers it she says "Cigarettes" in a hoarse whisper and hangs up.

He has no more ration cards for ersatz tobacco, and it isn't ersatz tobacco she wants. It will take hours of following whispered directions to restaurants and bars on streets where the Métro no longer stops, but he will find cigarettes for her. Black-market Turkish cigarettes. It's how they and the rest of Paris live now. It takes up everyone's time and energy, day after day, looking for food, drink, cigarettes; supplementing the rationing, just getting by. *Le système D.*, they call it.

He might find cigarettes in a bar on rue Cujas, he remembers, as he walks through Beaux-Arts's *cour vitrée*, with its immensely high, vaulted metal-and-glass ceiling. He can't help but admire the hall, filled with statuary and architectural fragments: colonnades, pedestals of ancient churches and châteaux, their discord creating a striking unity of form. Beaux-Arts seems permanent and unshakable, unlike everything else around him. The dimouts hadn't kept the Germans away, nor did lighting the streets at night with faint, sinister blue lights. But it's over now, there were never any bombings in Paris. Only an armistice and plenty of talk of collaboration, for the good of a unified, harmonious Europe.

Drôle de guerre, phony war. Now everyone goes on as if the Germans have always been here. Nothing is what it was before; hotels, theaters, and municipal buildings are offices for the German bureaucracies, their compound names printed on the black-and-white signs that clutter the streets. He walks through the courtyard and out the iron-grille gates onto rue Bonaparte, wondering if the Germans will keep the school open. He can't understand their evolving aesthetics or their bureaucracy, the Einsatzstab Rosenberg, an official organization of professional looters who are stockpiling the "degenerate" artworks of Klee, Matisse, Picasso, and others. They burn the art in ritual bonfires outside the city. He wonders when the Germans will decide his art and his teaching job must go, too. Or he could be arrested for his work with Défense de la France. He can't get used to the secrecy, the silences, the involuntary trust in strangers.

In the days before the Germans arrived, Paris had become a perpetual crowd scene gone out of control. Thousands of people were on the streets trying to flee. Cars, trunks, suitcases littered the boulevards, and entire houses, offices, factories were abandoned. He heard rumors that, in some hospitals, fatal injections were given to patients too incapacitated to flee, and that several government officials committed suicide as the occupation began. But Lenore didn't want to leave Paris. The occupation and the war wouldn't last, she told him, and Hitler wouldn't conquer the world, either. No one ever had.

•

There are no lights on in the apartment, but this isn't unusual. He and Lenore have closed off most of the rooms, unable to pay the exorbitant heating bills. Cramped and cold, they feel like refugees. But Kally has much worse to fear, with mass arrests and deportations, and, for those who remain, the many anti-Jewish ordinances; every kind of humiliation. The presence of informers saddens him, citizens writing letters to the German officials, reporting Jews who violate the regulations. He's glad that Kally remains as defiant as ever, refusing to wear the yellow star and continuing to go out to the cafés with Lenore and their friends from the dwindling Left Bank community.

He steps into the living room, where wads of newspapers burn in the black slate fireplace, giving the entire room a faint amber glow. Lenore is sitting on the sofa pushed close to the fireplace. She wears one of his flannel shirts over her dress. Her long hair is tangled. Unable to find peroxide, she has let it return to its natural brunette. Startling, still, not to see the familiar glow of platinum. The radio is on, heavy static and barely audible voices from the BBC reporting on the war. The British are fighting against the Germans in Egypt, apparently winning. He tosses his topcoat on the sideboard, sits with her on the sofa, kisses her. She barely looks at him, and as he holds her, she cringes and clutches the flannel shirt around her. He takes the cigarettes from his pocket.

"Could find only three cigarettes. National tobacco," he says, lighting one and handing it to her. "Where's Kally?"

Lenore doesn't answer. "Bay leaves and parsley," she says after a few moments, puffing on the cigarette. "I'm sorry there's no more cognac." She puts the empty bottle on the floor, kicks it toward the fire with great disgust. It isn't like her to be drinking so much, and so early in the evening, or to neglect the translations. He takes the cigarette from her and pulls deeply on it. He decides to keep silent, let her talk to him.

She gets up, paces the floor, lights the two white candles on the mantel. "Curse the candles *and* the dark," she says, sitting back down beside him.

"What's wrong?" he asks, taking both her hands.

"I've been drinking too much and I'm freezing." She unbuttons the flannel shirt and her blue crepe dress. "But I don't need more clothing, I need you," she says. She grasps him tightly and kisses him, digs her fingernails into the back of his neck. The pain is so unexpected and sharp it makes his eyes water. One of her wooden shoes falls and it sounds like a clap of thunder on the threadbare Kashan rug.

He pulls away from her and gropes for the cigarette, burning a hole in the sofa arm. "Not now, Lenny."

She looks at him, not seeming to agree or disagree, or even to be listening at all. She takes the cigarette and puffs on it, pulling the blankets around her. Her eyes are red and he realizes she has been crying. "This is how they destroy us. One by one." She gets up and looks through the side-board, finds an unopened bottle of Scotch. Her hands shake as she fills two highball glasses, hands one to Sterling. She sits cross-legged beside him on the sofa, holding the glass on her knee. "I was there when it happened," she says, about to cry again. She reaches for her handkerchief on the table. "I tried my damnedest to sit here like any other night. But I wouldn't be here all alone like this, would I?"

"Kally," he says as he embraces Lenore. She cries for a long time, blotting her tears with the handkerchief. He thinks of how poorly he'd gotten along with Kally over the years, the tensions rarely easing between them, despite their efforts. He can't believe she's gone.

"The Germans came to Pasteur and arrested her. They

said she'd been seen in public without her star. They started to rattle off their horrible rules, and now they've sent her away." She reaches for the cigarette and Sterling lights it for her. "What can we do? They're going to deport her, aren't they?" She exhales a cloud of smoke that lingers around her.

"I've heard talk"—he says, picking up the other cigarette, but he's too anguished to smoke—"about those camps in Germany and Poland."

"Tell me."

"There's nothing we can do to help her, that much I know. We don't have any friends in high places."

"But we've got to do something, Crönchen!" She drops her glass and it shatters in front of the fireplace. He mutters platitudes to her that sound lamer to him than ever. What everyone says about war, courage, and survival. Lenore barely acknowledges them. She looks at him so irritated that he stops. "She'll escape. I know she will," she says suddenly. He sees how hard she's trying to believe what she says.

"Twenty-two years I've known her." She leans against him. "I hear her telling me not to worry. My Kallischen, Kallischen," she whispers, crying.

•

The streets were as quiet as the countryside; there had been virtually no cars in Paris since the Germans seized them. There was snow on the ground; it fell during the night, covering thousands of bicycles, taxi-cycles, and rickshas casually parked all over the streets and sidewalks. Snowdrifts were everywhere, full of well-worn foot and bicycle paths that turned to ice overnight. There was no glamour or beauty left in the city. He couldn't even find canvas anymore, so he painted on wooden boards that he and his colleagues obtained on the black market. The oils were from Spain, ersatz products of nearly liquid consistency. He had to learn to paint all over again.

He and Lenore stayed up late every night translating and

typing intelligence reports on microfilm and packing them in tin candy boxes with hidden bottoms. The next day Lenore took the microfilm to an apartment on rue de Seine. Kally would have appreciated their tenacity, she always told him. When she talked about Kally, it was as if she were remarking on the foolhardiness of an explorer gone far out of radio contact. She didn't cry anymore; she was constantly absorbed in her work, but with a sadness that made her methodical and unenthusiastic.

Tonight he finished translating messages and sat in front of the fireplace, bundled up in blankets. He was waiting for Lenore. She sometimes disappeared for hours at a time in the evenings, returning minutes before the midnight curfew. She would only tell him she was helping to recruit and dispatch couriers for Cohors, setting up pickup and drop-off locations, distributing money. He believed what she told him, but he wished she would talk to him more freely. And there was his own guilt: he should be the one out in the streets risking his life, not her.

He tried to put aside his worries. He was sketching with charcoal on the emulsion side of the photographic paper he couldn't use anymore. He hadn't been able to photograph Lenore in the laboratory at Pasteur as he used to, late at night when no one was around but the two of them, and sometimes Kally, who in a spare moment would help him set up the photofloods. Now there were pages of new regulations and German officers who could recite them all. It took weeks to find film and darkroom supplies, and most of the time he was too cold and too hungry to search.

He cranked the Victrola and put on another record. Toscanini and the NBC Orchestra playing the Beethoven Seventh. Some of the record sides were too scratched to play and he sat in silence, remembering the lost passages. It was five in the afternoon and almost dark. He got up and pulled down all the window shades. He hated winter, hated the nighttime.

•

Lenore gathered up the blankets by the wing chair where he had fallen asleep. They were fading, full of dangling threads, dangerously close to the fire. This is how they kill us, patiently letting us freeze or starve, she thought. This is the real *Blitzkrieg*.

He opened his eyes slowly and reached out a hand to her. "It must be late," he mumbled. He was overjoyed to see her, but he knew better than to tell her so. She'd go on at length about why she had to do what she was doing, no matter how risky.

"A quarter past midnight and, by Jove, I've missed the curfew again. That'll get me interrogated at the rue des Saussaies so fast I'll lose both my glass slippers." She kissed him, got up, and poured two glassfuls of Scotch from a bottle stashed in the credenza.

"I don't know what you're doing. I don't think you know, either," he said, taking the glass from her. She buttoned her gray wool sweater and folded her arms tightly as she sat with him. He couldn't keep silent, not tonight. "Lenny, Cohors needs you to translate, not stalk all over Paris half the night. You're risking—"

"Risking what? My life?" she said, pushing back her hair. She stared into the waning fire, white ashes floating up the chimney. Not everyone died in those camps, she thought. There were always survivors. Sterling's pessimism was becoming unbearable. Sometimes she doubted he'd be with the Resistance if it weren't for her. She took off her shoes. They were wooden, like all the new shoes in France, either fanciful-looking with platform heels or inspired by peasant clogs, as if they were Paris chic, not another hardship of the war. She doused them both with Scotch and tossed them into the fire. They flared brightly in tall yellow flames. "Don't you understand? The sooner this war is over, the sooner Kally and the others can come home," she said.

"Darling, you know better than that," he said, as softly as he could. The courier Jan Karski had just returned from Poland and reported what was going on at Belzec and the other camps. Sterling, Lenore, and their Resistance comrades were gradually learning unimaginable truths about the war and the Nazis. He hated to see Lenore still trying to delude herself. He put his arms around her. She had become so thin he was afraid to hold her tightly; her bones seemed to him as fragile as porcelain. He himself felt more and more fragile, old, inept. "It's looking grim—" He couldn't continue. Of course she knew what he was going to say.

"Then why doesn't somebody do something?" she said. Churchill and Roosevelt seemed to do nothing but make speeches on the radio. On the BBC all she heard about was the Allied invasion of Morocco and Algeria. She was silent for a while, feeling powerless and fearful. She'd been missing Kally so much lately she'd started crying at Pasteur again, nearly every day. "This is V. The Victory," she said, bitterly. She picked up her Scotch, took a sip, and tossed the rest of it into the fire. The flames hissed and sparks floated everywhere in the dark room. She lay across his lap and reached up to stroke his face.

"I still dream about her every night, Crönchen. Every single night. Just ordinary little dreams. Mostly about how we lived back in New York. All we worried about were our studies and where and how to get the best liquor. Real liquor from Canada." She and Kally should have stayed in New York, she thought. But no, they left, looking for their vision of bohemia, of freedom, and they couldn't find it in the cafés and speakeasies of New York. They never would have believed how much the world was about to change, how oppressively irrational nations would become. "I shouldn't drink. I shouldn't run on like this. The Resistance is what keeps me going. Some nights I lie awake, trying to sleep and hoping I won't wake up," she said, tugging at the stray strands of her hair. She felt the comfort and the weight of

194

her words, as if talking about dying would keep her alive.

"Don't you ever say that again! Ever!" he shouted, pushing the blankets aside and grasping her firmly by her shoulders.

"You can stop shouting at me, Crön. You know I don't mean it." She stared at him until he released her. She took out a cigarette from her case. He lit it for her and they took turns smoking it, silently. She was so shaken she could barely hold the cigarette. She didn't want to tell Sterling just how often she thought of dying, how sometimes it didn't frighten her. "National tobacco," she said, pretending to cough. "And to hell with this goddamn curfew. My work doesn't end at midnight."

He put out the cigarette. "Never mind the curfew. *I* want you here at midnight. Before midnight." He drew her closer, started to unbutton her blouse. Her skin was warm against his dry, cold hands.

"Times have changed," she muttered with a soft laugh. She leaned closer to him and kissed his neck. "You'll do anything to keep me at home in the evening. I should thank the Nazis for saving my marriage."

She is freezing as the layers of clothing come off. It's too much, what he's doing, and she wants to touch him everywhere at once. Her touch is a frantic, fearful staccato. She is used to feeling fear all the time. She has to rush through the city carrying secrets, smile at the German officers and soldiers, and pretend she can speak their language only brokenly. All the while knowing she could be arrested, interrogated, sentenced to death. When she and Sterling talk about the Resistance, they talk abstractly about freedom and solidarity. He does his part for the newspaper, *Défense de la France*, typesetting the words of others on old and failing equipment in the basement of a decrepit apartment building near the Champs-Élysées. He sends the photographic plates by courier to Crémieu, where the newspaper is printed in the basement of a house. Thousands of copies of each issue are printed and distributed all over France by couriers who lug them in heavy suitcases, on foot, bicycle, train. So much order and logic to the Resistance, she could almost forget the danger.

She feels grateful when she and Sterling don't speak. He is the lover he never was before, with a tirelessness she knows better than to mistake for passion. Neither of them has the strength for passion. They have to make love slowly, the way they drink wine, eat bread, smoke cigarettes, and savor every other scarce necessity. Hours pass and they are unable to speak. She notices that his hair has turned completely silver and it gleams in the faint light coming in from the street lamps. Her own hair is becoming darker, like something ripening. It shocks her that they are both growing older, changing along with the world, which is also growing older and decaying, faster than they are. She's afraid they will both collapse and shiver helplessly through the long winter. Even the sunlight on the windows is white and cold.

•

It was raining fiercely outside. Raining on top of the gray snowdrifts that formed small mountain ranges all over the city. The large windows in the parlor rattled and she hastily resealed them. In the spring she would have to spend hours reopening them, chipping away at the powdery white putty. But now she and the rest of Paris were immobile, waiting for the snow to melt away. She had to deliver microfilm to the rue de Seine drop-off location tonight. She would have done it yesterday if it weren't for the snowstorms. She would go, not Sterling. She'd hidden the microfilm from him last night, knowing he would try to deliver it himself. She went to the living room, where she sat with him on the sofa, as always pushed too close to the fireplace.

But he felt neither the heat nor the drafty chill which floated supernaturally through the apartment. He had been fighting with her for hours, his voice was strained from shouting. He didn't believe that he stood a greater chance

196

of being caught than she did. He resented her implication that he was incapable of making a simple delivery across the city. Her Resistance work was making her inflexible and aloof. He tried to understand her, listen to her, but he was angry at himself for resenting her sad delusions about Kally.

They sat silently and she fastened her black wool coat, many sizes too big, like a costume. She took an ersatz cigarette from her case, struck the match against her wooden boot heel. She was afraid he'd start shouting at her again. "I'll be back before midnight. Wait up for me?" she said, stroking his chapped hands, kissing them. He didn't answer, just took her cigarette and puffed on it. His overprotectiveness not only angered her, it was foolish. Too much at stake, she kept telling him, too many lives. She took the cigarette back from him. He wouldn't even look at her.

"See me out the door at least," she said as she kissed his forehead and got up. He turned off all the lights. The foyer's hurricane lamp put a dim shaft of light across the floor. She leaned against the door frame, smoking and staring at Sterling's trio of photographs of her along the wall. The assiduous woman she hardly recognized. Too starved and restive to remember how she used to sit and concentrate on her research well into the early morning. It was five months to the day that the Germans had arrested Kally. She could hardly get her work done at Pasteur, listening to the BBC on the sly. She kept wondering about Kally, what it was like for her being imprisoned for so long. She had to believe Kally was still alive, but it was becoming more and more difficult.

She turned and he was leaning against the door and grasping the doorknob firmly. "You're not going, Lenny."

"Crönchen, please." He was shivering in the draft, looking as if he could barely hold the doorknob. Her cigarette sent its wafting smoke between them. She put her arms around him. He didn't move from the door; she could almost have cried for him right then. For a moment she remembered

197

every argument they'd ever had. All of them were futile and regrettable. "It's just like any other night," she whispered soothingly. "I won't even deface any propaganda posters. Promise."

He took her cigarette and put it out. He tried to change her mind one last time. She listened quietly, but impatiently glancing at his hand still on the doorknob. "We'll both go, then," he said. She shook her head. An unwritten rule: couriers always traveled alone. She smiled at him and kissed both his cheeks ceremoniously. "Listen, comrade, when I return you'll have the rest of the night to show me just how much you missed me." She put her arms around him and he held her for a long time, kissed her.

She walked out the door. He stepped outside as she turned on the *minuterie* light and dashed down the stairway. She blew him a kiss from the first landing and kept going. He stood by the door, staring at the banisters until the light turned itself off.

•

He had heard the same news about so many others. When he heard it about Lenore he could do nothing but sit and stare out the window in the dusty attic of a large farmhouse just outside Toulouse, stare at the morning fog that was beginning to burn off. It was a safe house whose three and a half stories were crowded with fellow escapees who hid quietly in their rooms during the day and sat up half the night in the cellar, smoking and talking. But he kept to himself, worrying about Lenore, waiting to hear word of her.

He had been here for weeks, waiting for organizers of the Brandy line to help him escape south through the Pyrenees and on through Spain to Gibraltar, where he would wait with other escapees, secret agents, aviators, and soldiers for passage to England. He couldn't think about the long, nearly impossible journey he would make in a few days as he listened to Lenore's friends. The two men were patient, sitting on the wooden packing crates that served as furniture and sharing their Turkish cigarettes with him. They belonged to Cohors and called themselves Max and Stephan. They were divinity students; Sterling recognized and craved their pastorly benevolence. They were passing through Toulouse on their way back from Tarbes, dressed as farmers in their faded gray trousers and flannel shirts.

For the past two months, Lenore had been forced to work twelve hours a day at a munitions factory and at the airfields near Ravensbrück. He knew her parents had been trying, through the U.S. State Department, to have her freed. But now she was dead. Shot by firing squad for helping to organize a work stoppage at the factory. Max and Stephan told him exactly what happened, in more detail than he wanted to hear. They told it as if it were a story from the remote past and Lenore a martyr and saint. His guilt for not stopping her from going out that night hadn't begun to overtake him; he couldn't yet contemplate what could have been. The strong tobacco and weeks of not eating or sleeping properly were making him lightheaded and numb. But he kept listening as Max and Stephan talked about her for hours and ran through the pseudonyms of all their fellow members of Cohors, wondering who the informer was.

Two days after her arrest, two unbearable days of being followed everywhere he went, of being unable to do anything but teach his classes and return home to the empty apartment, a Cohors courier delivered false identification papers to him at Beaux-Arts. Sterling went home and packed a Pullman suitcase. Evading the Germans as he'd been instructed to do, he headed to Gare du Nord, where he boarded a train to Toulouse.

•

He doesn't remember much of the rest. He is in a sanitarium in a district of London he's never heard of, far away from the city's landmarks. All the lights are turned off at night in the city because of air raids. He hears the sirens all night and he can't sleep anymore.

The grueling days of travel through the Pyrenees and the Spanish countryside and his grief have left him with pneumonia. Hospital rooms are scarce in London and there was nowhere for him to go but this tuberculosis sanitarium, where he's confined to a room with gray walls and a window way above eye level. When he stands on the bed to look out the window he sees nothing but row houses beyond the sanitarium grounds, which are overrun with weeds. The electrical power is faulty and the nightstand light bulb increases and decreases in brightness as if the light itself is coughing and choking, like the people he hears around him night and day. It seems extraordinary to him that people are still dying of ordinary diseases.

A photograph of Lenore is on the nightstand. When the nurses check on him and the orderlies give him his meals, he points to the photograph and asks in French, Where is Lenore? Where is Lenore? But he isn't listening for an answer; he lulls himself with the question, with staring for hours at the photograph. He took it some six years ago in the ordinary incandescent lighting of their apartment and with the Vacu-Blitz flashbulbs he had been experimenting with. The flash was blinding, neither of them used to it. She looks back at him from the photograph, uneasy, straining not to blink.

He has clutched the photograph so much the glass frame is gray with his fingerprints. Most of the other photographs of her are in New York, where he sent them a few months before the Germans came to France. He has a letter from T. R. Ruffec, Ltd., a London gallery that represented his work before the war, assuring him that all is in order. Ruffec himself has paid for Sterling's room here at the sanitarium.

There are other letters, almost a dozen. He hasn't read them. The BBC broadcasts tell him Roosevelt and Churchill are meeting in Casablanca. He doesn't believe the war will ever end. Sometimes he doesn't believe Lenore is dead. He closes his eyes and tries to imagine her dead, but he sees nothing at all.

He looks through the letters again and finds one from Moholy. A long letter in English, typed on onionskin paper. He holds it close to the weak, flickering light.

Moholy tells him about the war effort in America, how they have to learn to get by with shortages of materials and to develop substitutes, like mattress springs made of wood parts cleverly interconnected and glued to create elasticity. Chicago officials have asked Moholy to devise a method to camouflage the entire city. He plans to analyze visual elements, illusions, and the psychology of color perception to do this.

"Holy Mahagonny," he says, wanting to leave his room, leave England to see his friend, talk over these ideas. Mahagonny, he called him, years ago, punning on his name.

In Chicago he will be an American again. He will teach photography and film at the Institute of Design, the school Moholy has founded. He will talk about color and form, help Moholy camouflage Chicago. Or the entire country. He's tired of his sadness and grief, of sitting alone in a room, barely able to speak.

Second City

HE HAD BEEN IN CHICAGO for months when it occurred to him one evening that he was a two-hour drive away from where he was born, a dairy farm in southeastern Wisconsin. It was sold when he was ten; he remembers the two auctioneers standing high above the crowd on a hay wagon, their mouths blurring words and numbers till they were humming sounds that floated over the rain-soaked land. People signaled bids and he tried to watch the land disappear. When the crowds dispersed, he looked for the people who had taken the land, wondering how they would carry it with them. The farm would soon be gone and he and his father would soar like birds overhead.

But it didn't happen that way. He and his father rode everywhere, first in horse-drawn carriages, later in the motor buggy his father had ordered from the Sears, Roebuck catalogue. His father was a kind of backwoods Dale Carnegie precursor, a young-looking blond giant around whom people flocked to listen to him speak in his singsongy Germanic voice. He talked about the power of the mind and sold universal tranquillity as others sold tonics. He took Sterling to mysterious meetings in a Minneapolis town house where men and women dressed like Pilgrims, but with touches of finery: gold pocket watches, strings of pearls, diamond brooches, exotic bird feathers on their hats. They sat in a circle around lighted candles, speaking in warbled, tense voices he could barely understand. Later, Sterling found out these were mediums, through whom the dead spoke.

Airplanes, cars, movies, and radio were brand new back then, technologies progressing the very same years he was growing up and wandering the country with his father. Now Sterling is back in America, trying to adjust to Chicago and a new era. He lives alone on the South Side in a ground-level Calumet Avenue apartment, one of the two bedrooms converted into a painting studio and the walk-in closet a darkroom. He lives quietly, teaching the motion-picture class and helping out with the photography classes. He spends long hours in darkrooms and film-editing rooms, as he did before the war, doing what he imagines everyone expects former Bauhäusler to do, producing and directing his own short films on weekends and writing screenplays full of sketches and storyboards, not words. He closes his eyes and sees the film images, shadows cast by sculptures he has made out of Plexiglas. He and Moholy have both been sculpting with Plexiglas, but Sterling uses his sculptures only in his films, sometimes painting them with a natural sponge dipped in titanium-white acrylic paint. The sculptures are elongated, abstracted figurines with limbs of triangles, circles, and free-form shapes. Their shadows dance fluidly in the films, swirling transparencies, concentric shadows, and glowing fragments of light.

They remind him of the day the war ended. He was in the Loop with thousands of others. Strangers celebrating, jumping, shouting, standing on top of cars and lampposts, momentarily becoming each other's family and friends. He wandered through the crowded streets, pushed along by the strangers. They were all motion and energy, like his figurines, and the war seemed more unreal that day than ever.

He has been this way for months, hardly believing the war is over, not understanding how. No one has found him and taken him away. Not the Axis, not anyone. His father died not long ago, in a nearby Des Plaines nursing home. He told

Sterling the war would never end, that the Nazis would let a huge cloud of nerve gas float around the world which would cover the sun and leave all the dead sprawled on the ground. He dreams about this from time to time; he is the war's only survivor, walking through fields covered with the dead. He's looking for Lenore. He doesn't find her. Instead, every dead person he finds has a mask, a horrible, smiling caricature of Lenore.

Now he talks about Europe and the war to anyone who will listen. There are plenty who do, students who have never left the city, some aspiring to Hollywood or Madison Avenue and some believing in art the way he used to. Everyone he knows lives in a tense euphoria; laughter and smiles are like nervous tics.

A winter night in his apartment. It's still strange to him, living alone again. He picked a tiny apartment with barely enough space for himself; he doesn't want too many rooms to wander around in. Low, plaster ceilings, a sunken living room with a white-mortared fireplace. He has arranged all the rented furniture against the walls—royal-blue sofa and ottoman, director's chairs—leaving the gray linoleum floors of the room's center empty. His newer paintings cover the sky-blue walls. Canvas is abundant again; he can paint in large scale.

When he reads *The Chicago Beacon*, the NAACP newspaper for which he's preparing the mechanicals tonight, he doesn't understand or remember America being like this. Cross burnings and fire bombings in Cicero and other Chicago neighborhoods. A family's possessions thrown out of windows and heaped onto an enormous bonfire. In the South, segregation, mob violence, lynchings. He has never been down South to see the WHITE and COLORED signs hanging over restrooms, water fountains, and separate entrances to bus and train stations. It makes him think of the Paris the Germans ran.

And Lenore. He doubts that five minutes ever go by that

he doesn't think of her. *She loved justice and freedom even more than she loved science*, he said in an essay for the conference proceedings of the International Society of Virology. They asked him to write about Lenore, and he described how she and her friends raised funds for the Left in Spain, and did the same when Hitler invaded Poland and Czechoslovakia. He wrote about her work for the French Resistance, for which she was awarded posthumously the Medal of Resistance and the Cross of the Liberation. When he opened the large leather-bound volume, he found that whole paragraphs of his essay had been edited away.

The country that will one day suspect him of being a Communist is offering him nothing now but giddy illusions: parades, cheery radio announcers and programs, and swing music for dancing. And there are too many celebrations and parades in the city. The war veterans, the labor unions, all sorts of groups march on State Street, playing jubilant band music, waving large flags. He has been away too long. But the NAACP makes him feel at home in a way he can't completely understand. He doesn't go to many meetings, but he works closely with the small newspaper staff and a few of the subcommittees. Some of the members are lawyers or teachers who moved up North and speak among themselves about the Jim Crow South. He tells them his stories about the war.

He likes the feel of the columns and headlines of type, the paper slick and smooth like a thin vinyl. Sitting at his drafting table, pasting up mechanicals, makes him think of the old days. He looks over the mechanicals, stacks them in order. Times Roman type and headlines, razor-thin rules delineating the five-column pages; a few display ads for local South Side businesses. In two days, the newspaper will be all over the South Side and mailed around the country.

He packs the mechanicals in his portfolio case and bundles up in the same Donegal wool coat he has had since Berlin, and later in Paris, when he couldn't go anywhere without getting offers for it: chickens, rabbits, cigarettes, winter squash. Bitter cold outside, the winds gusting off Lake Michigan.

He walks to the printer on Wabash Avenue, down the deserted streets, almost running. Habit. Just as he looks over his shoulder every few seconds as he walks, forgetting that the old dangers are gone. The print shop is a storefront with hand-painted Old English letters, MAGNUS J. COOPER PRINTING COMPANY, forming an arch on the glass window. He rings the buzzer and waits for Magnus J. Cooper himself, a stocky man in gray industrial clothing, thinning salt-and-pepper hair, conked and side-parted. They sit and talk about typography and new printing technologies, raising their voices above the loud clamor of the printing presses and *Your Hit Parade* blaring from the radio.

Sterling leaves the print shop and takes a South Park jitney to the Persian Ballroom. The ballroom is a mysterious oval, with crystal chandeliers hanging from a silver-painted ceiling and grayish-blue draperies covering the walls and the stage. The dance floor is crowded with people he can barely see in the soft lighting. Eddie Heywood and His Orchestra play "C-sharp Minor Jump." He sits alone, sipping Scotch, leaning back in the velvet-upholstered side chair, wishing he had someone to talk to. He leaves his regal chair and table, finds a phone booth downstairs, and calls the man who is still his best friend in the world.

•

Berghoff's Old Heidelberg Room is full of color and noise. High, beamed ceilings, walnut-paneled walls, checkerboard ivory-and-sienna marble floors. The conversations of fellow late-night diners screen out the traffic and congestion of the Loop. The waiters in their black coats and bow ties rush about with an orderliness that reassures him. He keeps looking at the fresco on the opposite wall—Grecian temple and a gold sky above townspeople in Victorian garb. It's a place he would like to visit but can't, like the Berlin he remembers. In the newsreels there is nothing left of Berlin but monumental piles of rubble.

He and Moholy talk about film. The celluloid itself, how fragile it is, the silver nitrate shrinking invisibly. Motion pictures and the persistence of vision. They think of the hundreds of thousands of frames creating continuous motion on the silver screen. One day, Moholy tells him, films will have 144 frames per second and the images will be so luminous people will confuse them with real life.

They never tire of talking about art, philosophy, or politics. They laugh at puns, at the peculiarities of the English language, at words with too many meanings. Sterling speaks it poorly now, puzzling over irregular verbs and grammar as he and Moholy are laughing, drinking German beer in porcelain steins. They sit with portfolio cases at their feet, wearing dark suits. They stare at each other like young children and burst out laughing.

●

Later, in Sterling's living room, the air heavy with cigarette smoke. The dim light that shines through frosted-glass ball lamps hanging in the center of the room makes the smoke look darker and grayer than it is. He empties the chrome ashtray, returns it to the table, pours more Scotch into the glasses. He sets one down for Moholy, who sits uncomfortably on the sofa, his suit jacket rolled up beside him, round nickel-rimmed glasses tossed on the end table. The console radio blares Count Basie and His Orchestra. Sterling lowers the volume, stares for a moment at the coarse, tweedlike cloth that covers the speaker. He touches it, feeling on his fingertips the sound that has traveled all the way from the Edgewater Beach Hotel Ballroom. He finishes the Scotch and refills his glass.

"Living my life a certain way. Must it continue? I almost understand the painters," Moholy says in his careful,

Hungarian-accented English as Sterling sits opposite him on one of the director's chairs. He has been cryptic like this all evening. Something has happened to him. Maybe the constant news of war, the names of battles, cities bombed, reminds him of the previous war. Of suffering in the overcrowded Odessa Military Hospital, thinking he would die from his wounds. The new war has changed everyone. His friend of more than twenty years, since the Bauhaus, and years, places, and people which no longer seem real.

Moholy runs a hand through his dark hair, which he has always worn combed straight back from the front. It is streaked with gray now and his face is softer, rounder; the stark, angular features and enigmatic gaze are gone. He's like someone's neighbor or father, with a garnered look of wisdom and stability. Tonight he trembles, not humanly, but like the afterimage of a bright color.

"What are you saying, Laci?" It is at least the tenth time Sterling has asked him and he no longer expects an answer. He has never seen Moholy drink or smoke so much. He puts sentences together with a syntax Sterling finds more and more baffling.

Moholy taps a cigarette against the end table and lights it, cupping his hands around the match flame as if the strong Lake Michigan winds have knocked down the walls. He drags deeply from the cigarette, rolls it around in the ashtray until the ashes form a pyramid at the tip. "It's how we all live. All the changes. The new technologies: color photography, Technicolor film, long-playing phonograph records, television. They are altering our perceptions. We can't even see it all now, what's to come."

"I hate to say it, but what's to come will be more of the same." Sterling sips his Scotch, thinking that he's drinking more than he should. He's having trouble choosing his words, forming his sentences around these new pessimistic opinions of his. "I just read the other day that mankind has

208

made and broken more than eight thousand treaties since 1500 B.C."

"But we have more than treaties. We still have the knowledge and the ingenuity we've always had. We're controlling technology, not the other way around," Moholy says with a sudden exuberance, in his speechmaking voice. "Crönchen, you didn't really expect utopia overnight, did you? It was a terrible war." Moholy crushes out his cigarette, lights another. "But I still have those dreams about the future. We'll all get about and communicate so much better. It makes sense to me in the dreams. But what I thought I understood vanishes with the dream." He takes a deep drag on the cigarette, exhaling with almost a gasp. Looking up at Sterling, he smiles wearily. He has always smiled easily, now it is an afterthought.

"I don't understand," Sterling says.

"I'm talking about emotion. It's all we have, as humans, as artists. It links us together, bonds us, all of us. We'll never lose it. No matter where the industries and the technologies take us, we still have our humanity." He puffs on his cigarette and chuckles. "I must sound sophomoric, talking about what you've known all along."

Sterling shakes his head and rests his glass on the chair arm. He stares at the warm amber of Scotch and reflected light. "That's what put me in the sanitarium: giving in to my emotions instead of doing my part for the cause. I should have put aside my grief. It's what she would have wanted."

"Don't be disparaging. You're lucky to be alive. We both are," Moholy says, making an X with his forefingers. He means his X-ray treatments of a few months ago; he still talks about them, fascinated by the process, hardly mentioning that he almost died.

"Turn the radio off. Put on some music. Something different," Moholy says.

Sterling finds an old Billie Holiday 78, puts it on the Victrola. *A fine romance, my good fellow.* Moholy nods his approval and Sterling sits with him on the sofa. He hears the scratches of the overplayed record, but still the voice has the same mournfulness as his own. If he could sing.

PART THREE

DO NOT TURN TO GHOSTS

The world is now too dangerous for anything less than Utopia.

BUCKMINSTER FULLER

Body and Soul

EARLY SATURDAY MORNING, too early to get up and too late to go to sleep. So Wanda keeps sitting in the living room, listening to "Embraceable You" over and over. The singer and the band are unknown to her but popular in Berlin Sterling told her when he gave her the recording. He'd heard her humming the song enough to know it was one of her favorites. In the past several hours, she's probably heard it a hundred times. She wants to dance in her studio, but she would cake her bare feet with the plaster of Paris and sawdust she can't bring herself to clean up. And she doesn't want to dance alone.

Nothing distracts her, helps her forget that afternoon. She still wakes up seeing Bradley aiming the gun at her forehead. They stared at each other until he turned away and put the gun on the counter. He paced around the table as she stooped beside her father, who'd fallen face down. A painful fall, she thought, but he was already dead. She knew it even before she tried to find a pulse in his neck.

She stood up and opened the window wider. Someone's television was blaring. She sat on the windowsill, draping her skirt, her legs dangling above the floor, the rain pouring in on her. She leaned her head against the window frame so hard she knew her forehead would be bruised for days afterward. Bradley put a hand on her shoulder. He wanted her to look up at him, to understand it was an accident. She had to call the police, speak in a controlled voice that wasn't her own, give a street address and a description of what happened. She had to call them quickly, before Bradley changed his mind and decided to kill her, or himself, or Sterling when he showed up. Bradley might even try to escape. But he didn't. He sat calmly, waiting for the police.

She still hears the gunshots ringing out, louder and more terrible than she could have imagined. Sirens wailing outside, throwing red-and-white light into the loft. Blood on the floor and the counters. The homicide detectives, the police photographer, the forensics experts. The morgue attendants zipping up the body bag, wheeling it away. Later, she hired a cleaning crew of unemployed actors. But the kitchen is still full of unnatural sounds and an ammonia odor that doesn't fade away.

Bradley is uptown at Payne Whitney Psychiatric Center, staring out at the East River. His calmness has become an inability to speak or recognize faces. His parents have hired one of the best criminal defense attorneys in the country. A tall, exuberant man, with stark white hair and round tortoiseshell glasses, who uses his Brooklyn accent to persuasive ends on local television news programs. But there might never be a trial. Bradley could spend the rest of his life being diagnosed and treated and institutionalized until nothing remains of him. Either way, she doesn't care. He's ruined his life thoroughly, taken another. She hates him now, but the hatred is a dull, lukewarm disgust.

She tries to stop filling up her hours with regrets, with wondering what she might have done differently that afternoon. Could she have taken her father to Festhaus or changed her door locks sooner? If she'd called her father as soon as she found out he was in the city, they might have had their confrontation and then ignored each other, or even reestablished ties. Bradley would have known who Charles was, not thought he was some white lover of hers to shoot to death. Or even if she'd shown Bradley a photograph of her father ages ago. She shouldn't have tried to deny and hide her father's existence over the years. She starts to cry and doesn't hear Sterling coming downstairs. He steps into the living room quietly, sits next to her on the sofa. She shuts the music off. She hasn't heard the rainstorm until now.

She wipes her tears with a Kleenex. "I can't stand this place anymore. The kitchen smells and there's always a cold draft. Haven't you noticed it? It's as if Charles is still there." She can't stop thinking about her father. She hardly believes how much she misses someone she'd hated and hadn't seen for years. She doesn't have fond memories to relive; she often tries to remember something favorable and pleasant about him but can't. Only a few half-playful political arguments she had with him some years ago. Even after she grew up and he visited her at Harvard and she went to see him in New Mexico, she remembers nothing but his long-winded criticisms of her.

"Your father was a brilliant, cultured man. We had some enjoyable talks. But I could tell he was a man who didn't care much for his own life." Sterling puts an arm around her shoulders. She toys with the cuff of his gray satin robe. "I'm sorry for you," he says.

"Don't be. I'm all right." She still has trouble believing that Sterling had befriended Charles all those weeks. She doesn't ask him why. No reason to now. She strokes his hair, translucent instead of silver in the faint light. "It's just that I've been missing you."

He has been watching her intently, following the gestures of her hands, looking into her eyes like a lover. There are shadowy circles under her eyes and a slight tremor in her face. "I don't mean to upset you." He draws her closer to him. "I'm just an old man who needs to be alone." He says the words without knowing what they mean. He can't make her understand, can't put the pain and complexity into words. His memories are clearer and more real than the world.

"You're going to leave me, aren't you?" she says. He's been hinting at it for days, refusing to answer her direct questions.

He doesn't say anything. He knew she'd confront him like this, asking him the one question he can't possibly answer. Not *if* he's leaving, which she already knows, but *why*. Why does he live anonymously, letting the world think Cronheim is long dead? It's painful and unproductive, but he can't help himself. How can he tell her this? She's already grieving and he's doing nothing to help her. But these nights of sitting up with her, comforting her as she cries, will end. She will no longer need him, she will find another man whether he stays here or not.

"I've started figuring out some things," she says, stroking his hair again. He looks up at her, startled. "What's important and what's not. Who's important and who's not. You understand, don't you?" He doesn't answer, but she knows this is the way to talk to him—talk about importance and understanding, not love or caring. Large, honorable abstractions and ideals. She kisses him and he kisses her back, lingeringly. She could believe it's desire she's feeling, except for the way she clutches his shoulders, as if she's drowning. He reaches up and turns off the uplighter.

"You'll be all right. We both will," she says. Slowly, she decides, they are bringing each other back.

●

He awakens first and packs all his bags. He has no doubt about what he's doing. He spends a long time packing, searching the loft thoroughly for what belongs to him.

"What are you doing?" Wanda asks him as she comes down the steps. She's wearing the same kimono she wore last night, now full of wrinkles.

He doesn't have an answer for her, only a strained and

unbearable silence. She starts to cry. She goes to the living room and sits on the sofa. He follows her. "I'm sorry, Wanda. I have to," he says. He can't say anything else.

She turns on the shortwave radio to kill the silence. She finds a broadcast from Ghana, contrapuntal voices fighting in the dark. She is getting an unbelievably painful headache—flashes of light start to move from the corners to the center of her vision. It's from nights of not sleeping, from deliberately leaving the windows wide open during air-quality alerts, and most of all from trying so hard to pretend he'd never leave. She reaches for her handkerchief on the end table and wipes her tears. There has to be something she can do. She can't let him walk out now. The radio voices are gone and there is polyphonic music: timbres like champagne glasses filled with water, rims stroked to form the notes.

He goes to the kitchen for his luggage. The radio is turned off and after a few moments he hears "God Bless the Child." Billie Holiday's remastered voice floats through the loft. When he returns, Wanda is still sitting on the sofa, her arms folded tightly. She looks up at him with immense, violent pain. As he meets her gaze he knows he will never see her again.

"There's nothing I can say to change your mind, is there?" She should be shrieking, crying, she thinks. She feels as if she has lost her voice, lost consciousness, as if she has already awakened hours later aware of nothing but how painful it is to speak, to move.

He kisses her lips. "We'll see each other . . . somehow," he says. He slips out the door and into the slow, creaking freight elevator.

•

Hours later, when she can't cry anymore, she picks up the phone headset and calls her mother. Francine should be home, working on a speech for the New York Association of African-American Mental Health Professionals. The ringing on the other line goes on forever. Finally, Francine answers. Wanda is startled that her mother is so coolly chic in an aquamarine blouse, hair pulled back, pearl earrings. She doesn't look grief-stricken at all.

"What can we do for you, young lady?" Francine asks, sounding absolutely effervescent.

"Just wanted to talk, that's all." She looks away from the viewphone screen, toward her studio, the corner where Sterling had set up his photogram work. Everything is gone, even the black curtains he used to string up to block the light. But it's not Sterling whom she needs to talk to her mother about. "Why didn't you tell me you and Charles were talking about getting back together?" She's been meaning to ask her mother this ever since he died.

Francine leans back, and her image blurs momentarily, then refocuses. She doesn't seem to know what to say. "I couldn't do anything for him," she says finally. "And getting back together was the last thing either of us really needed."

Wanda thinks of her father's burial at Arlington. Of walking behind the casket-bearing soldiers of the Old Guard and their team of horses marching with haunting precision in the bright sunlight. Charles's mother, in a white bouffant wig and crippled with arthritis, gave Wanda and Francine hate stares through her mourning veil and thick eyeglasses. She has never accepted "the coloreds" into her family.

Francine tells Wanda she had hung up on Charles the night before he died. He had never tried so hard to talk to her. He kept smoking his pipe and wiping his face with a large handkerchief. If there were tears, he caught them before they fell. He wanted to see her, he was naming days and times until they were shouting at each other. She was telling him no, finally ending the conversation, watching him fade to the slate-gray color of the view screen. Francine thinks Charles didn't commit suicide mainly because he didn't want to deprive her and Wanda of the insurance money. A generous sum, but Wanda would spend every cent of it to track down Sterling. And fail to find him. What use is the money? Her life won't change.

"I just got off the phone with Karin not too long ago," Francine says. "Mind you, I haven't spoken to her in more than twenty years. She wanted to know what I did to her brother."

"What did you tell her?"

"Wasn't a thing to tell and she knows it. I said that, if anything, I should ask *her* that question, and I hung up. Of course you and I are getting blamed for what happened."

"I can't get it out of my mind."

"You might want to find another place to live."

"You've been saying that forever." Wanda picks up her glass. "It's water, in case you're wondering." She gulps it down. "I don't drink anymore. It was giving me nightmares." And it gave her blackouts she doesn't really want to admit to herself. She's all alone, not even Sterling to help her to bed those nights when she collapses in the living room. She doesn't want to die like an old and lonely alcoholic, tripping over furniture, hitting her head, bleeding to death.

Wanda can't think of any clever ways to continue the conversation. She and her mother sit, watching each other relive their pasts.

"Why don't you come see me next weekend," Francine says. "Reggie ought to be back from the Freedom March by then and we can all go up to the Adirondacks."

"I'll think about it," Wanda says. The tears fall suddenly; she turns away from the screen.

"What's wrong?"

"I'm all by myself now," she whispers, dabbing the tears with her kimono sleeve.

"Cronheim's gone?"

She nods. It was the first time her mother had ever called him by his name. "He had to go. He had to . . . Can't talk anymore," she says, hanging up abruptly. She really is alone now.

What I Desire

TELEVISION IS SUPPOSED TO ISOLATE, break up community and family life. But Wanda turns it on, feeling no danger, tunes in the Socrates Channel, where Beryle Danner's panel of guests, college-age grass-roots activists recently out of jail, are seated with her in the familiar library studio set. Danner is talking about progress and technology: space exploration, solar power, global communication, all diseases cured. The world running smoothly and never failing, or the entire human race traveling through the galaxy in multigeneration ships, leaving the dying planet behind.

This is death, not progress, Danner says, speaking directly to the camera in a tight close-up, *death masquerading behind dazzling, high-tech luxury for the elite while seventy-one percent of our world's people are malnourished, lacking adequate medical care, or without shelter. Luxury bought at the expense of the extinction of hundreds of species of the animal and plant kingdom every week. Yes,* hundreds *every week.* She pauses and the camera pulls back slowly to a wide shot of her guests, sitting attentively.

Wanda switches channels. She finds a German silent film on Kino-Universal: a lonely juggler turned beggar wandering through shadowy streets. The sound track is full of andante passages with startling, jazz-like progressions. She clutches her kimono tightly around her. She can't watch Beryle Danner without being reminded of Bradley, any more than she can remember him as he used to be. If she were to talk to him he might blame her for everything. After all, wasn't he content to live as he always had, letting everyone assume he was white? Wasn't it her fault he felt compelled to embrace his true heritage? And didn't she betray both him and her heritage with first Cronheim and later with the man Bradley couldn't believe was her father? All her fault, everything. She hates him now, just as she should.

•

The next morning she doesn't think of Bradley at all. It's Sterling she's still looking for, futilely. The stacks of photo-grams are gone. The sketchbooks, notebooks, everything. She can never prove he was here. This is how he wanted it. To disappear all over again, to be back with the dead.

She goes downstairs to the kitchen and takes a bottle of Absolut out of the freezer, clear liquid among frosted packaged entrees. She fills a large tumbler with the vodka and sprinkles it with freshly milled black pepper. *Embrace me, you irreplaceable you*, she sings in a dark voice, and swirls the pepper with a spoon handle. She once lived for a week on this concoction and all she felt was a burning in her nose. The phone rings. She hasn't answered it for days; she's used to hearing it ring and ring. Most of her conversations are awkward now. Family members, colleagues, everyone tries to offer condolences and, even worse, tries to make decisions for her. Like her supervisor at the Consortium who insisted she take this leave of absence. They all seem to think she's going to crack up.

She picks up her vodka and goes to the living room to unplug the phone. She thinks of her father. What she experiences is closer to fear than grief. Her whole body feels as if it's collapsing from its own weight, and gravity is suddenly lethal. Maybe Charles is still in the kitchen, in front of the window where he died, invisible mouth wide open, swallowing all the air and light. She'll never know what else he might have said to her. In her dreams, she will always try to continue the conversation.

She picks up her glass of vodka, takes it to the kitchen. Sterling would expect her to pour it down the sink. She does. Next, she pours out the entire bottle and dumps it in the garbage can. She turns on the telescreen and flips through the clutter of early-morning televangelists, global news updates, talk shows, Chaplin and Keaton films. From the Ebony-Jet Channel she finds out that the Freedom March will reach Washington tomorrow afternoon. She's been missing Reggie.

On the Art, Architecture, Antiques Channel three New York architects discuss their plan to revitalize Lower Manhattan by turning it into a canal city. They are slightly older than she, two women and a man dressed in corporate grays and dark blues. Their finely detailed presentation drawings fill the large screen. The twin towers of the World Trade Center, the three mirrored towers of the Neil A. Armstrong Aerospace Center, and other skyscrapers rise up from the shimmering, imaginary blue water cluttered with motorboats and water taxis.

But the ocean will take Manhattan no matter what anyone does, and its buildings will become small mountains of petrified stone and wood. She reaches for the teletext, punches in the channel's link-up number. The de Stijl–like logo of parallel lines in primary colors appears on the screen. She thinks about the logistics of turning city streets into waterways and the impossibility of accomplishing this in Manhattan as she waits her turn to speak.

"Manhattan is one island. Venice is many islands" is all she says.

•

The commuter bus rolls south on U.S. 202, winding past ruined, abandoned farms and faded, rain-damaged derelict billboards and the quizzical Burma Shave signs. THIS CREAM IS LIKE A PARACHUTE . . . THERE ISN'T ANY SUBSTITUTE. The bus engine makes a soothing, lulling hum. He starts to write her a letter and tell her why he had to leave. But all he can do is imagine he stayed. He tries to convince himself he left for her benefit: to shield her from all his sadness. But other people survive grief, aloneness, so why can't he? Years ago he could only tell his friends he had changed. It was the war, he'd sometimes say, no one he knew was quite the same after the war.

He closes his eyes and imagines himself back in Philadelphia. He had been afraid of all the spaces—his generously large office at Penn, his three-story Italianate Villa house, the Schuylkill River and Fairmount Park, where he would ride his bicycle for hours. People never saw his fear. They always marveled at his leanness, fitness, youthfulness. Some of them, both students and faculty, idolized him and developed crushes on him. He dreaded seeing his admirers crowding around him, touching him with their many hands.

Outside his office window, foggy hints of sunlight, rain pouring down on the campus; the grass and trees a flat, dismal green. Students scurrying with their umbrellas and raincoats across muddy paths between the ivy-covered buildings. If he were a realist (and he had toyed with realism, making tiny color-pencil sketches of mountains and landscapes full of reds and purples), he would have spent the rest of the afternoon painting this view. But he had paperwork keeping him occupied, and all his regrets. He should have known how to help William, what to say to him, those few months before his suicide, when he called nightly from Cambridge, unhappy with his new position with Gropius's Architects Collaborative. Sterling thought he understood the strife, the struggle, all about race relations. He'd spent those years in Chicago trying to help, was still trying to help in Philadelphia. He couldn't understand why William was giving up, not even trying to fight. William, a coddled member of the black Canadian upper class no one knew about. All his life, he had the best of the best. But William's professional life wasn't causing him pain; it was the strain of living in racist Boston, being picked up and harassed by the police, being chased by gangs of white youths. Sterling was afraid that, in his own way, he was just as much a racist as anyone else, for thinking all blacks were valiant and noble like the civil-rights leaders and their coalition of organizers, boycotters, marchers in the South.

He was always trying to get away. There were the trips to New Hope when William was still alive; later, the trips alone. Traveling meant casting off his charming, academician self and meeting strangers along the roadside, in restrooms, in deserted parks. Going where no one suspected he was going.

Now he's traveling again. Traveling when he should have flown to Berlin as he'd intended. It is still early when he arrives in New Hope, and the Delaware River sparkles with sunlight. Restored Victorian houses and storefronts converted into antique shops and specialty boutiques, crowds of people all around the bright green lawns and narrow, picturesque streets. He remembers the mule-barge rides he and William used to take, drifting down the narrow, muddy Delaware Canal, flanked by tall trees on either side. The trees were so thick he could believe they were part of the original forest covering the New World. But mostly he would marvel at William, an astonishingly handsome man with the perfect physical characteristics of classical Nubian statues. His skin was very dark, darker than his eyes, which were the translucent golden brown of apothecary jars. Sterling would look down disparagingly at his own hands, chapped and ashy white. He always hid them from the sun.

•

He wakes up next morning, sweating, the blanket and bedspread heavy against him. He forgets where he is, jumps up suddenly, and looks around his inn room. White enameled rattan chairs and tea table clustered in front of the bay windows, which overlook the river and smoky-gray clouds edged in red. He turns the radio on and finds WFLN, "the Good Music Station" he listened to years ago in Philadelphia. A Bach cello suite is playing. He doesn't know what separates him from what he was. Philly is nearby, still. He has seen photographs of the city and doesn't recognize it. New buildings trying to crowd out his memories. The Bach ends and there are commercials. Everyone wants him to buy something, know something, leave the country, leave the planet.

He counts out the money he needs to pay for the room in crisp fifty-dollar bills and puts it in an envelope. He sits by the window and stares out at the river. He has no place to go now. No place he wants to go.

He recalls a scene from a film he saw years ago. The shadows of two men, clandestine lovers, against a basement cinder-block wall. Frightened, whispering voices on the sound track. The shadows lean toward each other, merging. The camera pans slowly past a water heater, an emergency generator, and a pile of mops and rags, to the opposite wall where the men should be. The men are gone. Fade-out.

Sunlight pours suddenly across the room, bright shafts shimmering with dust. A cold wind slips in through the windows. Sterling opens the envelope and takes out one of the bills. He tears it into tiny pieces. He picks out another and another, tears up each one of them. He scoops up the bits of money on his lap and lets them fall to the floor, their authenticity holograms sparkling like jewels.

He starts to laugh. He laughs so hard he's choking. He puts his head down and begins to cry. But he hasn't cried since the war and he doesn't remember how. He heaves and gasps and pounds his hands against his knees. The room is moving, taking him somewhere, and he imagines he feels William's arms around his shoulders, hears sounds he believes are words. He tries to answer, but the words come out loud, unmodulated. He closes his eyes and the sounds turn into colors.

•

Wanda sits on one of the stone benches on Fifth Avenue along the edge of Central Park. It's dusk and the trees are beginning to turn a sinister, medieval green. The park looks more dangerous and forbidding than ever. The wind blows sheets of newspaper all around her. Across the street a trash-can fire is burning in front of a legendary apartment building, the gray-uniformed doormen and the richly dressed pas-sersby ignoring it. Wanda's been walking most of the day, drifting in and out of memories.

She remembers the Apollo banquets her father took her to when she was a teenager. The grainy television pictures of the astronauts planting the U.S. flag on the moon. Singing all the verses of the "Star-Spangled Banner" and "America the Beautiful," and listening to members of Congress make long speeches and tell old jokes. Worst of all was having to meet her father's friends and colleagues, mostly middle-aged white men who smiled at her a little too much and shook her hand, holding on a little too long.

Her father took her, not her mother, to the banquets. She hated the excuses he'd make when she asked him why her mother wasn't going. Still, Wanda believed in the future, not a future of space exploration, but one of the harmonious and cooperative society human-rights leaders always talked about. She really thought everyone would be like her some day, neither black nor white, but something in between. It might take decades or even centuries, but it would happen. And sooner than that, racism and the concept of race itself would become completely obsolete.

In a few days, the winner of the Abbott's Quay competition will be announced. She's already working on sketches for upcoming competitions: a railway station in Oakland, middle-income housing in Minneapolis, a new civic center for Baltimore. But these projects and their accompanying publicity obscure the real problem. The infrastructures of cities are decaying fast and the money and energy for rebuilding are lacking. Water mains break and flood entire neighborhoods; overpasses collapse, killing motorists and pedestrians; derailed elevated trains and subway fires kill dozens. The disasters are numbingly routine.

Next week she'll return to work at the Consortium. It's time to imagine what it will be like to see her buildings constructed, become part of the skyline. She wants to build, as Sterling once told her he wanted to—to make a contribution to the world. She still would like to design low- and middle-income housing, not high-rises but elegant town houses people will be proud to live in. Everyone will see her work and know what she does. Not like her father, who answered his phone with the last four digits of the phone number and, when asked what he did for a living, mumbled something about aerothermodynamics.

She's still thinking about going to the Metropolitan Museum this evening to look at Old Master paintings, but she doesn't think she can. Sterling used to go to the Met to sketch in the Asian Art galleries and she knows she'd start looking for him all over again.

She dreamed about him last night. He was still dean at Penn and he'd never disappeared. He wasn't the Cronheim who spent several hours every day in front of the telescreen bidding for art. This Cronheim was at peace, part of the world. Every Friday after work, she would take the Metroliner to Philadelphia's Thirtieth Street Station to meet him. He'd kiss her hello and talk about how years ago the city officials had permitted the demolition of the majestic and perfect Broad Street Station. They'd talk about art and architecture. She would visit his office at Penn, marvel at his vast collection of books. In his beautiful, historic house—

room after room filled with paintings, photographs, and drawings by his friends and contemporaries—they'd sit up late, old friends, side by side, talking and talking.

•

Sterling goes to the Metro Palace, the only film revival house in Philadelphia; Dietrich, Garbo, Bogart, and others peer at him from grainy, faded posters in glass cases on the lobby walls. It truly was a movie palace, would have been suitable for world premieres: sweeping spotlights, scores of movie stars stepping out of their limousines, stopping at a microphone in front of the entrance to say hello to the radio audience. Now the Metro Palace's double features of classic films play to small audiences of film students, tourists, and sleeping derelicts. Today *The Strange Love of Martha Ivers* and his *Night Without a Day*.

The first film is nearly over and he closes his eyes and remembers the other time he saw it, with Moholy back in Chicago. Afterward, they walked along the Lake Shore and the sky was a strong, solid gray, as if the air itself, not the light, were visible. Dark factory smoke poured from the buildings. They were walking slowly, in their unbuttoned trench coats, arms linked, saying nothing for a long while. In the newsreels, Churchill was in Fulton, Missouri, and he said an Iron Curtain had descended upon Europe. The phrase struck them. He and Moholy had believed the exaggerations, that the cities were rubble and people built bonfires in the streets and plazas and lived around the heat and light. But no, there was order, the order of the new governments; police governments, Churchill called them. Europe was far away from the Lake Shore and the brisk late-afternoon winds gusting around them and bending the newly planted willow trees at the water's edge. The gray waters rolled toward them like a shallow ocean tide.

The movie is over, the lights come back on slowly in the

theater, and the gold velvet curtain descends on the screen. He reads the program notes for *Night Without a Day*:

A gripping story of obsession and murder . . . One man's descent into the dark side of the American dream . . .

Moholy had died a few years before Sterling directed the film. Moholy had been talking optimistically of his future plans and making exquisite, free-form engravings by hand on his Plexiglas sculptures a few days before he died. The man who wanted to paint with light and build cameras with optical principles different from the human eye's trusted his art to his own hand one last time. A few days before Moholy died, he and Sterling spent a long afternoon talking about reincarnation and disembodied spirits. They were neither cheerful nor somber. Moholy looked as if he had aged twenty years in a matter of days. He had the serene face of someone who had lived alone and seen visions both terrifying and comforting all his life. His smiles, his laughter rich and vulnerable, as he held the chair arms, as if to keep himself from floating away. He was shivering, even with his royal-blue electric blanket draped around him.

"*Guter Freund*," Moholy said, mimicking his own formerly poor German. "I've been remembering."

"What do you mean, remembering?" Sterling asked.

"I remember when you and I went walking along the Lake Shore. There were willow trees. Little, spindly trees, just planted. They reminded me of how weak I was." He clutches Sterling's arm tightly. "And it got so windy we had to carry our hats in our hands."

"Mahagonny," Sterling whispered. Mahagonny, one of Moholy's many nicknames. Sterling knew right then he wouldn't see him again. His friend of more than twenty years. Moholy, sitting with him, taking off his nickel-rimmed glasses and tossing them just out of reach on the end table, as he always did. He smiled widely and laughed his old and easy laugh.

They talked about the light. Sterling tried to believe in the eternal soul, but he kept seeing the death, the funeral, hearing the eulogies. When Moholy died, Sterling became acting director of the Institute of Design for several months. He changed everything around in Moholy's cluttered corner office: Cesca chairs, hinged-top writing table, drafting table, paintings and photographs, piles of books and old art journals, *Der Sturm* and *Aktion* from Berlin, and *Ma* from Hungary, film cans stacked so high they were like large pneumatic tubes stretching toward the ceiling. All this would go into the new Moholy-Nagy archives he was helping to establish. He spent sixty or seventy hours a week teaching, working, searching for a permanent director. He felt at ease with his students, experimenting with new media, but he was no administrator. He worried about everything: utility bills, the new pay-as-you-go tax system, the board of directors and their many conflicts.

By then Billy Wilder wanted him as art director on his next film. So he resigned from the institute, signed a contract with Paramount, and worked with Wilder and other directors for a few years, finally directing *Night Without a Day*. He was living alone, in a bungalow in Glendale, his living room converted into a painting studio and one of the bedrooms a darkroom. He stayed far away from the Hollywood glamour that could never replace his old life. Still, Hollywood was suffocating, like living in the richly furnished house of a relative he despised.

Masterful chiaroscuro lighting . . . complex stylistic and thematic tensions . . . clearly rooted in the German Expressionist tradition.

The opening credits, against a still of the Chicago skyline at night. When the film begins, he tries to pretend he has never seen it. But instead, he remembers what happened years ago when he went to the Busch-Reisinger Museum at Harvard. He'd heard about the museum's Bauhaus archive and he passed himself off as a Berlin professor so he would be able to leaf through the old manuscripts, letters, and journals.

But he never made it to the archive that day. He was on the main floor of the museum, high-ceilinged, dimly lighted, and full of imposing entablatures, stained-glass windows, and colonnades recovered from German cathedrals and monasteries. Beyond the medieval and Renaissance galleries were four of Moholy's paintings, grouped together in a corner, and his *Light Space Modulator*, a structure made of polished steel and glass, approximately one and a half meters high. Machine as much as sculpture, with its disks and rotating screens and spirals throwing patterns of light and shadow. The motor was fragile now, according to the exhibit card, and was switched on briefly at a specific time once a week. Sterling strained to read in the faint light, faint everywhere, to preserve the works of art. He turned and looked up at the curving marble stairway to the mezzanine. Moholy was standing at the top of the stairs. He wore a gray suit, white shirt, black tie loosened. He folded his arms and looked into the distance, as if waiting for someone. He vanished as quickly as he had appeared. Sterling felt the air turn suddenly cold. He rushed up the stairs and searched for Moholy all over the mezzanine, its walls and free-standing partitions covered with the paintings of Kandinsky, El Lissitzky, and Malevich. He leaned against the balustrade where Moholy had stood. But he couldn't find him.

The Kino-Universal film archivists dug through vaults at Paramount, UCLA, and elsewhere to restore his film. Sterling has never seen the entire film uncut. And will not do so now. He folds up the program notes, slips them into his shirt pocket, and leaves the theater before his film is even half over. He dashes out quickly, down the marble stairway, past the giltwood mirrors he avoids looking in.

●

The city air shimmers. Everything about Philadelphia is different. He watched the demolition of the Broad Street Station years ago. The masonry viaduct, the soot-blackened Chinese walls, an immense city landmark collapsing, the dust hovering for hours. Wilson, Furness and Evans's minor architectural miracle, he used to tell his theory of form classes at Penn. A radical and modern building for its time, with an absence of symmetry and architectural axes.

He walks inside this new station of non-majestic cinder-block walls, concrete floors gutted from numerous floods and fires. He gets his bags from the cloakroom, buys an Amrailpass, and goes outside to the tracks. The trains are bullet-nosed, chromium steel, streamlined, just as they were years ago, when designers first began to apply aerodynamic principles to all modes of travel. His train is arriving, its headlamp bright even in the sunlight. He boards the train, the San Francisco–bound *Gold Rush*, and the porter checks his Amrailpass and shows him to his sleeper. He sits by the window, drawing the matchstick blinds shut. The rosewood veneer interior painted with Navajo and Hopi motifs in muted colors is lighted with annoyingly bright recessed fluorescent strips. He turns them off and sleeps.

•

For all its elegance, the train is oppressive. He doesn't know where he's going on this train, traveling five hundred kilometers an hour on rebuilt tracks. Sightseeing in the West, he tries to convince himself, the West he always wanted to see. When he took the *Twentieth Century* to Los Angeles years ago, he passed the time sketching, not looking out the window. Now he travels past Chicago and his green Wisconsin childhood, looking at the overgrazed, drought-stricken plains. Desolate, treeless land, monotonous kilometers of lifeless shades of brown, outside the panoramic windows. The glass is non-glare and its polarized coating intensifies the red sunset.

232

What was he sketching then? He can't remember, but he assumes he was making sketches of Lenore and throwing them away. He has none of these sketches, he's certain. He takes out his charcoal pencils and starts a sketch of Lenore. He draws with his eyes closed for hours. Finally, he gathers up the sketches and tears them to pieces. He wants to dream about her tonight. He puts the sketch down and turns off all the lights in the steel room and looks out at the darkness where the land should be. He believes there is nothing at all outside, only Galileo's vacuum, and the train is a feather, falling fast.

•

He gets off the train at Green River, Wyoming, and takes a bus north to the clear wide lakes and scorched land of Yellowstone National Park. Yearly forest fires have left the promise of ecological renewal, but all he sees are the dead, charcoal-black trees scattered among foothills and moun-tains, geyser basins and dust. Gray dust swirling every-where—old dust, he decides, remembering the scientists who have proven that we breathe the same air the ancients breathed. An ancient is what he's become; time and place are completely unreal to him. He walks slowly through the dust that hides the colors. Before, it had been the whirling of industry, the rush-rush of big-city life, the black-and-white of newsreels, newspapers, and photographs that blurred all the colors into gray. Moholy and he had known this while they were still in Germany, contemplating the colors and where they had gone.

Mahagonny, you can't imagine all this dust, he whispers to his old friend. Porcelain Basin they call it, a big attraction for tourists with their fully automated 35 millimeter cameras. And the smell, like eggs rotting in the sun.

He thinks out loud now and talks to people who can't hear him as he walks through the geyser basin's thick, rising steam. Clouds pass over the sun and the light around him is gray. He grips the cast-iron railing on the boardwalk around the basin. A young dark-haired man in white coveralls stands next to him, three cameras hanging from his neck. He is meticulously composing his shots. Sterling wishes he were taking photographs here; the burned-out mountain ranges just beyond the basin are like nothing he's ever seen. Colors of ruin, dark and formless, as if someone has doused all the fires of hell. Nothing is left but the steam that rises through the dead trees. This must be what Ravensbrück looked like, a terrifying, dead land where women prisoners filled the swamps with sand, built roads and airfields, Lenore among them, spending her last days readying the land to yield destruction. The tears sting his eyes but do not fall. He looks for Moholy in museums, but out here, in the dust and steam, it's Lenore he hopes to find. It's been so long, he whispers to her. She should be stopping by right now, rising from the hot springs, full of life. He will marvel at how strong and beautiful she is after all these years.

The photographer places a Polaroid print in Sterling's hand, says a few friendly-sounding words in a foreign language, and walks away. Sterling holds the print by a corner. It is grayish and shadowy as the colors slowly fade in. The print is dry; it was never doused in developing trays. It has gone on without him, knowing like a living creature how to get about in the world. He is the one who forgot how to live, how to stop thinking of people he would never see again. He watches the print develop. Lenore is not in it and he lets it fall from his hands. The wind blows it into one of the hot springs, where it curls up and sinks slowly. The hot springs seem bottomless, but they are far from the center of the earth. Even Porcelain Basin, volatile and roaring, is not the molten heat of the earth but a large, encrusted scar. The whole surface of the earth is scar tissue over the life and heat of its core, the steam escaping into the sky. He truly understands he is changeable like water, passing from solid to liquid to vapor.

He is watching himself die. In the middle of the geyser basin, dust, light, and heat cover him. His own death seems so insignificant next to the deaths of others. No one is left to listen to his dying words. Still, he calls Lenore's name again and again. A white light, glowing, covers him slowly, benevolently, and he experiences a tender euphoria as his pain leaves him.

He looks down at the ground where he's fallen and the people trying to revive him. Streaks of reds, whites, blacks, greens, blues where he's fallen, all the colors he's ever known flowing like blood from his fingertips.

Do Not Turn
to Ghosts

THE TELETEX FROM TORONTO tells her that she, Wanda
Higgins Du Bois, has won the Abbott's Quay Arts and
Cultural Center design competition. She sits at her terminal
and prints up a hard copy. The airmail-grade paper feels
like nothing in her hands. She opens all the windows, letting
in the cold air and the sounds of traffic, and paces the long
corridor from her studio to the living room. She circles the
Ionic columns beside the steel bookshelves, where shafts of
strong, late-afternoon sunlight coming through the Venetian
blinds make the floor warm under her bare feet. She can't
be dreaming, not with "Purple Haze" blasting so loud the
speakers begin to rattle.

She will call the Abbott's Quay Foundation back, hope for
real faces and voices instead of the answering console with
its fifteen-second summary of the life of Wilson Ruffin Abbott
and the importance of the new Abbott's Quay Center to
Toronto's cultural life. It must be four or five in the morning
in Guam, but she still wonders why the brothers haven't
called.

The groundbreaking will take place soon and a blitz of
publicity even sooner. Sterling might see her on one of the
art channels and press his fingertips against the screen,
forgetting he can call the channel to talk, forgetting he never
had to leave her. Cronheim, famous artist, pioneering Modernist. She keeps having the same dream about him, that

236

she's lying in bed with him, the way she used to, listening to him breathe and feeling his arms around her. The dream isn't comforting. She wakes up tired, believing she hasn't slept at all.

She wants to walk around in her Abbott's Quay Center right now, a promised land, enclosed to keep her from losing her way.

She picks up the phone headset next to the sofa and punches in the number of the Hilton Genève. Francine is attending an international symposium on anxiety and told her to call. Greetings in four languages, bright graphics of waving flags and snow-covered Alps on the small oval screen. Tiny, neutral Switzerland is shrinking, people moving away, the Alps eroding, turning to desert. Sterling could be there, in Geneva. She could call him at his house. But she knows it's not that simple. He's gone. Not to Geneva or Berlin, but somewhere else entirely.

She leaves a long message, pulling her shawl tightly over her kimono, knowing how well her mother reads her every gesture. She tells her the good news and talks about everything she can think of. How glad she is to be working again on new projects at the Architects Consortium, the increasing number of air-quality alerts, the latest flash floods. She doesn't mention how much she misses Sterling. She ends the message, and the screen fades to its murky gray. She didn't mention her father, either, whom she thinks about as much as Sterling. Or Bradley, whom she almost never thinks of anymore. She doesn't know or want to find out what is happening to him now.

She closes her eyes and feels the faintness she knows to be part of her grief. For her father, for the whole world. Winning a major design competition has made her happy, but she still feels as if she will start crying and never be able to stop. She can't explain to anyone how she feels. Not to her mother or Reggie, and not to Tyler, who cried so loudly at the funeral that her own mother and sister gasped quietly.

It was an inexplicable waste, not seeing her father for five years, as pointless as all the family feuds she's ever heard of. She can't remember now why it all started. She'd been disgusted with him for years but somehow managed to tolerate his occasional visits with her. Now she will never see him again. She doesn't cry anymore, but she has nightmares of being trapped in flooding basement rooms or of being left abandoned in a cold desert at night.

She doesn't forget how impossible her father was, how impossible to know or to talk to. He was always indignant, always shouting at Francine, as if she had gathered up strangers to stare and curse at them and burn crosses in their yard simply to annoy him. Wanda always thought he wanted her to discover the advantages of being part of the majority and leave her mother far behind.

When she saw him five years ago he was still trying to persuade her to believe in everything he believed in. She'd gone to Oberlin College for a week-long national conference of Architects, Designers, and Planners for Social Responsibility. Charles was visiting the Lewis Research Center in Cleveland and he arranged to see her before he went back to New Mexico.

She'd come to the conference alone; her friends from school were all too apathetic or despairing to attend.

She remembers the third morning of lectures on the ecological disasters in the world, after which she went to Tappan Square and sat under a large maple tree, its roots thick and vein-like above the ground. She was wearing a white halter dress and matching bolero, too preoccupied with reading to care about grass stains or the terrible heat and persistent mosquitoes. She arranged the flyers and pamphlets she'd been collecting in a coherent order. She skimmed through pages and pages of grim statistics about current and impending environmental crises that experts were trying to prove or refute. Days of discussions, debates, tutorials on the campus with its Victorian residence halls, interspersed with red brick dormitories that looked like housing projects. Acid rain had darkened all the masonry, and what little ivy was left was yellowed and dying in the heat.

"Had enough of the doomsayers?" It was Charles, putting down his oxblood leather briefcase and sitting on his newspaper. He had leafed through *Aviation Week* and nodded off during the lecture, and she knew he'd follow her out here. He was shivering in his gray pinstripe suit as he sometimes did in hot weather. His face was a healthy, ruddy red, as if he had been living outdoors, thinning white hair that he made no attempt to comb across the bald spots. He was cheerfully talkative today. She felt guilty that he was so kind to her. He'd never stopped bickering and fighting with Francine. Wanda would sometimes try to pick fights with him to keep him away from her mother. Otherwise, current events were all they talked about, arguing amicably like old political adversaries.

"Don't you ever have nightmares about the end of the world?" she asked, not expecting a real answer. She leaned against the tree trunk.

"I have all sorts of nightmares, don't you?" he said, lighting his pipe. The smoke was thick and mystical in the dense green shade. "That's just part of life."

"You didn't answer my question."

"I know a trick question when I hear one." He was frowning, loosening his tie. "You need to get away from these extremists. Harvard is overrun with them."

She laughed. He started talking about his upbringing, the hard times. English wasn't his first language and there was no bilingual education back then. He was teased mercilessly by other children because of his accent. Of course, Southerners weren't fond of Germans in those days.

"I know, I know," she said the moment he paused. She closed her eyes. What she was about to say she'd said too many times. "You had polio and it took you years to recover, no thanks to your alcoholic mother, who used you for target practice. And your father was always at the Space Center."

"It's quite a joke to you, isn't it? That I might know a little something about hard times."

"Don't talk hard times to me. You make good money doing what you do. And your second wife is six months younger than I am. Six months to the day."

"Now, whatever possessed you to make a point of remembering Unah's birthday?" Charles laughed and tapped his pipe against a tree root.

"It's not funny," she said. She changed the subject and started arguing politics and history, social justice and unfavorable Supreme Court rulings, Central and South American wars, how globalism was imperialism updated. He disagreed with everything she said.

He had tried to ruin her mother's life; now he was working on hers. She saw him in Boston a few months after the conference and he took her to Quincy Market. He told her that every year more people visit Quincy Market than Disney World. He had accumulated an incredible number of these surprising facts and smiled when he told her what he knew.

He bought her a scarf that looked like a piano keyboard. She talked about music with him as they wandered through the warehouse-like building, dodging the tourists with their paper plates piled high with ethnic food. Richard Wagner and Scott Joplin were his favorite composers; the combination always seemed fanciful and contrived to her. He could quote long passages from the *Ring* cycle libretti and he had a small collection of first-edition sheet music of some of Joplin's rags.

He told her Unah had been angry with him a few nights earlier and she had destroyed some of his compact discs, etching them with a steel nail file.

"Why didn't you stop her?" Wanda asked.

He looked at her as if he couldn't understand what she was saying as they stood in a crowded postcard boutique.

He dropped his handful of Renoir and Degas reproductions and turned away. "She only got as far as the H's. Haydn, Hindemith, and Hampton," he said finally, leaving the postcards on the floor, walking out.

She began to hate him that day. She hated him for leaving her mother to marry a woman who hated him even more than she did.

But she can't believe he's dead. She keeps believing she's choosing not to see him.

•

She wakes up looking at the bedroom walls, depressingly bare without Sterling's photograms. Their abstract forms were like shadows of creatures hiding from the modern world. The stagnant air is full of the dust of the city. The teletex is still on the nightstand.

The news feels more unreal than ever. But winning this competition is saving her life. She gets up, opens the blinds, and laughs. Finally something to celebrate and she doesn't want to drink anymore. She turns on the radio and *Morning Edition* tells her about the gloom in the world. An interview with a Los Alamos physicist who's just published a critically acclaimed novel about Impressionist painters. She remembers him clearly. He had pasted newspaper clippings about art forgeries on his office walls and tried to invite her out for a drink.

She used to wonder about her father's isolation: more people in one crowded New York elevated train than in Los Alamos, New Mexico, where he lived and worked. He socialized only with his project team at the laboratory. She heard stories about Los Alamos, that the entire staff constantly joked about death and genocide. She really thought they would be monstrous, smiling at nothing, truly mesmerized by their research, too young or too old to care about mortality. Her father once took her to the directed-energy laboratory where he worked. High-ceilinged rooms, white and hospital-like, with clerestory windows, heavily filtered sunlight streaming in. Most of his associates were her age or a little older, in jeans, and T-shirts with wry and cynical slogans. She talked with some of them and they were just ordinary people, not monstrous at all.

She finds a tailored shirtwaist dress to wear. A wartime dress, with a short hemline and an uneven maroon color from rationed dye. She wonders what she would have done in those days. She might have been poor, in a sharecropper's family in the South like her mother, fighting for an education. The family might have thrown her out because of her light complexion and blond hair. She'd think she had no choice but to go up North, go to school, become a nurse or a teacher, change her name, marry a white man, and spend each pregnancy suicidal, worrying about what color her babies would be. She's heard nothing but sad stories about women like her.

She showers and puts on the dress, with black seam stockings and patent-leather wedgies. She walks down the steps to the kitchen. The German version of "Falling in Love Again" is playing. A scratchy old recording that she doesn't have. She's afraid, but keeps walking, slowly, cautiously. Someone is in the kitchen already, humming along with the music, running the faucet, opening and shutting cabinets.

It's Lenore, standing by the stove, waiting for the teakettle water to boil. She is astonishingly thin, wearing a gray skirt and a peach-colored blouse with a faded lace collar, and she takes careful, short steps. Bright morning sunlight makes the mobile of prisms and holoreflectors by the window throw its rainbow colors all over her.

"What took you so long? I've been up for ages, waiting for you," Lenore says, sitting down at the kitchen table, two juice glasses filled to the rim and a pile of halved-orange peels beside her. She's stacked them like bowls on a large platter, the way Sterling used to. "You're so gloomy and angry at the world. Who'd ever know you've just won a

242

major competition. You're a brilliant architect. You won't be like my old friend Lilly Reich. She was so talented, but totally hidden under Mies van der Rohe's shadow." Lenore makes a gesture with her hands to indicate an endless skyline.

Lenore should be the bitter one, but she's cheery and still beautiful in a stark, emaciated way that Wanda couldn't have imagined or expected. Her face is so pale it's translucent and her elbow-length hair has a startling phosphorescent glow. This is how she looked at Ravensbrück, moments before the firing squad, Wanda thinks, as she sits down opposite her. "I should be trying to cheer *you* up," Wanda says.

"You don't have to. Say what you want to say. I know you hated those people tiptoeing around you, afraid to talk to you after your father died. Now you're doing me the honors." She gets up to put another record on her Victrola, Louis Armstrong playing and singing "When You're Smiling." The teakettle whistles and Lenore takes it off the cooking unit.

She smiles sadly and touches Wanda's shoulder. "You want me to tell you it gets better from here on out. Well, if it gets much worse no one's going to be around to see it. I don't see how any of you live, knowing you've got nothing left, no air, no water." She pours the hot water through strainers full of fresh peppermint and into two large turquoise mugs. "What I want to do is go back to my research. Do something about these deadly viruses mutating all over the world." She laughs as she leans against the stove, and it seems to take up all the energy she has. "Here I am trying to cheer you up and I'm talking about viruses." She sets the mugs on the table and sits down.

"You know what I want you to talk about," Wanda says, covering her face with her hands, trying to stop herself from crying.

Lenore puts an arm around her. "Of course I do. I can't believe he left you like that. But Sterling's always been a confused man. He never got over the sheer astonishment of being alive, or that his being alive might matter to someone else."

"What about you? Don't you ever miss him?" Wanda asks her. She wants Lenore to say she's forgotten him completely. She wants to know it's possible. But Lenore is silent. She looks as if she will faint from pain and hunger. Wanda reaches across the table for her hand. There is black dirt under her short, brittle fingernails.

●

Going to work, Wanda will not think it remarkable that her loft is full of memories and ghosts. The Brothers Guam will call her. She will meet them in person, eventually, as the Abbott's Quay nears completion. She will have several hectic and exhilarating days of congratulations from everyone at the Consortium, calls from the press, her mother, Tyler, Reggie, and a few old friends she didn't know she still had. Tonight, after celebrating with her colleagues, she will come home and tune in Global News Network and the Art, Architecture, Antiques Channel as she usually does.

Both channels will have the news about Sterling. He has just died in the middle of a geyser basin in Yellowstone National Park. He was carrying all of his original identification papers. Maybe he'd had them all along, wanting the world to know who he was at the end. She will sit all alone for most of the night, leafing through his books. She will look through the loft again, searching for something, anything he's left behind.